UNDER THE BLOOD RED MOON

BOOK ONE IN THE BLOOD RED DUOLOGY

EMMA BOXER

Cover design by Coverjig

ABOUT UNDER THE BLOOD RED MOON

Thank you so much for reading my debut novel Under the Blood Red Moon!

Being an author has always been a silent dream of mine and after rediscovering my love of reading in 2022 I made the decision, inspired by so many indie authors, to finally follow said dream.

I have written in my lunch breaks from work, in the quiet hours of the morning, and the stolen hours of dark nights. All to culminate in this final vision which I have immensely enjoyed creating.

I am sure I still have a lot to learn about writing and developing as an author but I hope you enjoy my very first finished book, and thank you for coming on this journey with me.

CHAPTER ONE

When you've buried enough bodies, you find that each one has its own specific aroma. Like a decaying perfume range, if you know what you're smelling for, you can pick out the subtle differences. Like how when they're too fresh they still smell of iron and blood and even a little like themselves. All people have their own smell. But if you leave them too long, they start to develop layers, a sickly sweetness that only comes with decay and rotting flesh.

Maybe that's just me.

They all have their own distinct sound when they drop into the grave you dig for them too. Depending on how big they are; how stiff they have become. It's all about the little things you know. And I would know, tonight I dig my one hundred and twenty first grave. I have a little pocketbook back at the house, tonight when I get home and wash the blood and decay from my body, Ill pull it out and add an extra mark in pencil. There have been far too many to track mentally, if I hadn't written it down, I doubt I would have any idea what number this was.

I look behind me to assess number one hundred and twenty-one. He is around 6"2 and 230 pounds, he wasn't easy to move here, but I've had practice. After the blunders I made with my first few bodies I became a quick learner. Got myself a nice makeshift tarp with handles, washable so I can reuse it, clips together on top so that as I slide the victim they don't fall off. Getting them in and out the car is usually the hardest part, that's why I switched to a van with a wheelchair lift, takes some of the pressure off, you know. I've managed to dig a hole that will be big enough for him. Out here in the forest no one would find him anyway, no one hikes or camps here, I picked it for a reason. Over five hundred thousand acres of forest. With at least over one hundred bodies already 6 feet under it, although who are we kidding, we've all watched true crime, there's probably at least a thousand bodies out here.

I slide number one hundred and twenty-one over the makeshift grave and unclip my tarp, grabbing the handles along the right-hand side I pull and roll him into his new home. I get a mouthful of his scent before I hear a thud and see him face down. I carefully fold up the tarp and place it in the bench locker I have installed in the back of the van, making sure it is sealed to keep the smell in. Number one hundred and twenty-one was dead for three days before I managed to move him. Master wasn't happy. But you must make sure the time is right, can't risk Debbie from down the road seeing me drag a corpse into my car. I need to move when its quiet, and I can't leave during the night when Master is awake. Finding the perfect time during the day to not be seen, isn't so easy as he would think.

Now I need to fill in the hole and cover it well, just in case. This will take me another couple of hours and my arms already ache but it's important to do the job right. At least I won't need to go for a run today, I've already got my workout in.

As I work, I take in the scenery around me, its noon, and a beautiful day for Alaska. For mid-June the weather is pretty nice, a balmy fifteen degrees that had me choose my light coat today instead of my usual parker. Sunlight streams through the forest canopy in angel rays making the landscape look ethereal. Towering trees here remind me of Christmas, tall, piney green spruce trees that have probably been growing since even before my grandparents were born. They stretch out in expanse across the forest floor, littered with their needles and the leaves of other trees. Everything around me bristles with a light wind, carrying with it the sounds of scurrying animals, flowing water, creaking branches.

It's the most peaceful place I have ever experienced. Not so different from my original home in the lake district of England, as much as I can remember it, I was only four when we left to come to Alaska. My first impressions were always that it was like home but just so much bigger. I still feel the same.

As I continue to shovel loose earth onto the back of one hundred and twenty-one, I think about the day we arrived here. My mother used to always say she didn't believe I remembered it because I was too young, but she was wrong. I remember everything about it. It was the first time I had been on a plane, and the last. It took over a full day to get from Newcastle to Alaska and two different changes, in London and New York. My parents had told me much about we were going to start a new life, an adventure across the sea. I had dreamed the whole flight of the amazing new land we would be going to see, deep in my fairytale books, the only thing to entertain me and pass the hours. I thought of Mulan and the beautiful pictures of a green sprawling China, rice fields and great temples. I thought of sleeping beauty and landscapes covered with great castles. I even thought of the little mermaid and her underwater city. Imagine my disappointment when I arrived in Alaska, and it barely looked removed from home.

My mum had always reminded me of my first words when we landed, and she asked what I thought. *That it hadn't been worth the trip*, I responded. I don't feel that way now of course, coming here changed my whole life.

I finally pat down the last remnants of loose earth to make sure I have sealed number one hundred and twenty-one in nicely. Then, gathering some pine, leaves, and twigs, I spread a camouflage over top.

Happy with my work, I knock my shovel off against a tree to get rid of as much muck as possible and toss it in the back of the van. It will take me about four hours from this point to get home, not too close to cause suspicion, but I enjoy the drive. Connecting my phone and playing my audiobook, I head back out onto the road. I still have six hours before Master wakes up so I should be back in time to prepare everything for him. He will be pleased regardless, now that one hundred and twenty-one is out of the house. He won't need another for a good few weeks but he likes the trash taken out in a timely manner. As I settle in for my drive, I allow my mind to go blank and just focus on the soft rhythmic voice of my audiobook. The body cooling off in the forest won't cross my mind again, now he is buried. I don't feel any guilt, that stopped a long time ago, I don't really feel anything now. It's just the way life is. For now.

CHAPTER TWO

Pulling into our suburb I am greeted with the usual sights. Children play on their front lawns and spill into the street. They laugh and squeal with the unadulterated joy of being young. At this time of year, the sun is up about eighteen hours of the day, not so good for Master but the families here love it. Children will stay out until their parents drag them home by the scruffs of their neck. Families take the opportunity to socialize more. There's always BBQs, birthday parties and football game gatherings. Perfect for your average American family, kind of a nightmare for a serial killer.

I've gotten smarter with passing through, and I go mostly unnoticed. I'm just the woman who lives in the creepy house at the end of the road. I did try and be friendly when we moved here, I smiled, I waved, I complimented people's lawns. All the correct etiquette for an American suburb. But soon people were avoiding meeting my eye, they told their kids to not play near the haunted house at the end of the road. We didn't even get trick or treaters, which had thoroughly disappointed me. To my surprise it had disappointed my Master too. He loves Halloween.

But the families here knew that there was something wrong with us. Though they never saw Master, only me, they didn't like that they couldn't understand me. I dressed normal, looked normal. But I didn't work, I seemed to live all alone, and all my windows were boarded up from this inside. I never came out during the day, except once every few weeks, in which time I drove my child catcher looking van out and came back almost a full day later. It freaked people out enough to know something wasn't right, but no one suspected what I was. Or if they did, they didn't care because I didn't target them. People, on the whole, were simple. They may think there's something wrong with me but as long as they are safe, they would rather play ignorant. And they are safe, I would never choose someone in this neighborhood.

Don't shit where you eat as they say.

I would never target anyone in the community, even though I had to learn quite a few lessons when I first started killing, I was never that stupid. So, they avoided me and now I avoided them. It worked, albeit it was lonely.

As I roll slowly down the street the kids playing move aside onto their lawns to let me pass. They keep their eyes down, only the brave few stealing a glance at the van they fear. I wonder what they say I am, a witch maybe? If only they knew. As I round the corner at the end of the cul-de-sac our house comes into view. It is exactly like every other house on the block other than the boarded-up windows. I always make sure to keep the outside spic and span, as well as the lawn. Honestly, I think the people here would be more upset to have a poorly maintained garden littering their street than a serial killer. I would probably have the homeowner's association asking for my head before the police. I pull the van up the drive and the garage starts to open automatically for me. I had a sensor installed that picks up my van. I pull in and the door starts to immediately close behind me, shutting me in darkness. I take a moment for myself before I have to get out and get ready for Master. A deep sigh escapes my lips. It's been a long day. A long year. A long life. And I'm only twenty-five.

I only allow a minute to feel sorry for myself then swing myself out of the van. I'll worry about the tarp tomorrow; the van already smells like death, cleaning it tonight won't make too much difference. As I walk up to the main door to the house, the retinal scan display clicks to life with a red glow. Master takes his security very seriously. All the top of the range equipment was installed before we even moved in. Only he and I can open any of the doors in this house. Unawares to those outside, metal plating is in place behind all the boarded-up windows. The boards were my idea, I thought having metal casing visible to protect your house may make us look like drug dealers. Looking like a creepy witch is only a slightly better alternative I suppose.

"*Name*"

The system demands.

"Sabine Riley"

I reply.

"*Sabine Riley, voice activation accepted. Please present left eye for retinal scan*"

I place my left eye over the camera and try not to blink as the red-light slides over my vision.

"*Retinal scan detected. Present hand palm down for fingerprint analysis*"

I place my hand over the scanner and watch the small LED line slide up and down as it tracks my prints.

"*Fingerprint scan verified. Access granted, Sabine Riley.*"

There is a series of clicks and sliding noises of metal on metal as the series of locks open to allow me access. Finally with an electronic hum the door slides open, and I step through. Hairs bristle on the back of my neck as the door firmly slides shut behind me, causing a breeze that feels like a breath on my back. I complained to no end when we first moved in about the reaction time of the door, Master forgets I'm not as fast as him. He lacked sympathy of course. *Move faster then,* he had told me.

The decor inside the house is quite the unexpected considering the modern security system. It reminds me of when we used to visit small castles at home in England. Lots of red, lots of plush velvet surfaces, lots of old paintings of men riding horses. Master unfortunately did not move with the times when it came to his taste, he prefers a more … vintage look. The carpet below my feet is uniform throughout the house and has the feel of a Persian rug, with a maroon base and variety of intricate patterns. It clashes slightly with the lighter red wallpaper that covered the walls, separated only with a cream runner on the bottom third. The decor matched with the complete absence of natural light makes an oppressively dingey atmosphere.

Dragging my feet down the hallway I notice all the small things that make this place feel so oppressive. Cleaning and dusting is a part of my role here and I take it very seriously, but no matter how much I kept this place dusted it never truly feels clean. My parents old place had hardwood floor and a lot of smooth shiny surfaces. My mom would spend hours polishing and mopping until my reflection would stare back at me. Plush carpets and cluttered surfaces here required vacuuming and feather dusting but no matter what, there was no sparkling, no reflections.

There would be a lot of cleaning going on today is all I can think as I feel the caked mud dropping off my boots as I trudge to the bottom of the stairs. My room is immediately at the top of the stairs, by design, I'm the first port of call should someone make it up there. My Master was at the end of the hall, theoretically protected by me. I would be the first in the firing line if someone got into the house. I'm sure this was the idea when he selected where we would be staying, though honestly I'm not sure why, if someone did break in here he would be much better prepared to deal with them than I would.

With each step my clothes are disturbed and I am reminded of the God awful smell I'm doused in, all I can think of is a nice scalding shower. Though nothing would make me happier than stripping off and cleansing myself of the smell of decay, I don't have time. It has taken longer than I thought to get home and I'm way behind schedule for the night. Master needs to be woken at precisely eight PM and it was seven fifty-six when I turned off the van. If Master isn't woken up on time, he won't be happy especially because tonight he has guests to prepare for. So instead of what I really want to do, I shrug off my jacket and throw it into my room before slamming the door and heading to wake him. My room was absolutely stink later but it's nothing that some bleach and open windows won't be able to fix.

I open his door without knocking and walk straight in. His room itself is completely barren, a stark contrast to the rest of the house. Other than of course the closed steel bed compound in the corner of the room, sealed against any light or air. If it hadn't struck you yet, Master is not completely human. I wouldn't become a serial killer for any average man. He requires my services and so I am of use, but that's not all. This is also an interview, a decade long test to prove that one day, I can be worth more than I am to him currently. Over the past ten years serving him, I like to think that I've done well, made him somewhat proud.

I don't kid myself into thinking this creature has any exceptional fondness or attachment to me. No more than a farmer would for his dairy cows, maybe even less. But when a creature cannot be out during the day and requires a constant supply of fresh *blood bags* as he calls them, he needs assistance. Yet one day, if I show I am of use, perhaps the cow will be given a chance to move up in the world. I like to think that though I am just a human familiar to him, I have come to mean something in his life, I doubt he would have suggested that I could one day join him in his immortality if he didn't care for me just a little.

My boots not yet removed I'm conscious of the dirt tracks I leave on his carpet as I make my way to his resting place. Most people think creatures like Master sleep in a coffin, not completely true. My Master sleeps in a perfectly normal bed. With an automated, lockable, steel cover. It's easy to see where the rumors came from, it does resemble a final resting place. But this is much higher tech and much more spacious, a king bed size at least.

Although the entire room is blocked from natural light, he still prefers this extra precaution whilst he sleeps, just in case. A window stretches directly above his bed, the same steel that covers his bed also covers the glass opening that would allow any visibility to the outside world.

I go to the electronic panel on the side of the sleeping chamber and repeat the process from the garage. Master wouldn't allow just anyone access to him whilst he sleeps. He can escape without me letting him out, the man is smart he wouldn't not put a failsafe in, but he does prefer a wake-up call. Due to the complete lack of natural light, he needs me to be there to give him the all clear. God forbid he let himself out when a stream of sunlight is present. My eye is scanned, my palm approved and with a click and slide of the motor the case retracts to reveal him. My Master, the vampire.

He is already awake. This isn't good.

"It is about time." He snarls.

Though he is likely thousands of years old, he looks no older than his mid-thirties. Deep black hair falls just past his ears in short waves, a dark shadow of stubble trimmed into perfect straight lines perpetually covers his face, though I have never seen him shave. And his eyes are piercing, they bore into me as he speaks, ice blue, with almost no color it looks inhuman, which of course he is.

"My apologies Master, I was disposing of the victim." I bow my head slightly as I speak to him even though he is below me. Respect is paramount, especially when he looks like he could eat me alive right now.

"I do not want your apologies; I want you on time. You are aware we have visitors today." He rises as he speaks to me, one fluid and quick motion and now he towers above me.

It never escapes me how unsettling it is when he moves like that. He can choose to move slowly, match my human pace, and most of the time he does. Except when he wants to intimidate me, when he wants me to remember that he is to be feared. At only 5"5 I'm not exactly substantial but Master is at least 6"5 and it makes me feel miniscule, especially when his defined muscle pulls at his clothing. Even if he wasn't a vampire, he would still be able to put me down with one hand. With his inhuman strength … he could probably do it with one finger.

"I'm aware Master, I thought you would want the house to be removed of the … smell." I suggest.

It is true, he has been talking about the guests who are coming tonight all week, and he has mentioned the smell number one hundred and twenty-one was making for two days in a row. Today was my last opportunity to remove the problem, and my first opportunity. I can only move bodies when the street is quiet, and the first two days that one hundred and twenty-one was sitting in the garage, there was a series of street parties.

He flexes his broad muscular shoulders and steps out of the coffin. He is completely naked, as he likes to sleep but this doesn't concern either of us. I'm used to it, and he sees me as the family dog.

"True," he allows "I will dress now; they are expected within two hours. We will require sustenance." He throws over his shoulder as he walks towards his closet. The normal number of words I have come to expect from him. He talks to me, about he what needs me to do, but small talk isn't exactly in his repertoire. I wonder what it would be like to have him inquire to how my day was, or how my body disposal went. But right now, that isn't the top of my lists of concerns.

"Already Master? But you only fed this week." I startle, it is usually much longer between hunts, and I usually have time to prepare. Its already dark, and I smell like a literal dead body. Trying to hunt tonight is going to be a literal nightmare.

"But our guests may have not, a good host always has something to drink on offer, no?" I hear the smirk in his voice, though his back is turned. The doors to the closet thrown open he fingers through his clothing looking for something specific. The muscles in his back ripple as he moves, more slowly now.

I have no choice, I will have to hunt, and do it quickly, he will expect the man back here before his guests arrive which means I have two hours to make myself presentable, drive out to find and retrieve someone. I always want to make him happy, its literally my purpose in life, but tonight it's even more important. These guests are the first I will ever host here and it's for a reason. My immortality will be a topic of conversation tonight. It isn't the time to fail.

"As you wish Master, I must leave now if I am to return in time." My left foot takes one step back, he would usually expect me to help him dress, to prepare the room for visitors, to entertain him. There's no time for that tonight, if I even give up thirty minutes to helping him prep, I might not be back in time with victim number One hundred and twenty-two.

"That's a good familiar, do not let me down." His hands freezes over a suit jacket and his head tilts slightly. Not enough that he's making eye contact with me but just enough to make me momentarily freeze.

A suggestion? A threat? Who knows, honestly who cares. When you have been a vampire familiar as long as I have, you learn to live with a certain level of discomfort. It's like your body is aware it is in the presence of a predator and the fact that you ignore it must just dampen your natural fight or flight. Though I always find him somewhat terrifying, I know he won't really hurt me. He never has before, never so much as lifted a finger to me. He's like a distant father who just doesn't want any problems.

It won't be easy to find a victim tonight, but I will, I always do. Though my Master has put a roof over my head these past ten years, familiars can be replaced; I know that all too well. My consideration for immortality relies on me being invaluable to Master so that is what I'll be.

He turns back toward his clothing and continues his quiet contemplation. That is my cue to move my ass. I don't need to be told twice, my feet pivot and I turn my back to him before racing towards the door. My steps quicken as I turn and have to curse myself as I pass the hall mirror. A rumor that holds no weight is that vampires do not have reflections, they do, and in my experience, they spend a lot of time staring at it. I currently take myself in, I'm small but curved, muscle built from lots of hours in our home gym, softness on top curtesy of my love for chocolate. My figure isn't the issue I'm looking at, my hair and clothes however need a lot of work before anyone would look twice at me.

My ebony hair, usually past waist length is pulled into a messy bun, which after today's outing looks more like a bird's nest. My green eyes, though quite alluring if I do say so myself, hold no makeup to make them pop. I'm dirty, I'm a mess and more than anything I s*mell.*

As quickly as possible I speed up and sprint to my room, the entire MO of my murders requires me to look presentable. I need to be wanted, and right now I doubt I'd even be let into a bar. That shower I had been wanting becomes a necessity rather than a pleasure, though I don't have time to let it heat up to scalding like I want. Instead, I rinse down with strawberry soap under the tepid water to get the thick of the grime and smell off. I won't be able to wash my hair, I don't have time to dry it and drowned cat isn't the look I am going for. As I towel dry myself off, I opt for the next best thing than a wash and blow dry, dowsing my hair in perfume to cover any smell lingering there. Pulling it into a loose but neat braid that falls nicely down my back I move to my wardrobe to select something appropriately… inappropriate. Braiding it will keep it out of my way enough but also show off its length. Men like my long hair.

I haphazardly apply some concealer to hide the bags under my eyes, thick liquid black eyeliner that tapers into ticks and some blush. It doesn't have to be perfect, the bar will be dark anyway. Finally, I gloss my already plump lips and evaluate where I am at.

Wiping off the condensation on the en-suite mirror I look much more put together now but I will have to overdo it with the clothes to make sure I'm successful. I go back and find the skimpiest dress my wardrobe has to offer. A green velvet corset top dress that hugs my figure and stops above the knees. Master likes this dress too which is a bonus, he says it compliments my eyes. It will do for the guests when I return if I don't have time to tidy myself up further. With their heightened senses I'm sure they will get a nose full of sickly sweet death under my perfume but that can't be helped. Decay has a nasty habit of settling in hair.

Finally, I pull on a pair of black heels to bring me up a couple of inches, men like short girls but the stilettos lengthen me in a way that draws the eye. Then I'm back out. The stairs force me to take my time to make sure I don't topple over in these ridiculous heels, but as I hit the bottom floor, I quicken up again. My feet sink into the deep pile carpet as I run. I repeat the same security procedures to get back into the garage, pulling open the van door. Forgetting the smell of the tarp I left there earlier, I'm unexpectantly met with a thickness that makes me pull back and gag. My own damn fault, I should have taken it out to air the van. I'll pay for the mistake now; it won't be a mistake I make again. No time to cry over spilt blood. I jump in the van and roll all the windows down, hoping the wind will air it out slightly. I will have to find a different way home though, no matter how drunk, no guy is going to step foot in here and still be in the mood. The mood is important.

The garage door opens as I back up and I pull out onto the now dark street. Thankfully, most of the kids have gone inside now, probably having dinner around tables with their normal families, having a normal life. How nice it must be. As I set off towards the nearest bar, I think about the first time I realized I could lure men with my body to feed my Master.

It was my first solo time hunting; he had told me to bring someone alive and I had absolutely no idea what to do. At only sixteen I had little life experience and even less murder experience. Being a small town, entering the local bar without any I.D hadn't been that hard, even though I probably looked even younger than I was because of my small stature. I had wandered around, pulse racing and throat tight. I'm not even sure what I was really planning to do, I had a steak knife from our kitchen slid into my dress. Some guy had asked to buy me a drink which I refused but he was persistent, he bought me one anyway which I luckily spotted him crushing a pill into.

In that moment the guilt and worry I had been feeling left my body. I knew I would be able to lure this man to his death and not think twice about it. I asked him if he wanted to come back to my place, told him I lived alone. When we got back to the house I didn't even need to do anything else, Master was waiting and descended on him the moment he saw him. Terrified, I had ran, locked myself in my room until I could no longer hear the screams and noises of struggle.

Master had came to me after, stroked my hair and told me what a good job I had done. It was one of the only times he has ever given me physical affection but it made my heart sing to be given crumbs. *Keep up the good work,* he had told me.

So that's what I did, week upon week, month upon month. I mixed up which bar I went to just in case people got suspicious. But tonight, I didn't have time to peruse the options, the rocking 9's was the closest and I was in a rush.

My M.O hadn't taken me long to develop, killing wasn't something I took pleasure in. I had to find a way to live with what I was doing, and quickly. So I always took bad men, men who were harassing women, men who spiked drinks, men who hung around in dark alleys by the bars until the early hours looking for prey. I didn't always get lucky and find someone bad, but most nights I did, there was enough of them.

When it got tough I convinced myself I was like batman, a vigilante justice protecting the women who no one else would. We have all seen the stats and arrests following sexual assaults, it isn't like the police were lining up to round up these men. So, I would, and I did, week by week Usually if I saw no one I came back another night or tried a different bar. I wouldn't have that luxury tonight; I'd have to be quick and confident.

My wheels crunch on the gravel as I pull up into the bar's carpark, I make quick work of rolling all my windows up and parking in the darkest corner at the back of the lot. I jump out and give myself a quick sniff, not too bad, hopefully the smell of sweat and degeneracy from the bar cancels me out some, though I can feel whisps of hair falling around my face. Pulled loose from the braid by the wind of having the windows down.

Wobbling slightly in my heels on the uneven floor, I start to walk towards the bar. As if a gift from god has been presented to me, I notice a guy coming out holding up a barely conscious girl. He's wearing jeans and a plaid shirt, with a cropped mess of blonde hair. The typical football kind of guy who is probably approachable, looks trustworthy, except for the victim I suspect he's dragging along. Surely, I couldn't be this lucky, I'd have to put the lotto on tomorrow. As I slow down to better assess the situation, I can see him twitching. He looks worried, he looks like he's checking for witnesses. The girl, a blonde pretty thing, too young to be in a bar I suspect anyway, she mumbles to herself nonsensically as she stumbles to keep upright.

"That your girlfriend?" I shout to him.

His eyes flash to me, a mixture between furious and terrified, maybe this is his first time assaulting someone. Lucky me.

"Mind your business." He spits and drags the girl quicker, heading towards a grey corolla.

"Don't you want someone a bit more conscious, someone with a bit more experience?" I try my best to appear sultry, adding some smokiness to my voice.

He hesitates. Though I don't know if its because he actually is interested in me, or if he's now worried I could be a witness.

"She's plenty conscious, just had too much okay. I'm taking her home." Yeah, that's bullshit, and I know it is. He doesn't handle her the way you would if it were a friend who drank too much. There's no care behind his touch, she's slung against him like you would expect to see the dead carcass of a successful hunt.

"Hey, I'm not judging." I might not be able to get into this guys car, but I would stop him hurting this girl still if I could. I hold my palms up and walk toward him slowly closing the gap. "But I don't think you know that girl, and all I'm saying is rather than get to know her, why not get to know me?" I try to sway my hips sensually as I walk, the words make me sick as I say them, but I know I'm doing good here. Not only am I saving this girl, but I'm also permanently removing this guy from the equation if I can.

I see his eyes darken, then flit between the girl and me. He has a choice to make, regardless of whether he wants me or not, I've seen him now, he can't take this girl with him and leave me behind as a witness.

Looking me up and down he makes me feel more frightened than Master even would. The threat here isn't just for show, it's real, and if I give him a chance he will act.

Suddenly the body of the poor girl slumps to the ground as he lets her collapse, and I try not to wince. She mumbles slightly letting me know she is still somewhat awake though I doubt she has any idea what is going on. Lying in the dirt her dress is hiked up leaving her with little dignity and modesty, making my heart ache for her. But I can't show too much sympathy, me and asshole here have a little game to play, and it doesn't work unless he thinks I want him.

"So, you would rather me take you home for a good time?" He drawls, stepping over his discarded victim. It takes everything in me to not take a step back in response, but I'm used to this, I won't let his intimidation tactics ruin this, I've only got one shot here.

"Take me to my place, I live alone, I only came out tonight to find someone to show me a good time. You up for that?" I know his ego won't be able to resist the challenge in my words. And hopefully the going to my place won't be an issue.

Instead of taking another step toward me he takes one step back and I'm worried I've blown it. Thankfully he turns and extends a hand towards his car.

"Well then, your chariot awaits, tell me where your place is and I'll show you the best time of your life. "The smirk on his face makes me want to punch him, I hope Master and his guests makes this one suffer.

My eyes flit to the poor girl on the carpark floor one more time.

"It's fine, she wasn't here alone, her friends will come find her." Douch bag assures me. An admission, he isn't the friend taking home his poor girl who got too drunk. Hopefully, her friends come for her soon and pick her up off the floor. I can't afford to waste any more time, or risk losing him, by getting her moved. So instead, I plaster a seductive yet meek smile on my face and head toward the passenger door of his car.

"Get in then princess and tell me where we're going." He unlocks the car but waits for me to be firmly in the passenger seat with the door closed before he follows.

I tell him the address and he starts driving. At this point I've used about an hour of my two-hour slot, we should be back in plenty of time. I breath a sigh of relief, hoping he doesn't read too much into it. My van can be picked up another day, Ill grab a taxi to come get it. Hopefully in the meantime no one investigates it because of the smell. It's not like there's many other scents that dead body can be explained away as.

"You live alone?" His voice cracks as he asks me. He definitely hasn't done this a lot, he's too nervous. Plus, I've already told him that I do. Not wanting to put him off I ignore this little fact and instead smile demurely at him.

"Sure do." I say breezily.

The next twenty minutes pass in tense silence until he comes closer to the house. He doesn't attempt small talk so neither do I, I can tell from his direction he isn't trying to pull anything and take me to a dark alley somewhere. We are heading home and I'm not going to say anything to spook him. His knuckles turn white and they grip the wheel and I can feel the tension in his shoulders. Strange, as far as he's concerned, I'm a willing participant in this, which means he's probably still intending on hurting me anyway if he's so nervous. Scum.

"It's this one up on the left, pull close into the garage it'll open for us." I say as I pull out the sensor I pocketed from my truck and tucked under my dress.

He listens and rolls slowly into the bay as it opens for us. With the lack of streetlights we are suddenly plunged into darkness as the door slams shut behind us. I don't waste any time and jump from the car, racing to get the security system unlocked.

“That seems pretty intense what are you a drug dealer?” He laughs as he gets out the car and saunters up behind me. His laugh seems off, nervous, the system is throwing him off.

“Don’t worry about it.” I shoot back. This is always the hardest part, the security system makes them distrustful, more than one has tried to run at this point. But our guy over here is too dumb for that apparently and a few words from me relax him enough to come so close behind me that I can feel the breath on his neck. It makes me feel sick.

I’ve never had a boyfriend, but I’ve had plenty of these fake interactions. Luckily, it has never had to go further than brief touches and nuzzles against my neck, but it has still given me an aversion to physical touch. Not that I am offered any other than by those I hunt.

“You gunna get us both a drink?” He asks as the door slides open.

“Sure, this way.” I lead him past the stairs and to the study where there is a built-in bar. Its rather impressive, the old-fashioned décor in here matched with a full mirrored wall holding any liquor you could think of. The other walls are covered in bookshelves blocking the wallpaper but giving the room a regal feel, which is enhanced by the wing backed velvet armchairs that are placed facing inwards around a large mahogany table. Everything in this room is likely priceless and irreplaceable. The worry about breaking something that's been here longer than I've been alive is the only thing that usually keeps me out of this room and reading every book Master owns.

Victim one hundred and twenty-two helps himself to one of the most expensive whiskies on offer and pours me one too, without asking what I drink. Handing me a crystal glass he waits until it is firmly in my grip before clinking his to mine in a cheers. I cringe as I hear the noise, hoping to God that it didn't cause a chip or a crack.

Master won't be happy he's touched the pricey stuff, but he'll have plenty to drink in return. Lifting the glass to my face I can see small bubbles rising to the stop of the liquid, the tail end of an effervescent reaction. He spiked my drink, and smoothly, I didn't even notice him palm the pill in. Good thing I always check. Perhaps he has done this more than once before after all.

"Cheers." He says and lifts his glass in the air toward me again, as if reminding me to take a drink.

"To a good time." I reply and raise my glass in

response, avoiding touching them together again just in case. It strikes me at this moment he doesn't even know my name. And I don't know his, he will simply be one hundred and twenty-two. I tilt the glass to my lips but take none of the liquid in my mouth, instead I merely swallow emptiness momentarily.

Happy I have taken the bait he tilts his head back to down about one hundred dollars' worth of whisky and I reach under the table. I always keep at least three syringes of ketamine under here. I have the same routine each time and I like to be organized. Sometimes, in this moment, I feel as quick as a vampire. Before he can swallow his drink, the needle is in his neck and the plunger down. I stand in front of him, death wrapped in a bite sized package and stare up into the eyes of a man who will never again assault a woman.

"What the fuck." He spits and stumbles back, the needle still sticks out of his neck rather comically before being wiggled free by his frantic movements.

"You crazy fucking bitch you stabbed me!" He frantically palms at his throat trying to locate the source as if he can remove the huge ketamine dose coursing through his veins.

"Yes, I fucking did." I smile as he collapses to the ground.

He moans and tries to thrash but he is too sedated. He won't be unconscious, oh no he'll be awake to experience all of this. But he'll be subdued enough that Master and his guests can all feed with minimal mess. A job well done if I do say so myself. I glance at the clock, thirty minutes to spare.

I gather the glasses and move them through to the kitchen before heading upstairs. I'll tidy myself up a bit more before the guests arrive. It's important as a familiar to impress, like a well-groomed poodle. Tonight, I am going to be judged, a day I have been waiting patiently for, and I do not want to come up short.

CHAPTER THREE

A car engine sounds in the driveway as I leave my room, my hair rebraided, my make up much more neat and in place. Tonight, we will use the front door, this can only be opened from the inside and only by Master. I will stand behind him, silently, I will listen, and I will serve and I will speak only if spoken to. Visitors are something we have never had before but he has gone over some ground rules with me in preparation for this.

"You should be seen but not heard unless I request it from you." Master says as he sits in his study, a quiet game of chess being played against himself.

"Of course." I reply head dipped.

"You will have your chance to prove yourself Sabine, but first impressions are everything. They should be aware that you are subservient, loyal and would make me a fine companion."

The word companion sparks something in me. Our relationship would change when I was no longer a human servant, but his vampire companion, though what that meant I still wasn't sure.

"Creating an immortal is no small notion, we have rules in place, it is why we designed the trials the way we have. Each of our guests will be entering one of their own familiars for consideration also. This isn't just a chance for you to prove yourself to me. It is to show others that we are strong, formidable." He moves a pawn across the board and then rotates it to play his counter move.

The trials are what I must endure to prove my worth, they have been mentioned time and time again. That familiars are given the chance to compete, that the victors will become immortal as their reward. And finally, it is my time. My chance. Though he hasn't told me what the trials entail I have prepared in my own ways over the years. Running, weight training, boxing drills. All on my own of course, a familiar doesn't exactly have friends.

"I understand Master," I nod to him. "I won't let you down"

He moves his knight and knocks the opposing pawn straight off the table. Landing softly in the plush rug, he considers it for a moment, his silence stretching into eternity.

"You better not."

That had been a week ago and his words were the last thing I heard before I went to sleep and the first thing that rang in my mind when I woke up each day. The familiar trails were something I had thought of and worked towards for ten years now. I may not know what I will be up against, but I'm no weakling. I can do this. And this started tonight, started with being the good and obedient familiar for Master and his vampire friends.

It used to bother me so much at first. The do not speak unless spoken to. I had the strange and stupid assumption when I first came here that he was going to become my new family, he would never replace my father but he could be a father figure. I was only a teenager when he first took me in, and I had a lot to learn. Quickly I learned reality, that he was my Master and that I would always be an employee, but even then in the beginning I guess I thought it would be like you see on TV with an employee and their boss. We would make small talk and ask just enough about each other's lives to get to know each other, but not too much. I thought I would be able to ask him questions about being a vampire and he would tell me stories of his past.

I knew he was old, and old people usually like to talk about the good old days a lot. Not Master though, not to me anyway. We had never really gotten past formalities and discussing tasks and duties. He was always respectful though and I was grateful for that, he asked for things in a polite way and quite often even thanked me. We became used to each other and that created comfort and familiarity. He would be there during the nights, and I would be around for anything he needed. During the days, when I was awake, I could do as I pleased. Working out, watching television, passing time.

Heavy footsteps behind me wake me from my trance, I stand at the top of the staircase now, looking down at the front door and wondering who will walk through it tonight. Master was making noise for my benefit, if he did not want me to hear him coming, I wouldn't. Turning away from the door I face him and dip my head in a sign of respect.

"I can assume we have refreshments?" He trawls.

"Yes Master, sedated in the study." I reply. He looks stunning and lethal as always tonight, in a black velvet suit with a maroon paisley shirt underneath. He certainly had a unique sense of style but if anyone could rock it, it was him. His short waves are slicked back out of his face, falling behind his ears.

"Lovely, fantastic job as always Sabine thank you." He murmurs as he passes me and begins to descend the staircase.

I did not say you're welcome, but merely dipped my head again slightly in a bow, my own thanks for his recognition, as I follow closely behind. Halfway down the stairs, a knock finally sounds at the door, firm and intense. My head begins to create possibilities of who is behind that door, what he looks like.

Master drops his human slowness and is at the door in an instant, leaving me to quickly get down the stairs so that I can be in place behind him before he opens the door. He lifts his palm to the security tab and leans in for the retinal scan to release the locks. I tense in slight excitement. We have never had a visitor before, I know I will not likely speak but still, for someone living such a lonely life any company was a welcome respite. Perhaps it would be like you see on TV when old friends unite, they will sit and talk about stories from their past, reminiscing on good times. And I may finally get some insight on who my Master was before he settled into his quiet life here in Alaska.

The door swings open and I have to remind myself to keep composure as I slide into place behind my Master, where I belong.

"Melchior!" A Russian sounding accent exclaims. I know this is my Masters name, but I do not use it, nor do I hear it and so it shocks me initially as the vampire's face comes into view. He is just as tall as Master, but with a shock of white hair, white eyebrows to match and a strange red tint to his eyes. If this was not enough to make the new creature stand out in a crowd, he is dressed as though that's 70-show chewed him up and spat him out. Wearing a corduroy suit with bell bottom pants, and a flower power turtleneck underneath the matching jacket. I cannot help but allow the small twitch of a smile as I drink in his appearance.

"Alexandru, my old friend." Master steps forward arms open and grasps the vampire in a deep embrace. I'm assuming old friend means a lot longer in vampire years than it does in human, but I am still surprised to see Master giving affection so freely. Even his voice sounds warm and familiar, it causes a small pang in my stomach that I can't quite place.

"It has been too long Melchior, I am beyond exulted that we should meet again, and for such an exciting time no?" Alexandru wiggles his eyebrows at Master in a suggestive and comical manner and it is all I can do to stifle a giggle.

"Come in my friend we have lots to catch up on, and lots to discuss. We still await Zaros I am afraid." Master steps back and holds his arm out in invitation as Alexandru steps forward.

"Oh, and surprised, are we? That man has the ego of a Transylvanian warrior my friend he must make an entrance, I am sure."

As I contemplate what I will be expecting of Zaros I'm caught by surprise as another man follows Alexandru through the door.

Slightly shorter but still towering over me, this man is decidedly human. His features though sharp do not hold the secret of centuries, his eyes though blue carry a vibrant color unlike the washed-out irises of most vampires. His dark brown hair is pulled up into a bun on his head, with stray curls escaping down his neck. My eyes follow down to see him dressed in a smart grey suit, very non-descript unlike the vampire in front of him. His eyes meet mine as he passes me and without word or acknowledgement, he looks away and follows the vampires into the study.

I am left reeling momentarily in the hallway. He must be a familiar also. Of course, why had I not thought. Vampires do not travel without their familiars, we are essential for caring for them, feeding them and protecting their bodies at night. I should have known Masters' visitors would bring them. And yet he barely noticed my existence. I know we aren't supposed to talk, but he could have smiled, nodded, anything.

Suddenly remembering myself I realize I now stand alone as the gaggle of men pass into the study, it will not bode well to embarrass Master tonight, so I hurry to join them. The two vampires are already settling onto the armchairs. They must have stepped over number one hundred and twenty-two as he is still thrashing gently on the floor, though no one is acknowledging him, not even the other familiar. He is positioned behind his Master, arms in front of him, hands grasped together. He looks like a lethal and poised bodyguard; I look down at myself and feel self-conscious immediately. He looks like James Bond, and I look like a hooker.

I move to mirror his position behind my Master and stand quietly, trying with all my will power to not look at him again but instead stair at my shoes.

"How long has it been?" Alexandru asks as he slides back into his chair.

"At least thirty years if my memory serves me." Master replies.

"Has it been that long? I suppose between trials we have become lazy at keeping in touch."

My ears perk up at the mention of the trial but I keep my head bowed.

"Well international travel is not so easy my friend, perhaps if you would move to America, we could have social calls more often."

“Ba! Live in America, the people here have no culture” Alexandru spits.

Masters’ lips twitch slightly at this, not in the same way as when he smiles to me, but in a genuine way. The smile you have when talking to a friend, this smile reaches his eyes.

“Americans have no culture you say and yet I must ask if this is the rage in Russia?” He motions to the 70’s getup.

“Of course, my friend!” He laughs “We have exceptional taste in fashion, not like yourself.”

The discourse is cut short when a knock sounds at the door.

“I will be back, this will be Zaros grand entrance.” Master raises his eyebrows at his vampire companion and rises from his chair. I cringe internally as he steps over number one hundred and twenty-two, and the man makes a weak grab for his leg.

Master gives him a firm kick in the side and laughs at the responding groan.

“Pathetic.” He spits and continues out of the room.

“And your name my child?”

I start as I look up and realize Alexandru is addressing me. He does not appear to be threatening nor does he make me uncomfortable, he merely looks curious.

"Sabine." I say with a small dip of my head.

"Oh, Sabine lovely name, I was expecting something like Charity or Banana or whatever the usual American girls' names are." The familiar behind him snickers, and my eyes meet his in surprise. To laugh at your master is not a small thing.

"Ah and Sabine this is Nikolas, he takes good care of me." Alexandru smiles back at his familiar in a genuine and warm way.

"Well, someone must Master or you should surely lose your head." Nikolas chirps back, the same strong Russian accent.

I cannot believe my ears; they are speaking as if friends. This is not how a familiar addresses his Master, the talk of losing heads would most surely result in decapitation for the familiar himself!

"My boy, I am much more important than you, I do not have time to worry about things like my safety or wellbeing that is your job."

Alexandru winks at me as if this is some inside joke, I am supposed to laugh at but I can do nothing but stare, mouth agape at what is unfolding. I did not even expect to be spoken to tonight, I certainly didn't think I would be invited to c*hat.*

"It appears this one is mute Master." Nikolas quips.

"Oh, merely frightened, Melchior keeps them on a tight leash, don't speak unless spoken to and all that. He thinks its trains good brides." He rolls his eyes, in obvious disagreement.

I almost choke at the mention of brides. It is not the same for vampires as for humans, bride is merely the term for companions, created from the blood of a vampire. But to create a bride is a rare and dangerous thing. Prospective brides are kept as familiars for many years before they are even considered, and then of course, they must pass the trials. Only a select few winners become a bride every fifty years.

"Well, she must find herself some gusto if she will be entering the trials or she will never make it to bride." The familiars sharp blue eyes meet mine across the room and I sense threat behind his words. Would this man also be competing to become a bride? Was he aspiring for immortality?

"Do not frighten the competition Nikolas, it is a cheap trick." That was a yes then.

"Alexandru stop speaking to the help."

My head snaps left as I feel shivers down my spine. The biggest man I have ever seen in my life enters the room. His complexion is washed out with the lack of pallor that centuries indoors bring, yet he clearly has dark skin. He wears a polo shirt showing off his extensively tattooed arms and large biceps. I thought Master looked muscular; this man could snap him in half.

“They might start thinking they are important.” His black yet ashy eyes meet mine and I immediately lower my head again, remembering my place. So, it is Alexandru who is the unusual one, not Master. I feel slightly better knowing I’m not the only one who has been treat this way. I look up and lean slightly back to see the familiar Zaros has brought.

“Don’t waste your time, I can feed and dress myself I don’t need a mutt.” He snaps at me. I immediately lower my head again.

“Now, now let’s not be argumentative, you are bringing down the mood.” Master teases as he ushers him into the room and into the remaining armchair. I have never heard of a vampire without a familiar but then again Master doesn’t tell me much, and these are the first vampires I am meeting other than him.

“I am not, I know you two need to have a human running around after you and that is why you have become weak and soft." he says this with a gruff laugh, teasing his friends.

Alexandru raises a hand to his mouth as he gasps in false shock horror.

"I am not weak Zaros how dare you, perhaps we should have a test of strength ey? It has been a while since we all had a good roll around with each other." The way his eyebrows raise suggestively at this I suspect he isn't talking about wrestling.

Zaros guffaws "I think we have that well out of our system by now Alex, if you wish to roll around do it with your arm candy." He motions towards Nikolas whose face is completely unreadable.

"I would not want to harm his pretty face my friend." All the men laugh, and I can't help but feel uncomfortable for the poor familiar standing there, being completely objectified. Not that it seems to bother him.

"Please. Let us first discuss business and then we can move to pleasure otherwise you degenerates will not allow us to accomplish anything" Master says forcefully, I sense that he is the unofficial leader of this small group by the way the two other vampires immediately silence themselves and face him.

"The trial has been diligently organized by the coven."

This was the first time I had heard Master discuss a coven; in my mind I think of witches not vampires. I begin to wonder just how many make up this coven.

“There will be three challenges, each in increasing difficulty, only the strongest will be able to complete the final challenge and so it has been designed to allow as few victors as possible.” I gulp at this as Master returns to take his seat, as few victors as possible, what are the chances that I come out of this on top and not get sent back to continue my existence as a human servant. “Each of the twenty main families have been invited to include their familiars and it is my understanding all have accepted.” Alexandru and Zaros exchange a glance and I wonder if it is unusual for all of the vampire families to take part in this.

“All families have a familiar they feel they could turn into a bride?” Zaros questions, slight disgust lacing his words.

“They do,” Master confirms, “It has been a long time since many of us have thought to expand our families and many of us have suffered losses.”

“Indeed.” Alexandru expresses wistfully “This is the smallest our coven has been in centuries, many of us are alone reliant entirely on our familiars, it is not the way it should be.”

"It would not be so difficult to expand our families had we not created this farce with the trials and were allowed to change who we saw fit." Zaros snarls.

Interesting. The man who seems to value humans the least wants to be able to change them as he see's fit. Perhaps he has someone in mind, someone who he finds less pathetic than the average human, I think to myself smarmily.

"And what would happen then pray tell?" Master slices back "Do you think if we allowed anyone and everyone to change who they wished, that we would have been so successful at keeping to the shadows? Do you think people like Vlad to be competent enough to properly screen and carefully raise a newborn?"

I imagine by newborn Master means a newborn vampire. The trial system means that humans live and serve their Masters usually for decades before they are turned, a strong bond is built and the character of the person decided. If I were to be successful in the trials and become Master's bride, he would be by my side to aid in my transition, though I have no idea what the process will be like. That will be explained should I be accepted.

"No, he would probably change every whore he met on the street and set them lose to enjoy the carnage." Zaros admits painfully "But one bad egg should not represent us all, if we find a human, we know to be suited it should be our right to change them."

I notice his fingernails beginning to dig into the wood of the armchair. This is personal. He has a human he wishes to change, but not a familiar. Perhaps it isn't humans he resents, but merely our subjugated state here. Raising my head I risk a look at Master, his face almost looks sad … regretful.

"I am sorry Zaros, I know you wanted her, but it is not the way of our people. She lost." Alexandru is the one who speaks, he looks sympathetically towards his friend in an attempt to diffuse the tension.

He had someone in the trial, she lost. My breath hitches, she doesn't seem to be here now, did he not keep her around because she wasn't deemed worthy of transitioning?

"I will not argue again with you Alexandru why she should have been allowed to live; I fear if we begin that discussion it may resolve with your head detached from your shoulders." Zaros knuckles turn white around his clenched fists. She died. In the trial? I didn't know much about them, but I had never truly considered how dangerous they would be. Could death be on the cards for me if I didn't win these vampires games?

“ENOUGH!” Master silences the room forcefully and I flinch at his raised voice. It carries the authority of many more years than he looks and I am not the only one clearly intimidated by his sudden show of force. “If you wish to change the rules Zaros you will raise it with the council during the trials, but the rules remain currently. You cannot change a mortal who has not lived as your familiar, completed the trials and been deemed worthy by the council.”

Zaros clenches his jaw and takes a deep breath. I wonder if he is contemplating tearing this whole room apart. I wonder who he thinks about as his eyes close, and his fingers unclench from the wooden arm rests, leaving deep imprints behind.

“As you wish Melchior, I will be raising it.” He opens his ashy eyes and they meet with Masters across the room, a promise written in them that this is not over.

Master nods ever so slightly as if to acknowledge he understands the intent within his friends, then swiftly moves on.

“As I said we have twenty familiars taking part, the trials therefore have been designed in such a way as to facilitate a quick but assessing reduction of the numbers early on to thin the heard.” I can’t help but feel my pulse quicken and my palms sweat at this. Thin the heard? I know we are thought of as less then by our Masters, but it is difficult to hear him talk this way. As if I am cattle off to the slaughter. Surely If I am valuable enough to become his bride, I would be valuable enough to not want dead?

I know that I must perform not only well, but the best and the longer I stand here and listen to these ancient beings discuss the trial my confidence wanes. I risk another glance at Nikolas to see if I can gauge his feelings, but he seems completely unmoved. His body language relaxed, he now rests hand on the back of his Master's chair, the muscle of that arm flexing underneath his grey suit coat. He slouches slightly to one side, head moving between the three vampires and listening to them discuss our demise, as if it were a discussion of types of wine.

Even against this one man I doubt my success, he's bigger than me, stronger than me, certainly more confident than me. Though it depends on the nature of the trials, surely this man isn't smarter than me and I have to use that. If I can't, be the fastest or the toughest I must be the smartest. Yet part of me can't help but begin to wonder what the other contestants look like.

"Hopefully by the final trial we will be down to less than a handful so that we can thoroughly test their worthiness." Alexandru examines his nails, long and lethally pointed at the ends.

"Indeed, and when shall the trial begin, soon I hope, now that everyone is having to reside in this hellhole you call home Melchior." Zaros snips.

"Of course, it shall begin at the turn of the full moon."

I barely have time to register the thought that the full moon is tomorrow before there is a blur of movement and a cloth over my face. I thrash, my fight or flight kicking in, but it is no use. As the world begins to go black around me, I hear the words of my Master whispered in my ear.

"Make me proud Sabine, I have high hopes for you."

CHAPTER FOUR

Pain, it is the first sensation I recognize. My head throbs in time with my racing heart, at first, I can think of nothing but it. It feels like the worst hangover of my life, I try to peel my eyes open only to be met with a fluorescent light that sends shockwaves through my already aching head.

I groan and try to roll over away from the harsh glare only to be met with cold concrete. I'm lying on the floor I realize as I place a palm flat against it to try and push myself up. My arms shake with the exertion, and I have to concede and allow myself to slide back, face flat to the floor. My whole world is spinning and I can't understand why, I don't drink, and if I did it is only ever one drink. I've never been hungover like his in my life. But that must be what's happening right? I try to piece together the last things I remember. I have buried one hundred and twenty-one, I had made it home, Master needed another for his guests.

The guests. The other vampires. The trial.

I begin to slowly remember the feeling of abject terror as my Master held something over my face and my

Masters last words in my ear.

I have to get up.

I fight with everything I have to push against the floor and get myself onto my knees. I sway slightly but manage to stay upright and slowly blink my eyes into focus. The light is blinding initially but my vision begins to clear, and I can take in my surroundings. I'm the first one awake at least.

Around me is a sprawl of other bodies laid unconscious in varying states of disarray. Another nineteen I would assume if I counted them. We all are squeezed inside what looks like an old prison cell. The walls and floor are a grey concrete, the far side wall is made of bars with a locked bar door in its center. Outside the bars, I see nothing but more endless concrete leading down a corridor, more cells perhaps?

There is a bench running along the back wall of the cell we are held in, and it reminds me of the holding cells you see on TV. Like on a sitcom where a character does something stupid and is held until someone can come make bail for them.

Though it is big enough to hold all twenty of us the floor is almost covered with bodies. Some overlap in places, an arm slung over someone's back, a body heaped onto another. Our Masters obviously didn't take much care when they slung is in here. I can't help but be a little offended on behalf of us all. I know our Masters don't see us as equals but they could have propped us upright at least.

I have to remind myself however that the point of this trial is to test us. All familiars are told of the trial when they start their service I know that much as Master told me when I started serving him. It is what draws many familiars to do what we do. We are told that in exchange for our devotion we will have the chance at some point to compete to be turned into a vampire ourselves. The gift of eternal life. I honestly didn't care that much at the time, I had just lost my mother and father, I was only fifteen, but Master took me in. He told me he was a friend of my fathers and had promised to watch over me. I never got more to the story than that but for a fifteen-year-old girl with no other family and nowhere to go I wasn't in a position to question.

The possibility of the trial was something I had given very little thought to until my twenty-fifth birthday last year, when Master had told me in one year, I would have the chance. I thought of it every night since then. If I were a vampire, I would be Masters equal, first name basis, I would no longer serve him but instead be truly considered his family, maybe even more if he felt so inclined once I was his bride. I didn't love him, I didn't think I did anyway, he was just all I had.

I glance around at my competition still deep asleep and wonder why I was the first to wake, perhaps Master did me a favor, gave me a head start with a slightly smaller dose. I smile at the thought. I sober quickly however as I take in the people around me. First of all, I'm the only one in a dress and heels. I silently curse Master for not doing me the favor of putting me in some leggings and trainers and can only hope we will get the chance to change at some point.

There is an equal mix of men and women, all at least my age but some older, in their thirties or forties. My breath hitches as I see one man with hair as white as snow in the corner, though he is face down his body looks frail, and I wonder what on earth someone of that age would agree to do this for. I look around to see if I can spot the other familiar from the house, Nikolas should stand out because he was bigger built than any of the men, I see around me. Towards the edge of the cell, rolled up against the bars I see the back of a grey suit and a mop of brown curls. He must have lost his man bun in the struggle I scoff to myself.

I start as I hear a moan from behind me and I swing to see a girl around my age beginning to stir. She tries to blink her eyes but has the same reaction to the fluorescent light bulbs and immediately tries to fling her hand over her eyes. Because she's so weak she ends up just slapping herself in the face with back of her hands which elicits another moan. She has strikingly blond hair, almost as white as Alexandru's, now in knots but it looks as though it was curled before. It spreads around her like a mane, and I can already tell, though her face is scrunched in discomfort, that she is beautiful. She tries again to open her eyes and immediately they meet mine. I stare back at her in silence unsure what my next move should be.

She extends a small hand in my direction,

"You gunna help me up?" She says in a thick New Orleans accent.

"Oh yes, of course" I start and move to grab her hand. As my hand slides into her I notice how soft her skin is, though her palms hold many callouses. I wonder where they are from as I pull her to her feet. Her hair falling in uncontrolled waves around her. She is much taller than me meaning once she's on her feet I have to tilt my head back to see her face properly. She has sharp features, and a wickedness in her blue eyes that both frightens and excited me.

She looks down at me with assessing eyes and I feel self-conscious about my dress again immediately. "Well, aren't you just a snack." she growls, to herself more than me, and I can feel my face begin to flush.

She notices and grins.

"Don’t worry princess not the place nor the time, but you're not making it easy in that dress." she winks at me as she turns away and begins to assess the room around her.

I can’t help but take note as she turns her back to me that she's dressed in a tight black tunic and high-waisted pants that show off her lithe but curved figure.

I shake my head annoyed at myself, this is what being essentially alone for years does to you, I'm in literal mortal danger right now and I'm checking out this girl’s ass.

"Sabine." the word is out of my mouth before I realize I have even said it.

She turns slowly, looking over her shoulder at me and raises an eyebrow, smile cocked to one side in question.

"My name is Sabine, not princess." I try to stand tall as I say it, knowing full well how pathetic I look. I can't imagine how inferior I'd feel without the heels helping me out.

"Sabine, I'm Andromeda, friends call me Drea." She

immediately turns from me again to survey her surroundings.

"Well, it's nice to meet you, Drea." I turn away from her to let her know I'm ending the conversation, but I hear her mutter under her breath …

"I said my friends called me Drea."

Well screw her I think, I thought perhaps another woman would be a good ally but turns out she's just a bitch.

Slowly one by one the people around us begin to wake up, I notice Andromeda has taken residence in the far back corner of the cell and is watching quietly.

I on the other hand start helping people up, I move from person to person as they wiggle and moan on the floor and help them sit up, telling them where they are to help orient them. Some are friendly and grateful; some tell me to go fuck myself or shove my hands away.

Almost everyone is up when I spot a tiny figure in the back corner opposite Andromeda and make my way over.

A small mop of mouse hair lets me know this is a girl, but she looks so small, not small like me. I may be short but I have all the curves of a woman, unlike this girl. I hope to the gods I am wrong as I get onto my knees beside her and place a hand on her shoulder. I roll her onto her back towards me and gasp. She can't be more than twelve years old; this can't be right; it must be a mistake. I have no idea what the trials have in store, but I know it's no place for a child. I look back at all of the muscular men now standing flexing their limbs. This little girl shouldn't be here.

"Can you hear me sweetie?" I gently shake her shoulder, but she seems dead to the world. I tuck my hair behind one ear and lean down to place it over her mouth. I see the gentle rise and fall of her chest and feel her shallow breaths against my face.

This girl is barely one-hundred pounds, whatever they used to knock us out, I'm betting it was way too strong for her. I look around me frantically but no one else seems particularly interested. They just circle each other with assessing eyes but not speaking.

“Can anyone help?” I call to the room “Is anyone like a doctor or anything?” I look back down to the girl hoping that will express everything that needs to be said.

“You're joking right?”

I turn to see Drea making her way over

“I don't think anyone who's found themselves here”

she motions around her “Has been to medical school” She places her hands on her hips in a nonchalant way, but I swear her eyes shine with just a tiny bit of concern.

“Fine,” I spit in no mood for her crap “Well does anyone have any idea how to help a child who’s been overdosed on chloroform?” My head swings around the room, but though some people do look sympathetic, no one speaks up or moves to help.

“Relax.” Drea cuts in again and moves to fold her arms leaning one shoulder against the wall “She isn’t going to die, it’ll just take longer to wear off for her than the rest of us, she’s only little.” her voice softens slightly on the last words and some of the tension in my shoulders immediately lessens.

“She isn’t your problem anyway.” A familiar Russian accent drifts across the room causing Drea and I to both turn to the male voice intruding on the conversation.

My mouth opens slightly in surprise to see Nikolas making his way through the crowd. All eyes are on us now but no one else makes a move to speak.

“Excuse me?” I say, sure I can’t have heard him right.

“She. Isn’t. Your. Problem.” He repeats slowly as if I’m just too dumb to understand. “She’s not going to last two minutes in here anyway, better for her to just not wake up I would think." He shrugs as if what he says is the only logical conclusion.

"What the hell is wrong with you?" Drea exclaims before I have the chance to. My head whips to her and I'm pleased to see even if she is a bitch, she isn't completely heartless, she seems just as outraged as I feel.

"Don't pretend like you aren't thinking the same thing." Nikolas starts walking towards her, slowly but menacing. Even though Drea is almost as tall as him, he is much thicker and more formidable. In a fight I have no doubt who would win.

"She's a child okay, and this trial is going to be cutthroat, there's no room here for sentimentality. Either she doesn't wake up now or she meets a gruesome end at the hands of one of us." He opens his arms and turns in a slow circle, making everyone culpable.

"It kind of sounds like you're saying to not let her wake up Nikolas?" I throw at him, hoping I'm wrong.

"That's exactly what I'm saying Sabine." He almost has the threat of a smile on his face, and I feel a wave of nausea hit me.

"You two know each other?" Drea cuts in.

“We had the pleasure but once.” Nikolas winks at her as suggestively as possible.

“Our Masters had a meeting the night before this disaster.” I flap both arms into the air exasperated. “And though I thought you were kind of a dick; I didn’t think you were a murderer?!” I scream at him as I stand. How could he possibly be considering this. She was a child, and she though she didn’t belong here, she certainly didn’t have to die here.

He turns to look at me and I suddenly go quiet. Feeling those ice blue eyes staring me down I can almost feel a hole burning into my skull. He takes a step forward and I instinctively shrink back. This makes him grin and he continues to advance in silence step by step like a predator until he is close enough that I feel his breath on my face. His hand reaches out and clamps me around the throat. I gasp and claw at his hand instinctively, but he doesn’t even flinch. He flexes his arms and lifts my neck and head slightly, enough to cause pressure, but not enough to completely cut off my breathing.

“Murderer? That’s rich, how many have you murdered little rabbit hmm?” He tilts his head to one side and tightens his hand a fraction, showing me how easily he could crush me if he wanted to.

“We are all here because we serve a vampire, we hunt,

and we kill and we deliver victims on a platter." He spits at me "And you're no better. So don't you dare stand there and judge me for wanting to put this girl out of her misery before it begins"

His hand suddenly retracts, and I fall to the floor, sprawling on my knees. I feel hands around my shoulders moments later and recognize Drea's voice in my ear asking if I'm okay. I can't respond to her; my throat feels so tight I don't know if I could talk if I wanted to.

"What the hell is wrong with you, you fucking lunatic!" Drea throws at him as I try to regain a modicum of composure.

"If you two bleeding hearts want to look after the child fine, but she's your responsibility."

As I watch Nikolas walk away, I remember everyone in the room was watching. Their faces now a mix of worry, fear, and disgust. They all however seem to realize one thing as they part like the red sea to allow Nikolas to pass. This man is ruthless and he's here to win.

*

I sit in the corner with the young girl's head on my lap, gently stroking her hair. As I watch the people around me assess each other, the feeling of being completely and utterly out of my depth crashes over me in waves. Drea is standing next to me, arms crossed, leaning against the wall watching everyone as well. I like to think she is standing to help protect me and the girl but that's probably my naivety talking.

One thing that strikes me is that no one here seems to know each other. They all watch with weary eyes, but no one speaks or introduces themselves and no groups form. I know we are all competing against each other, but I thought that people would have naturally gravitated towards each other, making partnerships. Perhaps it is too early for anyone to make that judgement, perhaps they want to see what we're made of first. I guess this first trial will be like our time as a familiar, an interview of sorts. No one wants to commit now, only to find out they have the weak link later.

Men and women are here in approximately equal amounts, I wonder if that is any reflection on their Masters. Though we aren't necessarily taken for romantic purposes all of the vampires I have met have been men, perhaps some here may have female vampires. The people here appear to have come from all over the world considering their attire, and all were taken without expecting it. While the minutes stretch ahead I make a game of guessing who people are and where they have come from. Musing to myself I wonder what story people would make up for me.

A woman as white as snow with hair to match looks around herself nervously, she is dressed in a series of grey and brown garments made of furs, with high soft boots to match. She must live somewhere with snow with her Master. Perhaps somewhere so remote she gets around using sleds and dogs like you see on TV. I'll call her Antarctica, God knows no one is lining up to actually introduce themselves. She must be absolutely sweating packed in here with all these bodies, but she makes no move to remove any of her layers and instead wraps her arms around her middle. Her head is bowed and she seems shy, though perhaps that is an act in itself.

Behind her is tall and athletic looking man with tanned skin and blonde hair, he's wearing board shorts and a graphic T with a rainbow-colored wave on it. Somewhere warm then, I think, maybe California. He seems approachable and maybe even kind looking as he glances at those around him, smiling every so often. Perhaps he hunts young women for his Master, he would certainly find it easy to pick them up. If I saw him in a bar, I wouldn't have targeted him. Most bad men, they give off a vibe, you can feel it from them that they have evil lurking underneath. This guy looks like a handsome version of shaggy from Scooby-doo.

California attracts some judgmental looks from a few of the other men who are mostly dressed in suits. Particularly a man dressed in a beautiful linen suit, pressed to perfection though the back is now crumpled from how he was dumped on the cell floor. He has light brown skin with black hair slicked back into a low bun and a perfectly groomed beard to match. He obviously thinks this man's attire is completely inappropriate from the way he looks him up and down. He has the initials AM on his suite pocket so that is what I name him.

I work my way through the room like this and can't help but think how I would fair against each one. I may be small, but I am fit, I'm used to carrying bodies and digging graves. On top of that I've always made it a priority to make sure I'm stronger than I look. I run almost every day and utilize Masters in house gym when he sleeps. I've never seen him use it though he looks as though he does. I always assumed it was for decoration, perhaps it was for me after all. I spent hours, deadlifting, squatting, boxing, anything I think I needed to be able to give myself the best chance. I never wanted to be caught in the situation where one of my victims spooked and overpowered me.

Still puny muscle aside I see now that whatever I was doing wasn't enough. Many of the people in here outmatch me by strides. There are a few who look nervous and unsure of themselves like me, but not enough to tip the odds in my favor. Skill is important, but it can only do so much against brute strength. If someone like Nikolas was head-to-head with me, I wouldn't have a chance.

Beneath me the young girl stirs slightly, and I look down to check if she's conscious. Her eyes are trying to flutter open, and I suspect she will be awake soon, there's no clock in here but everyone else has been awake for what feels like at least an hour. I sense Drea move into position behind me to observe what happens next as the girls' eyelids finally flutter and stay open.

Abstract terror. There are no other words for it, her tiny eyes are brimming with fear the moment they open. I'm not even convinced she actually sees me, but instead she looks through me, reliving some previous trauma. I know I should try to console her, give her some comforting words. But in the moment, I'm so shocked by the frozen look on her face, that I too freeze.

"Where am I? Who are you?!" Her tiny voice is so high pitched it comes out as a squeal. She scrambles away from my lap, scooting straight back into Drea.

As her back hits another person she yelps and swings around realizing she's cornered.

"It's okay." I say, palms raised towards her "My name is Sabine, you're at the trials?" I say the last part as a question as I'm still convinced this girl isn't supposed to be here. It must be some switch up where she was grabbed by mistake. Yes, our Masters are vampires but they aren't cruel, especially not unnecessarily, they can't have kidnapped and plan to change a child intentionally. Though one thing vampires certainly are, is secretive, and now that this little girl is here, now that she has seen this, I don't know that they will let her go.

Her frantic eyes take me in, so wide they might just fall straight out of her head.

"No, no, no, NO!" She scrambles to her feet and runs through the crowd of people to the bars, grabbing them as if she could bend them with sheer willpower. Her fingers barely wrap all the way around them.

"I said I didn't want to." She shrieks "I said I didn't want to do this; you can't make me!!"

The last words escape as a wail as she slides to the floor, hands still gripping the bars. She begins to sob uncontrollably, and my feet start moving before I realize it, rushing to her. A scoff sounds to my left and I swear its Nikolas, though I don't give him the satisfaction of looking at him to confirm my suspicions.

"I told you to put her out of her misery. "That Russian accent drawls, arrogant bastard, that is definitely him.

"If you don't shut up, I'll put *you* out of *your* misery!" I spit back at him. My sight meets him for just a moment as I fling my head in his direction. Amusement and shock are spread across his face, clearly, he wasn't expecting me to bite back.

Verbal sparring with him can wait though, right now my priority is the little girl who is collapsed in a distraught pile on the floor. I drop to my knees in front of the mousey girl who looks even smaller now she is falling apart.

"I'm sorry this happened to you … can you tell me your name?" I reach a hand to place on her shoulder, but she jerks away from my touch. I try not to take it too personally.

"Alice." She manages.

"Do you know how you got here Alice?"

"My mom, she worked for a bad man, he said he wanted to take her away to marry her." To become a bride, I think to myself. "But she didn't want to marry him I guess because she said he could marry me instead, but only if I got through his trials first."

Her eyes fall away from mine as she makes this admission, and I swallow the bile rising in the back of my throat. This girl's mother sold her out to save her own ass. How could anyone do this? And why did the Master of that woman take her daughter, I thought the prescreening process of working as a familiar was an essential part of being allowed to take part in the trials. Surely this undermines the whole process if a vampire is willing to change someone they have never met, as a trade.

Whoever this vampire is, he's a monster. Well, more of a monster than the rest of them anyway.

My head swings around looking for someone else to tag in on this conversation. I don't know who I am looking for but I'm completely out of my depth and I'm not so sure I have the words to comfort her in this moment. Thankfully yet surprisingly the first person's eyes I meet are Drea's who has moved to stand directly behind me. The look on her face is a picture-perfect reflection of how I feel.

Unfortunately, her mouth seems as empty of words as mine. I swallow and move to hold Alice's face in my hands.

"It's okay Alice, I'll look after you okay." I mean it, I have no idea why but I do. Whatever comes next, I'm not going to let this little girl get hurt.

"This isn't right, a child shouldn't be here, how old are you girl?" This time the voice comes from the man in the linen suit. He speaks with a distinct Indian accent.

"I'll be eleven next month." She doesn't look at him as she speaks but keeps her head to the floor. She isn't even eleven, bile rises in my throat, she is even younger than I thought.

"Ten years old." The man shakes his head "This is wrong for so many reasons; we must speak to someone."

"Who?" I ask him, and I mean it genuinely. Who the hell as we supposed to speak to in here. We have been dumped and locked in a group cell, no cameras, no communication, nada. I'm all for getting Alice out of here if he thinks its possible, but I don't see how we're going to accomplish that from here.

"My Master, as I am sure many of yours, would not allow this. I am sure they are discussing it already. We will broach to topic next time they interact with us." He nods the matter settled. He seems much happier than I feel. Speaking to them when they come to see us doesn't fill me with a whole lot of confidence. Perhaps he is right and the vampire responsible is being scolded as we speak, perhaps not.

"Yeah, I really don't think they give a shit." Nikolas. Again. His voice is becoming more and more grating every time I hear him speak.

"You know we don't always need to hear your opinion on everything." I don't even give him the satisfaction of looking his way as I throw the comment out.

"Sabine, most of our Masters eat people for a living. I'm pretty sure most of them have eaten children at some point. We are livestock to them; they don't care if a child is in here and they won't care when she gets decimated."

Alice flinches at his words and a fury rises in me. I stand and swing round to face him. I have to tilt my head back to meet his eyes, but I do my best to square my shoulders and seem intimidating.

"Well, she isn't going to get *decimated* because we are not our Masters and no one in here is going to hurt a child." My voice doesn't waver though inside I am terrified. If I'm being honest I shouldn't speak for everyone in here, I'm hoping that no one in here would hurt her but that's all it is. Hope.

"She has fire this tiny one." I hear laughing from

behind me as the man in the linen suit approaches. Before I can take offense at the condescending nature of that comment, he extends a hand to me.

"My name is Aashutosh; you can call me Ash." The smile on his face is genuine, and kind. My hand slides into his and he shakes it gently.

"Sabine." I reply with a returning smile. A smile that quickly fades as Nikolas opens his self-important mouth again.

"This isn't me being a dick Sabine, its reality. When we get into whatever the first trial will be it'll be every man for themselves. It won't have to be one of us who puts her down. She will fail and she could die. Its cruel to lie to her." His eyes almost look sad and part of me feels like he is fighting the urge to look towards the little girl whose death he talks of so callously. I don't dare to look at Alice to see how his words affected her, I can only imagine the terror she must be feeling, deepening inside her with every moment.

"It won't get to that, even if she fails, she can be extracted, I'm sure." Ash insists, I'm thankful that I am not the only one having to stand up for her here. "The Masters will pull her out of the trial I suspect before it comes to that regardless. They are not cruel"

Nikolas laughs his disagreement then turns away.

Conversation over, I guess. Ash relays the words I have already thought, they are not cruel. He seems to put more faith in them than I do but I guess none of that matters. As long as we have radio silence there is no point debating what the vampires will or will not do.

"Don't worry, you're right, ignore that prick." Drea put her hand on my shoulder and tilts her head towards Nikolas. Her words are what I should be focusing on but instead I am excruciatingly aware of the place where our skin touches, her gentle hand on my bare shoulder.

"Indeed, don't be afraid child, I am sure this is a misunderstanding. All will be well." Ash breaks me from my trance as his voice floats towards Alice offering words of consolation.

He smiles at her in such a kind way that Alice cannot help but smile back. I feel so reassured by him that I convince myself to agree. Any minute now I will see my Master, he will come with the others, equally disgusted. They will take the little girl and drop her somewhere safe. It isn't like they need to worry about her keeping secrets. Who would believe a ten-year-old anyway?

My thoughts are interrupted by a sudden series of dings coming through a speaker system I can't locate.

Attention candidates. The first trial will begin in 5 minutes. There are currently ***twenty*** *candidates within the holding cell.*

Momentarily you will be released into an enclosure containing a variety of weapons, traps and most importantly ten red flags. Claim a red flag and make it back to base by the end of the trial and you will be successful. Fail to gain a flag and you will be terminated.

Thank you.

Terminated.

It's the only word I hear, the only word I can think. Over and over again. Terminated.

I don't know what I thought would happen. I knew there would be eliminations, but Master never told me any information about the trials. Terminated to me means only one thing, though I hope to God I'm wrong. Death.

Everyone around me must have also come to the same conclusion as for the first time since we arrived the cell is filled with noise. Everyone talking over each other, questioning.

"What do they mean terminated?"

"Five minutes? Are they joking?"

"Are we not even going to be fitted with gear? I'm in shorts and slides for god's sake!"

I barely hear them all as they clammer over each other. The sound of my heart beating is all I can hear until one voice splits in particular through the crowd.

"You'll keep me safe though, won't you?"

Alice's eyes stare up at me with trepidation and she grasps onto the velvet folds of the bottom of my dress. Such trust in her eyes, barely masking the pleading and desperation that resides there too. This poor little girl who was abandoned by her own mother, now completely reliant on a complete stranger.

She is right, I did promise. A promise I have every intention of keeping The decision is made in a moment because it was never really a question she needed to ask me, I'll help this little girl as much as I can. Immortality may be my end game here, but I will not lose my soul to get it. I will get two flags, one for Alice first, then one for me.

"Of course," I grasp her little hand in both of mine and meet her eyes with steely determination. "You stick with me; I will get us both out of this okay." I nod and Alice parrots the motion, as if the little act creates a pact between us. A small smile tugs at her lips as she releases a slow breath. Though she hoped I wouldn't, I truly think part of her thought I might leave her just like her mother.

"You sure about this princess?" Drea's voice is questioning and lowered but I'm sure Alice can still hear her. "No one is going to hurt her, but taking her along for the ride? I mean honestly, can you even look after yourself?" She looks me up and down appraising me. No disrespect in her voice, just a genuine question. She doesn't think I can do this, and she thinks I'm adding a ball and chain to an already slow start with Alice.

"I'll be fine." The disappointment rings clear in my voice. I didn't think we would necessarily be forming any teams, but I thought from what Drea had said that she would have felt the same way about getting the little girl out of here as I did. I guess not wanting to hurt her, and not wanting to let her reduce your chances of winning are two different considerations.

Before she has a chance to continue the conversation I lean down and remove my heels. I grab the stiletto under one and pull until it snaps off, I repeat the process with the right heel then place them both back on. I stand somewhat unsteady on the new makeshift flats but it's better than trying to run in heels.

"Go get em." Is all she offers in reply without meeting

my eye and moves away, shuffling to the back of the group. Why would she want to stick close to the two dead weights I guess?

“It’ll be okay.” I reassure Alice “You need to stick next to me at all times okay, if I tell you to run, run. If I tell you to hide, hide. I’m going to get us both a flag.” No one else might have faith in me in here, but I need Alice to. I don’t want her terrified going into this, she needs to be somewhat levelheaded if we’re going to make this work.

Unfortunately, I sound about as confident as I feel as I again survey the room. There’s no comradery here. Everyone knows that only half of us are making it out of this and I don’t think anyone will hesitate to eliminate the competition. I think about Nikolas and his low hopes for Alice’s survival and part of me can’t help but acknowledge now that he is right. As if he senses my thoughts, I turn my head and see him looking directly at me. I may be wrong but there does seem to be concern in his eyes. He shakes his head briefly then looks away. He won’t be offering any help.

All I can hope is that we seem so unlikely to succeed that no one will bother wasting their time on us. Why chase us down when there are bigger fish to fry? Well, I would show them all by the end. Years of running made me fast and agile. My strength training might not be enough to save me if it came to hand-to-hand combat with one of these big guys, but it would certainly help me climb trees. I had my own set of skills that would get us out of this, and no one was going to get in the way of that.

CHAPTER FIVE

Five minutes may not sound like a long time. It's enough time to run half a mile or make an omelet. Five more minutes in bed certainly never feels like enough. If you were asked to comment on the usability of five minutes you would consider it an insufficient amount of time to complete any real important task.

Yet the five minutes we wait for the trial to begin are the longest minutes of my life. They stretch out in front of us in abhorrent silence. Tension building in the room until I feel it will have no choice but to break out in madness or violence. My hands begin to tremble, and my breath quicken, adrenaline working overtime to prepare me for what is to come. We are like racehorses kept in the gate and I am terrified at the thought of the inevitable stampede that will likely result.

People rearrange themselves within the cell and take what they feel is the most beneficial position. There seems to be no rhyme or reason though. Some move to the back, some push forward to the front. I don't know where strategically it is best for us to be, so I stay put at the door to the cell. We will be the first ones out, whether that is a mistake or not, well I won't know until it happens. And if it is, it will be too late to worry about the consequences.

Just when I think we can't possibly take any more of this torture the lights suddenly switch off creating a unanimous gasp. Almost instantaneously the floor becomes illuminated with blood red arrows running along the floor outside of the cells, the glow in the dark paint heightening my already ever-present fear. Follow the red blood road I suppose, looks like we need to go right once the door opens. With the change people immediately start edging forward. Where before I had space and room to move, I now feel the breath of others down my back. The people seem to be moving in slow but steady waves forward and I look down to the small girl who is about to be lost in this crowd.

"Get on my back." I whisper down to Alice. She looks up at me with momentary confusion, but when she sees people closing in on us, understanding dawns on her tiny face.

I'm short but luckily, she's young and tiny and I manage to maneuver her quite easily onto my back and secure my arms underneath each of her legs. She wraps her arms tightly around my neck and I have to remind her to let me breath. Running for our lives isn't going to be very easy with a tiny vice clamping my airway shut.

With a creak of metal on metal the door begins to slowly open I feel the push of twenty bodies in panic and it is all I can do to steady to my own heart. Luckily because I'm first I can slide out of the door before it is fully open, even with Alice wrapped around me. As soon as the first opportunity presents itself I pull her legs in tight and force myself through the new gap.

Sliding out and finding freedom in the hallway, it takes me a moment to gather myself for what needs to happen next. Before I get a chance to start my legs again I hear an uproar behind me followed by a bellowing.

"What are you doing?!"

Turning to face the door I can't believe my eyes as I see Nikolas, arms grasping the bars at either side blocking the exit for those behind him. The muscles in his arms ripple as they fight to keep a hold of exit whilst he is pushed from behind.

"Go" He screams at me, his eyes meeting mine over his shoulder "I'll give you twenty seconds at best."

This must be a trick, I think. The man who was so

willing to kill this child but an hour ago is now … Giving me a head start? Though he did say he purely wanted to save her suffering, could that be true? Did this apparent tough guy actually genuinely care about what is going to happen to this child. It really is the only explanation from what I can see, why else would he allow us to get out in front of them all. Including him.

Figuring out his motives can wait however, though I might not trust he is being solely selfless I won't waste the opportunity he is giving me. I don't need to be told twice and I swivel in the direction of the arrows taking off as fast as I can. It is more difficult than I thought running with Alice on my back, she bounces up and down, sliding with the movement. Though I am usually fast, I must never have realized how much I rely on my arms to steady myself. Now that they are pinned under the little girls legs I struggle to keep my balance. The makeshift shoes not helping the situation.

Still, I run faster than I should have been able. Fueled by pure adrenaline and fear. Before I know it, I'm at the end of the corridor, marked by a small rectangle of natural light. The thought of an exit has me speeding up and I feel my thighs groaning at me in protest. But the hard work pays off as I break through. Taking a moment to let my eyes adjust to the blinding light, I look around to assess the next move. I only allow myself a moment, I can't squander the head start I have been afforded. As I slowly glance around, I see a small grass clearing, surrounded by trees. There are no weapons here that I can see, and more importantly no flags.

Of course, there wouldn't be flags so close to the beginning, it wouldn't be much of a trial if you could immediately win. I take off again and dash for the entrance to the trees. Once we are safely inside, I slide Alice off my back and immediately feel one hundred pounds lighter.

"We'll be better off with you on your feet sweetheart I'm sorry." My words come out in shallow pants; I didn't realize how out of breath I was until I try to catch it again.

She merely nods and sets herself, ready to run. Perhaps being bounced around like a backpack isn't exactly fun for her either. But the main purpose I asked her to hop on is already accomplished, we didn't lose her in a stampede. I grasp her hand in mine and take off again deeper into the forest. Setting the pace at a light jog, Alice keeps up surprisingly well. I notice for the first time she is wearing little pink and white sneakers. More appropriate footwear than me at least.

As we plow forward, I have no idea what direction I am moving in or why all I know is that it's imperative we put as much distance between us, and anyone who might be on our tail. If this was just about surviving, I would scale a tree and hide until it was over. But we must find two flags so onwards we go. Alice is nimble and fast, and she doesn't slow us down. About twenty feet into the tree line, I hear the pounding of feet and some words being exchanged. That's our head start gone. If we all make it out of this alive Nikolas is getting one hell of a thanks for saving our lives. We need to make it out first though.

I keep moving forward trying to frantically come up with a plan but I'm too frightened, for Alice and for myself. As I start to wonder how long it would take for people to catch up to us, I catch sight of the beginnings of a wall slotting through the trees. It's a rocky surface that likely makes up the side of a small mountain or hill. I try to look up through the trees but the green canopy is too thick to see how face the rock face spreads up and beams of angel rays breaking through the foliage blur my vision. At least it's something more substantial to follow, if we have a wall to one side of us, its one less sided we are exposed on. I pull Alice close to the edge and keep moving, one hand running alongside the rockface.

My instincts must be working today because we soon

come to a large crack in the rock face, this I can use. I stop in front of it assessing the thickness. We can certainly slide through, even if I have to turn sideways. From here I can't see how deep it runs but I think it goes quite deep as it seems to fade into blackness rather than have a rocky end. As if it's a sign from God I hear the sound of footsteps approaching through the woods. The sounds of heavy breathing and snapping branches. There's definitely more than one, and they're moving fast.

I guess that's the decision made for me, if we don't move into this now, we're done for. Deciding against trying to explain my plan I just opt to shove Alice into the crack, she yelps slightly, and I smack my hand over her mouth. I can only hope it wasn't loud enough for anyone close to hear.

"Move Alice, as far in as you can physically push, we need to hide." I hiss as quiet as I can manage.

"It's so dark." She whimpers against my hand but after a moment I feel her feet shuffling and she slides out of my arms and further into the crack.

"I know Alice, you're being so brave." My voice wobbles as I say the words and I have to scold myself. I don't want her to know I'm pretty scared too. Hopefully, we don't get descended on by crawling, burrowing bugs.

My feet shuffle side by side for what feels like eternity in pace with Alice, I always keep one hand on her, making sure I don't lose her. The walls press in closer and closer as we proceed, and it begins to feel a little harder to breath. Where before I could just about slide without touching either wall, now my back is pressed flat against rock on one side and my nose almost touches the other. I won't be able to push much further if this closes in more. A few more steps and I'm scraping myself against the walls, fighting against the friction to let me just a little further. Silently I pray that I'm not going to get wedged in here.

I try to focus on my breaths, I tell myself to breath in through my nose and out through my mouth but that gets harder as the rock presses on my face, and I have to turn my head to the side to be able to continue breathing. My good intentions fall apart, and my breaths quicken exponentially. I start to wonder how Alice would ever get out if I wedged myself in here. Would I be the stone sealing her into this tomb.

I can feel my heartbeat in places I should not be able to, my ears, my tongue. Is this what pure terror feels like? I don't think I can say I have ever truly felt it until this moment. Even on the few occasions Master has been furious with me, I still can't say I have ever felt as though death is imminent like I do now. Just as I'm about to completely lose my mind Alice tugs my hand forcefully.

“It gets bigger! Sabine, it opens out!” Her words echo around me ominously, like they aren’t really coming from the voice of a little girl, but the ghost of one.

I don’t believe or even truly register her words until I start to feel the world open out. All of a sudden, the oppression around me lifts and I can’t help but fall to my knees gasping for breath on the floor of the cave opening we have squeezed our way into.

“Are you okay?” Alice strokes my back in soothing motions as I attempt to get my body back under control. It takes longer than I would like to admit but I finally manage to slow my breathing, I realize that my vision is not blurred like I thought but instead struggling in the almost completely black cave.

“I’m okay, sorry Alice” I struggle to my feet and try what I can to assess my surroundings. Embarrassment flushes over me, I should have been the one comforting her, not the other way round. I honestly would have thought myself brave before today, I mean I lured predators back home for a vampire! But I guess I’ve never been in a situation like this before and my body just didn’t know how to handle it. One thing is for sure, I can cross caving off my bucket list. I will not be doing this again. Ever.

My eyes slowly adjust as I look around our space and I start to get a sense of the size of the cavern we are in. It's around the size of a family room, there doesn't seem to be any other way in or out, but the floor is wet which means water must be coming from somewhere. A few seconds later as if on cue, a drop falls from the ceiling and makes a small splash in front of me. Following the line upwards I see more water pooling ready to drop from the ceiling.

"Hey look what I found!" I turn to see the outline of Alice next to the hall we used to enter. In her left hand she holds something, a piece of fabric. In this light I can't make out its color, but I don't have to. The excitement in her voice tells me everything I need to know.

"Alice … is that?" I don't want to get my hopes up, what are the chances that we found one already?

"A flag!" she waves it above her head, it's around the size of a tea towel and does have a dull red tinge to it that is barely discernable in this light. "It was hooked on the side here!" This girl is my good luck magnet. Unbelievable.

"Okay good. This is good, that's one flag down." Alice's flag. She is good now, so as long as I can find one too and we make it back, then we are home free.

Considering the next move, I get a sudden and sickening thought, can others kill her and take the flag? The announcement said there were ten flags, and you had to make it back with the flag to continue, that means if someone were to intercept us on the way back ... No. I couldn't think like that. Getting the flag is the hard part, I'm not going to let anyone take Alice's flag or mine. They will have to pry it from my cold dead hands.

I gulp. I guess prying it from my dead hands is kind of the point.

Moving forward I reach out my hands and take in the crack we fit through. There's no way anyone else other than us could fit inside that. Alice is tiny and I'm the next smallest person by far. If I almost got stuck, then no one else would get in here to reach her. And that was if we were unlucky enough for someone to decide to come looking! An immediate decision forms in my mind.

"Alice, I need you to hold onto that really tight and stay here okay."

I kneel to look her in the eye and see she is immediately panicked at the thought of me leaving her. I don't like it either, but it just makes sense. If someone out there is looking to pick a fight I really don't want Alice there to worry about. Once I have my own flag I can come back for her, but right now … she is safer here.

“Don’t worry you’ll be fine no one else is fitting through that hole okay, you’ll be safe”

“You can have this flag!” She waves it at me “Then we’ll go together and find another one for me.” This girl. How could her mother have done this to her, she is such an angel. Her eyes are filled with pride as she tries to stuff the flag into my hands.

I smile at her.

“That’s really kind Alice, but I promised you I would look after you and keep you safe and that’s what I’m going to do.” Pushing the flag back towards her I place my palm flat against her face and close my eyes.

“I’ll be back, don’t move, don’t make a sound okay.” There is no reason for someone to look for her here, she is going to be fine. I repeat the words to myself in my head, hoping that they will ring true if I think them enough.

She nods against my hand and without looking at her I stand and move back through the crack. It isn’t nearly as worrying this time that I know I’m not going to be crushed to death but it still makes me super uncomfortable as I force my way through the smallest section.

Stopping a few steps away from the entrance I tilt my head and listen to the wood that's now within view. I don't want to run straight out into the wrong end of someone's knife, they did say that there are supposed to be weapons hidden around, I wonder what kind and how many have been found. If I had thought I should have looked around the cavern more thoroughly, if there was a flag there may have been something else. Too late now, and I can't waste time going back. There are only nine flags left and I have to make sure one of those are mine.

Slowly emerging, careful not to make too much noise, I peep my head out first doing a sweep with my eyes. The coast is clear. I creep forwards trying to make as little noise as possible which isn't easy as I thought in broken heels on forest floor.

Each step causes more rustling and snapping of leaves and twigs, and I cringe with each noise. It shouldn't be possible for one person to make so much noise, even if they were trying! I'm going to have to move quicker than this if I want to stand any chance. If we have already found one flag with our complete ineptitude, I'm lots of others are already snagged.

Heading further into the trees I notice for the first time it seems slightly darker than it was when we entered the cave. We were only in there a handful of minutes so we must be pretty close to dusk for such a quick and noticeable change in the natural light. I look back and consider for the first time how on earth I'm going to find my way back here, especially in the dark. Heading in a straight line is going to be my best and only bet. Unless there is a compass somewhere along with those weapons, I can't wander too far and hope to find the way back. Worrying about that now isn't going to help me anyway, moving forward is my top priority or this game will be over without me. I continue on slowly for what feels like a lifetime but is likely only a matter of minutes. Stealing glances upwards through the green ceiling of tree cover I try to keep track of the time based on the waning natural light.

I suddenly falter as my foot hits something soft. A yelp escapes my mouth before I can stop myself and I immediately panic. Throwing my hands over my mouth to quiet the noise that escaped me, I close my eyes and wait. My ears on full alert, listening for any movement or noise that would suggest someone heard me. Gentle rustling is the only answer in line with the wind swaying through the trees.

My breaths finally slow and I scald myself for being so soft. My nerves are on edge yes, but I have to pull it together. If someone had heard that I could have given myself away. Finally, I allow my hands to slide from my mouth and my eyes to reopen. Recovering nicely, I look down to see what it is I just walked into. Unfortunately, the sight leaves me feeling sick to my stomach. The obstacle isn't a rotting tree stump or sleeping animal. No, a dead man lies on the floor in front of me. I vaguely recognize him from the cell, but I don't recall ever hearing him speak. He looks tall and muscular which surprises me considering the state he is in now.

His left arm is mostly detached from his body, blood, and raw sinew on show. It looks like some parts of muscle have tried to stay attached and I think if I tried to pick the arm up, I would find it still clings loosely to the owner. Whatever tried to remove it was sharp because the edges of flesh along the shoulder line and top of the arm are cleanly cut, just not all the way through. I can't tell if there is bone or not, the area is drenched in so much blood. I'm assuming, he was still alive when someone attempted amputation.

Unfortunately, the arm isn't the only wound. His face has also been split in two. Like his arm, blood and brain tissue covers the area and makes distinguishing features impossible. Everything is red and grey and despicable. I wouldn't know what color his hair was. The right side of his face has caved in completely from the pressure of whatever was used on it, but the left side is unnervingly intact. I can still see on open brown eye, still filled with abstract horror. His tongue lolls out of the side of his half-removed mouth, still open. Whatever last words or cries for help he had forever silenced.

I gag and place my hands over my face to spare myself the sight any longer. I've seen my fair share of dead bodies. I've lured them to their death, buried them, but this! This was different, this was beyond reproach. I always left a muted man for Master, and he always drained them quickly and cleanly. When I collected bodies to bury it was almost peaceful. They would look mainly untouched if not extremely pale. But never did I even see any blood. To see this man, so brutally pulled apart. To see his organs spilling from the side of his face. I simply can't bare it.

I turn on my heels not even know which direction I am heading, but I don't care. Wherever I'm going, it is away from here.

I don't even realize how full the air was with the scent of blood until I am clear of it. The fresh air clears my senses and my mind, and I begin to calm down. Someone must have done that to him. One of the other familiars in that cell destroyed that man in the most brutal way I could imagine. I momentarily chastise myself for not checking to see if there was a flag, he had been harboring but then I remind myself that is likely what his attacker was after and certainly wouldn't have left it behind. If nothing else, I now know that leaving Alice safely in that cave was the right thing to do. Though I'm starting to wish I had just stayed with her.

My pace must naturally slow and lighten as my body relaxes and my brain attempts shakes itself of the images that will likely forever be ingrained. I have never thought of myself as weak; I can murder if needs be, but I don't murder innocent people. No one in that room knew each other enough to justify an act of violence like that, even if someone was evil, that death was unnecessarily cruel. When I joined these trials, I may not have known fully what I was signing up for, that much is clear. But what I do know is that I never signed up for a slaughter of innocent people. What is the point in testing the limits of your familiars just to wind up with them all dead?

My footsteps become lighter again as I creep forwards through the forest, the daylight now seems to be waning by the minute, it will be dark soon. With a gut sinking feeling I realize I deviated from the straight-line plan. My shock had me running away in any direction I could from the horror show I just witnessed and now, I have no idea where I am. I swallow deeply and shake my head, a problem for later. The darkness is creeping in by the minute and I don't know how long this trial has left, I need to focus.

As I move, I hear a struggle nearby. There are no

words being spoken but there is definitely a large disturbance of leaves and the muted grunt of a man struggling. I don't know what possess me, but I move towards the noise swiftly and quietly as I can. I wonder to myself if I will see some maniac with an axe covered in blood, the culprit who created the last scene taking his next victim.

Imagine my surprise when I move behind a pine and spot two men in a small clearing ahead. One of which being Nikolas. He has removed his suit jacket and tie at some point as well as rolling up his sleeves. He stands now with his arms wrapped around the surfer looking guy, California. He has him grasped from behind one hand over his mouth and is struggling to keep a hold of him.

California thrashes wildly, attempting to shout and scream but falling short beneath Nikolas huge paw which holds in his breath. I consider stepping in, but don't need to. Nikolas manages to move his hands into position on either side of California's head and with one swift motion, snaps his neck.

I can't believe my eyes as the now dead man drops to the floor like a sack of old potatoes. Nikolas tilts his head to the side and cracks his own neck, the noise makes me feel ill. I chastise myself for being so weak around all of this. I never thought death would make me so nauseous, but I've never seen such cruelty. This man did nothing to Nikolas, he didn't even know him. As far as I can see from here, he is unarmed and doesn't even seem to have a flag. Was this just a case of taking out the competition? I refuse to believe the man who would risk himself to give a woman he barely knows and a child a head start, would also go out of his way to murder a blameless participant.

I dare not move as Nikolas wipes his large hands down his suite pants, there's no blood on them so I'm not sure what he's trying to clean off. Maybe saliva from having them clamped over California's mouth as he screamed. I swallow back bile as I think again of how quickly his life was snuffed out.

His murderer however seems completely unbothered as he turns and heads back through the trees in the opposite direction to me. I wonder if I was in that clearing if he would have snapped my neck. That man is a walking contradiction, and I think I best stay as far away from him as possible. His help is not worth it if his rath looks like this.

I take a step back to head away from Nikolas when I walk straight into someone else. A hand clamps over my mouth before I get a chance to scream, and I immediately begin clawing at it. Another hand slides around my waist and pulls me close to them.

"Ouch, okay princess relax."

The hand drops from my mouth but the hand around my waist remains firmly in place.

"Drea." I breathe a sigh of relief.

"Don't sound so relieved you don't know if I'm friend or foe yet." She leans he head down slightly so that she whispers directly into my ear. I feel tingles spreading down my spine in response.

"Well, I know you don't consider me a friend, but I don't think you'll snap my neck." Though she didn't step forward to help us when the trial started I had a gut feeling that this woman wouldn't actively hurt me or Alice either. She did back me when Nikolas suggested putting Alice down like an old dog and that speaks more to her character than anything else. With my life completely in her hands, all I could do is hope I was right.

Drea runs her nose up the side of my face and I feel her move even closer, our bodies pressed tighter than I have ever felt with anyone else. My body completely freezes in response, not the faintest idea of how it should react.

"Nah I think you're far too fun to off yet. I've got loads of plans for you princess."

I feel the heat pool in my stomach at her words and suddenly I forget where I am or what we're doing. All

I can think about is all of Drea's curves pressed against my back and her mouth against my ear. My breath hitches and she must hear as she suddenly laughs and slides away from me. I'm left suddenly cold where I wasn't before, and I hope my face doesn't betray me too much as I feel the blood rise in my cheeks.

"You are very easy to please you know, do you not get hit on by many girls?" She smirks, clearly very pleased with herself. Which means she can tell exactly how, distracted, she makes me feel.

"I get hit on plenty; I just never follow it up." I huff, attempting and failing to hide my embarrassment.

"So, no girlfriends? Boyfriends?" She raises an eyebrow. Her hair is now pulled back from her face in a pony making her features look even sharper and dangerous.

"None of those either, I don't know what you do for your Master, but I've been a little busy. I can't exactly bring someone home unless I want them to get eaten."

I decide the best way to end this conversation, which is completely unproductive, is to march past her and not look back. She cackles at the comment though in a way that makes me feel like I missed the joke.

"How old are you, like mid-twenties surely? Please do

not tell me you've never had a dalliance." Her voice as well as her feet follow me easily as I stomp away from her. Hopefully no one else is nearby because the whole being stealthy thing has gone out the window.

"I have not had any *dalliances*, and I am twenty-five." I continue marching. Alice might be safe, but I would quite like to not die because I was too distracted by a woman to find a flag. Even if my brain keeps returning to the thought of her arms around my waist. At least it isn't giving me images of the dead guy still I suppose.

"Well, take it from someone who has had many dalliances, you should try it sometime." Her voice carries a level of suggestiveness that I can't ignore no matter how hard I try.

"Can you stop distracting me I have a flag to find." I look around at the trees as if they will give me some clue as to where I'm supposed to be going.

"Distracting you? I thought I was seducing you." I can almost feel her eyebrows wiggling at me as she talks.

I swing around, my mouth hanging open to meet her eyes. They glisten with a sinful glee, and I can't decide whether she is genuinely flirting with me or if she is just getting enjoyment out of getting me flustered.

"Okay that's enough, you are not seducing me because we are both about to die so if you could focus or leave me alone that would be great." I genuinely mean it, even if I wanted her to flirt with me, now is not the time. She can pick this up if we both make it to the end of tonight. I cross my arms across my chest and try and show a front of confidence to back up my words. I finish quite pleased with myself until she pulls a red flag out of the back pocket of her tight black leather pants.

"You might be about to die, I'm not." As quickly as she removed it the flag is back in her pocket, not even a hint of red visible. She might be a pain in my ass but she isn't stupid, she doesn't want anyone else seeing that flag. I try not to think about the fact that she showed me it so easily probably means she sees me as literally zero threat.

"Oh well you've got plenty of time for flirting then go find someone else whose already got a flag!" I throw my hands up in the air exacerbated. I was quite confident she wasn't going to kill me anyway but now I know she has a flag I'm certain she has nothing to gain from snapping my neck like Nikolas did to California.

"What about pipsqueak?" Drea's tone suddenly shifts, and she almost sounds serious.

“Excuse me?”

“The kid, where’s the kid? Did you just dump her as soon as you got out here?”

“Of course not!” I’m offended she would even ask, and the look in her eyes shows me she is genuinely concerned about her fate.

“She’s safe okay, we got her a flag. She hunkered down until this is over. No sense dragging her around she would be easy pickings.” I don’t tell her where she is, I might not think Drea is a threat, but I still don’t fully trust her.

“She would be easy pickings? Unlike you?” Drea laughs. Its musical and I hate how it makes me annoyed and excited at the same time.

“Yes, I’m stronger than I look you know. I do a lot of weights.” Its true, I might not be skilled in fighting, but I could deadlift almost twice my body weight if I wanted to.

“You didn’t feel very strong when I had you from behind.” She wiggles her eyebrows at me, smirk playing at her lips.

“Maybe I didn’t want to get out of that particular situation.” I throw back, giving her a bit of her own medicine. I try to add the same teasing tone she has to my voice, but I can tell it doesn't quite ring the same.

She laughs, a gentle amused laugh. Not the reaction I was expecting. I feel strangely deflated though I'm not sure why.

"There you go, princess has got some spice after all. Come on I'll help you get a flag." Drea walks straight past me and doesn't look back. My feet stop momentarily as I see her swish away, her hair cascading behind her in an untamed waterfall.

"Why would you help me?" I ask, my feet wanting to follow but my head not allowing it.

"Because I think you and me are gunna have a lot of fun princess."

She pauses, then stops in her tracks, turning to me and giving me a serious look for a change.

"And because you were the only one who stepped up to look after that little girl. So, I think, though you're pathetic, you seem like a pretty good person. And I like to try and be one too where I can." Her voice rings true and I know that at least those final words were from the heart. She has her flag; she could go back right now and win this. But she isn't, she's going to stay and help me go back with her. This woman sure is something.

"Because the rest of that was really nice, I'm going to ignore the fact that you just called me pathetic." I walk on and straight past her, knowing she will follow. As quickly as it appeared the sincerity in her eyes disappears. Replaced with her usual sinful sparkle.

"Come on then I think I know where there's one left." she says as she easily overtakes me.

I have to do a strange sort of speed walk/run to keep up with her long, graceful legs. We walk until the daylight is completely gone and I struggle to see my hand in front of me. I hope Alice isn't too afraid in the cave. I hope she knows I'll be coming back for her.

I'm close to losing all hope when I hear the trickle of water nearby. We pass through a few more trees and come to a small stream visible only by the flecks of moonlight that have broken through the canopy and are reflected in its water. I look around to try and see why this was our destination but even if there was a giant red flag waving from the trees, I doubt I would spot it unless it was in front of my face.

"Up there." Drea points to a large tree on the other side of the stream. I can't tell how tall it is from here. As the trees rise, they all meld into one to create an ominous shadow.

"Up there what? Up the tree?" I ask.

"There's a flag up that big tree, I saw it earlier in the day light, but I already had mine. I don't know if it's still there now, but we won't know until you go up."

"You're joking right?" I look at her and then look down at myself. "I'm not exactly in tree climbing attire." I am completely capable of climbing a tree I know that much, but in this dress, with no real shoes. Its going to be a challenge.

"You can bring a horse to water." Drea mumbles under her breath and rolls her eyes. "You're really earning that nickname now aren't you princess. I'm not climbing up for you you'll have to get it yourself."

I look to the tree again and my resolve settles. I'm not going to die out here. There may or may not be a flag up that tree but it's my best option. I'm not going to down without a fight. I manage to hop over the stream not getting my feet wet. This elicits another chuckle from Drea in response to which I throw her a profanity. This accomplishes nothing by making her laugh harder. As I approach the base of the giant elm tree, I consider that I may have over egged my abilities in my mind. But surely I would be okay, how hard can it be?

I look for somewhere to get a hold onto, but the branches don't start until around a foot above my reach, and I'm immediately stumped. My options are limited by I need a rock I could move or another smaller tree I could climb and then jump from perhaps. Any plan I have likely is well past my actual abilities. Suddenly I feel arms around my thighs and I'm in the air.

"Fine I'll give you a boost princess but that's the last help your getting or you'll never learn how to do things on your own." I didn't even hear Drea cross the stream; my awareness of my surroundings has been severely lacking tonight.

I look down and Drea has managed to pick me up by my thighs and hoist me up at least a foot and a half. I try not to think about her touch on my skin or how my tiny dress covers not much of the area now directly in her face.

"Thank you" I swallow and reach for the first branch.

This is where my gym training will come in, I know I can do a pull up. My arms strength is surprisingly good for my stature. As I grab the branch, I tense myself and Drea drops her arms standing back. I swing my body and manage to pull myself up, swinging a leg over the brand that luckily is thick and solid enough to hold me.

"That's cheating! That's like a crossfit pullup not a proper pullup." Drea shouts.

"Shut up, if someone finds and kills us because you can't keep your smartass comments to yourself I will haunt you in hell!" I hiss down at her.

She laughs as I attempt to get my feet underneath me and balance enough to stand. I can barely see anything here and part of me starts to panic.

"How far up did you see it?" I hiss, making a point to keep my volume low.

"Like maybe twelve feet up, not far."

Sure, I think, not far. I continue to climb until I think I've reached the height Drea reported. I squint and try to make out a piece of fabric but other than the branch I'm on everything blurs into one. All I can do is feel blindly feel around hoping that I will come across something other than leaves and bark. I would be lucky if the flag was even still here since Drea last passed it. If the flag was ever here at all. I suddenly worry that I have blindly followed a wolf into the den. What if there never was a flag and this was all some sort of trick. But to what end? Drea already has her flag, and she gains nothing from leading me into danger. Unless this was just some sort of cruel prank, play with the princess until the clock runs out. That does seem like something she would do honestly. Though she has seemed kind in words her actions haven't spoken to her thus far. She didn't speak up or step forward to help Alice. That was Nikolas. Though after watching him snuff someone's life out, he isn't exactly the moral arbiter to compare to.

I don't know what to think or what to do. Maybe it would be best to stop talking to or interacting with anyone at all. If I do find a flag and get us out of this, I'm going to ignore everyone and everything other than Alice. Relying on others, I have a feeling will not give me success in here, it makes me too vulnerable.

As I continue to spiral, grasping frantically around me, something tickles my face. I stop in my tracks and move to brush the stray branch out of my face when I realize something. It isn't a branch nor a bungle of leaves but a piece of fabric. I grasp and secure my hands around it; it comes away easily. It must have just been draped over something not even secured. I can't believe it is still here. I suddenly feel absolutely awful that I doubted Drea, though I'm still not naïve enough to think she is my best friend, at least I know she wasn't lying about this. Though I still have absolutely no idea why she would want to help me. Maybe I'm not the only one feeling chemistry between us, I wonder if chemistry is enough to keep her from throwing me to the wolves if it came to it.

I twist the cloth around my hand and bring it closer to my face, ensuring that it is indeed red. Once I'm happy I push it down the front of my dress, currently lacking in the pocket area. I do hope we're given the opportunity to change at some point.

"How are you doing princess?" I hear.

"Got it." My voice is shaking as I peer down.

It was a lot less intimidating climbing up I find, but then I didn't have to look down. I carefully and slowly make my way back down. When my feet finally touch the ground, I release a breath I didn't realize I had been holding. I straighten myself and attempt some kind of dignity before pulling the red flag out of my dress. I wave it seductively as best I can.

"Well look at you, climb one tree and she thinks she's the bees knees." Drea laughs and I'm momentarily taken aback by how genuine and beautiful the sound is. Its light and musical and as she stops herself, I realize I'm smiling.

"I'm glad I amuse you." I huff at her, trying to regain some of my composure.

She tucks a loose lock of hair that has escaped her pony behind her ear and for once she doesn't look so intimidating. I am about to take a step toward her when a deafening bang sounds overhead. Drea's head snaps upward a moment before mine to see a firework explode overhead. I can feel my heart beating through my chest and up into my neck.

“What the hell?” I breath.

“That must be for us.” Drea throws back. “There’s no way they would bring us close enough to a populated area that this could happen. That is directly overhead, there can’t be anyone in these woods but us.”

“Do you think that means it’s over?” I ask her.

“I mean, it could be. How the hell would we know. I don’t want to head back to the entrance and run into some familiars without a flag if we aren’t sure.” Her face looks troubled as she considers her options.

“I wouldn’t even know how to get back to the entrance.” I laugh, showing Drea again how completely out of my depth I am here.

“Good evening familiars. Congratulations, you have reached the end of your first trial. Through infrared we have determined only eleven living beings are now in the compound. Please return to the starting point. If you do not have a flag, you will not be permitted entry and therefore terminated.”

“Guess we gotta go back.” Drea turns her back to me, her long hair swishing around her. I’m glad I’m not in her personal space or I think I would have been whipped in the face. “Good thing I did find you because even if you don't, I know the way back."

I take a step to follow her before my brain catches up with my feet.

"Wait!" I shout.

Drea turns her head over her shoulder.

"Yes?"

"Alice." I say, guiltily. It was just for a split second, but I forgot about picking her up.

"Ah yes, lets pick up sprout on the way. Chop, chop though princess I don't know if there's a time limit on us getting back." She holds her hand out in front of her motioning for me to lead the way. I look round and have to revisit my earlier fear. I have no idea where I left Alice.

I know it was in the crevice entrance to a cave but where to find it, I don't have a clue.

"I … I don't know where I left her." I whisper.

Drea's casual smile drops.

"Princess we can't randomly wander round the forest in the dark. If you don't know where she is, then … I don't know what to tell you. We'll have to go back."

"I can't leave her Andromeda! I left her in a cave okay. There was a rock wall thing, and there was a crack in it. We squeezed through into an opening." I look desperately to her as if she is going to have a light bulb moment based on my terrible description.

I imagine her saying *Aha of course! I know just the place, follow me!*

But that doesn't happen, she continues to meet my eyes, they look sad.

"Sabine."

I don't like that she's using my actual name, Its too serious.

"I can't leave her out there!" I shout at her.

"She might have heard the announcement; she might be on her way back already!" Drea throughs her hands in the air exacerbated.

"She won't! She was scared, I told her to wait. I told her I would be back for her." I take a step toward her and reach to take her hand. My fingers slide into hers and I grasp her more tightly than I should. Her eyes drop to our hands as if she isn't quite sure what's happening. She doesn't close her fingers around mine, but she doesn't pull away either.

"Ten minutes." I plead "Ten minutes and if we don't find her then we go back."

I have no intentions of turning round after ten minutes, I think Drea knows this, but it's harder to argue sparing such a short amount of time.

Finally, her fingers curl slowly over mine and she closes her eyes.

"God dammit princess I wasn't supposed to do this, I was going to kick this trials ass."

"Does that mean yes?" I wrap my other hand around our already clasped palms and pull closer to her. She opens her eyes to meet mine.

"Yes, everyone in here is supposed to be a merciless killer you know. It makes it much harder to say no to helping when your kind of a ... well… princess."

I laugh "I never said I was a princess you called me that. If I had to pick, I would call myself a disaster."

Drea snorts at this, I suspect in agreement.

"Okay, the land seems to rise over there." She points to our left and I have no idea what she's looking at. "I noticed it earlier I started going uphill so turned around just before I found you, that might be where we could find a cave."

I walk past her but keep my hand in hers and pull her in the direction she pointed. Poor Alice must be scared witless. I'm sure she will have heard the announcement; she's probably panicking in the tiny hole in the wall wondering if I'm coming back for her at all. I think about the look on her face as I left her. How worried she looked, but how much hope and trust were in her eyes.

We make our way forward in silence. I don't keep track of the time but I'm pretty sure we have been walking for more than ten minutes as we make our way through the forest. My palm slicks with sweat and I clutch Drea's fingers harder in mine.

"Sabine."

She used my name again. My breath quickens along with my feet. Maybe if I can ignore her long enough, we will magically come to the crack.

"Sabine." she says it more forcefully this time and yanks my hand to force me to a stop.

"I've let you go longer than we should already, and only because were heading generally in the right direction anyway. But we gotta take a right here to get back to the clearing where we started. You *have* to let this go." It's so dark now I can barely make out her face but I can only imagine the firmness there. I can feel it in her grip. She isn't asking this time. I drop to me knees and can't control myself as small sobs start escaping me.

"It can't have all been for nothing, I helped her. I got her safe. Now you want me to leave her in a cave to die?" I slide my hand out of hers and use it to cover my face, stifling the pathetic gasps I'm making.

"You did good princess, you did better than anyone else was willing to do." Drea crouches in front of my but I can't bring myself to look at her.

"Maybe if we go back, we can tell them where they need to find her. The Vamps will be better than us in the dark anyway, right? She's got a flag; they'll go pick her up."

I know the words are a kind lie but I don't really have any other option than to accept them. I'm never going to be able to find her again in the dark and if we don't make it back before dawn starts, they might not let us back in at all.

"Yes." I nod to myself "We'll go tell them where she is so they can pick her up."

Drea grabs me under my arms and tugs gently to urge me to my feet. I rise and wrap my arms around my waist. I think I've been running on so much adrenaline that I didn't realize how cold it was out here now it's night.

I shiver and nod to her to let her know I'm ready to follow. We make our way, steadily but quickly across the terrain. I don't know how much time passes but we finally head out of the tree cover and into the clearing. Here without the ceiling above us the moon illuminates the area and I see figures in the distance against the cell block wall.

I can't tell from here who made it, but all I can think of is those who didn't. I think about California, lying on the forest floor with a snapped neck. I think about the man who was decimated, who's name I don't even know. I wonder if Ash is amongst the living or the dead. He was the only other name I knew already. Perhaps I shouldn't learn anyone else's name when we get back, I think grimly, it'll be easier when they die. Eleven people were still alive, that's what the announcement said.

Minus me, Drea, and Alice. I count the figures, there should be eight, but there's not. I count again, and again, and again.

Nine.

There are nine shadows lined up in the distance.

I feel sick to my stomach, that makes eleven in total including us. Is she here? It could be Alice, I tell myself. It can't be though, none of the figures look smaller than the others. I feel my feet speed up as I move ahead of Drea. I get closer to the figures trying to look for a tiny girl. They move making it hard to get a good view of them all.

"Sabine!"

I almost fall to my knees as I hear a tiny voice from the gaggle of people.

"Alice?!" I shout into the crowd.

I feel Drea's hand at my back.

"Good thing I turned you around princess looks like she found her way back all on her own."

I see one of the figures clear as she moves through the crowd and runs towards me. I can now clearly see Alices outline. I remember myself and close the final gaps towards her. I open my arms as she jumps into them, and I close her in an embrace. I can't believe I feel so strongly for a girl I met less than a day ago. But with her in my arms I feel like what a mother must feel like when she finds her child after they wander away in the grocery store. The relief, the absence of dread.

"I looked for you." I promise her as I bury my face in her hair. "I didn't leave you behind I looked but I couldn't find you." I don't know if I'm reassuring her or myself.

"It's okay." She leans back, arms still holding me "I heard the announcement and thought I best come see if you needed help. Nick found me and brought me back. He said you would make it."

Nick. Nikolas. This is the second time he's saved her. I wonder if she knows he advocated for her culling. How many times does he have to save her life to make up for that? I'm not quite sure. I would feel slightly better about the whole situation if I hadn't seen him commit a cold blooded and seemingly pointless murder today. I stand up and take Alices hand in mind. Drea moves forward and I smile at her.

"Thank you." I smile.

She simply nods at me and walks off to join the rest of the winners. My heart sinks a little, we made a good team, didn't we?

We follow slowly behind her; I don't want her to feel like we are following her but we need to join the group. As we close in, I see Nikolas, he now has some blood splattered on his white shirt and whatever was tying his hair up has disappeared. It falls around his face to just past his jawline in tousled waves. One side has a leaf stuck in it. I can't help but wonder if someone else had to die by his hands today. I nod and smile to him none the less. He saved Alice and it's pretty obvious I want him on my side rather than against it.

As we take our place in the crowd, I pick out more and more faces. Nikolas is not the only one splattered in blood. A white woman in her thirties has blood smeared down her face. It looks as though she has been soaked and then tried to swipe whatever she can off, leaving harrowing streaks. She is dressed in black yoga pants and a green hoodie, much better than my attire. I can't help but think how out of place she looks. If not for the blood on her face she could look like a mom ready to pick her kids up from preschool. She stands in front of a young black man in his twenties, around my age. He's wearing jeans and a green hoodie, as if they were a couple who matched their outfits. He distinctly lacks any signs of warfare and I wonder if he managed to get his flag without taking someone's life.

Other than Me, Drea, Nikolas, and Alice that only leaves seven other opponents behind me. Ash who I met earlier is still alive which pleases me. He seemed kind and reasonable at least. Two of the remaining three are now the oldest of the group both men in their forties, both pale skinned with a mop of brown hair and grey speckled beards. They almost look comically alike. They both also wear jeans, but one wears a plaid shirt where the other wears a waterproof pullover. Neither of them have blood on them either. I must remind myself this doesn't speak to their innocence as Nikolas managed to end California's life without spilling a drop. The last is a younger woman closer to mine and Drea's age. She's white with jet black hair and dark eyes. She is halfway between mine and Drea's height making her the normal out of the three of us. She crosses her arms and keeps her head down so I can't read her expression. Lastly, I see the old man I had noted in the pen earlier. He must have kept mostly to the shadows as I never noticed him after that initial sweep. From here I can see he is at least seventy, bent over slightly in a way that seems permanent. Does he know immortality won't make him any younger? Does he want to be old forever?

Dropping from twenty to only eleven people feels like a worlds difference. Where before I saw a sea of faces now, I see people, individuals and we all feel somewhat closer. I suppose we have all overcome the first trial together. I'm sure I have read something about shared trauma bringing people together. I somehow doubt that will be the case here as I look around at the various crossed arms, averted eyes and general tense atmosphere. I don't know how I'm going to get through this. The next question though is … Who here doesn't have a flag.

CHAPTER SIX

Standing awaiting termination can't be an easy thing, whoever it is, is taking it very well. Eleven people stand lined up awaiting the verdict, were we successful? Everyone with a flag should feel confident, though there is a strong mix of emotions spread throughout the camp. Trauma I suspect being the main one. Yet no one in particular looks afraid. No one portraits that they are about to die and all we can do is wait.

After a while my body begins to come down from the extended feel of adrenaline. My legs begin to shake slightly, my eyes feel heavy and all I can think is how much I need to sleep. But sleep won't come as long as we are kept out here.

As my eyes begin to close and my head dips, I am awoken by an unfamiliar voice,

"Good evening, all!" I jilt upright again, my heart quickly remembering it should be beating overtime as it has all night.

"You have all done very well" The vampire who has

appeared in front of us is barely visible in the dark. Though he clearly has light ashy skin, he is dressed in what appears to be a long black robe causing him to meld into the background with the trees. "Ten of you have captured flags, but unfortunately, eleven of you have returned."

We were about to see what being terminated would look like. I wasn't looking forward to it. Grabbing Alice without a word I turn her to face inward, her head pressed into my stomach just below my chest. She doesn't protest and part of me wonders if she knows what is coming next.

After a moment of silence a small sob comes from the gaggle, all heads turning to see who the unfortunate soul is. My heart sinks as I see the old man drop to his knees, his cries coming soft but continuously. I try to convince myself this is the best outcome, at least he is old, he has lived a full life. But it doesn't settle my stomach or stop the tears silently rolling down my cheeks as the vampire approaches him.

All the other familiars take a few steps away from the man, giving space for justice to be delt, but also putting some distance between themselves and the vampire.

"Adrian, my poor familiar." The vampire sounds genuinely sad as he places a hand on his familiar's head. I suppose it makes sense that they would send the persons Master to take them from the game themselves. “I will make this quick, you have served me well. Now, you may rest well.”

The man, Adrian, says nothing. He merely keeps his head bowed and begins to whisper to himself. Though I cant hear his words I suspect he is saying a prayer, and before he can fully complete it my worst fears are confirmed.

With one fell swoop, the vampire lashes the man’s throat edge to edge with a sharpened nail on his index finger. My hands clutch tightly into Alices hair instinctively, hoping that she will remain unaware of the reality of our situation.

My heart breaks for the man who tries to continue his prayer in gargles and strangled noises. This was not a merciful killing, bleeding to death would be slow and it would be painful. Unable to watch anymore I close my eyes and try to ignore the sounds that comes next, one I recognize all too well. The wet and slurping noise of blood being drank.

*

Numb, it is the only emotional I can feel. If I allow myself to feel anything else, I will fall apart. We stand with the dead body of our fallen familiar for far longer than they should have subjected us to. And just as I think I may finally give up and collapse to the floor, the door to the entrance of the building begins to slide open.

"Thank God, any longer and I would definitely have hypothermia." I say to Alice as I steer her through them. Trying to keep the atmosphere light so that she doesn't understand the tragedy we all just witnessed.

Though the comment is true, I breath onto my hands trying to return some life to them. The fingertips are blue and I have a feeling my lips would be the same if I could see them. As the door fully opens, I steal a glance at the pre lit walkways, now heading in a different direction. We all push to get inside, I'm clearly not the only one so affected by the cold. Rather than the chaotic rush of leaving we all shuffle somewhat deflated down the corridor. I end up next to the young man in the green hoodie and I can't help but notice the look of deflation on his face. He seems to be absolutely beaten by this. I think for the first time that perhaps people have taken lives when they did not want to today.

I was lucky, Drea helped me. What would I have done had she been foe and not friend? I don't delude myself into thinking that I would have been able to beat her in hand-to-hand combat if that's what it came to. On the contrary I think she would absolutely kick my ass. But if I had the chance, if I was backed into a corner, would I kill her?

I have killed before but only bad people, and I hadn't really killed them, I had led them to their death. It's very different, I left them alive on the floor somewhere in the house and went to bed. When I came back, they were dead. In a peaceful, quiet, and clean way. I guess It's wrong, but I think deep down I have never really, truly accepted that I was murdering these people. I never put my hands around their neck or put a knife through their skin. Now I'm here I don't think I have the spine for it. Especially to people I know nothing about. I feel silent tears slide down my cheek. I really don't know how I'm going to do this.

"Were not going back to the cell?" Alices voice breaks me out of my stupor.

I look up and realize she's right, we're walking past the cell and following the corridor down to the left.

"I guess not." I say. I don't say the rest of what I'm thinking. That we could be headed straight for the next trial. They can't do that. We can't be expected to go straight into another task. We haven't slept nor eaten. I know our Masters are vampires, but they have all kept familiars if they have us in here. They know we need to sleep and eat. They know, but will they care?

I reach for Alices hand and grip it tightly in mine. Whatever is coming next, I have protected this little girl this far and I certainly am not going to leave her now.

Thankfully, my worries are quickly squashed as what we enter what seems to be a rec area.

We all move through the door and pile to a stop just within the entrance not trusting our surroundings. It is set up like a large circle with ten doors spread around the outside wall. The middle of the room holds everything a human would need. There is a kitchen area, with a fridge, an oven and even a microwave. Close to that is a large table and chairs, rather ornate which looks completely out of place in the concrete pen of a room. It is dark wood and has carving in it that match the ten chairs placed around it. Spread to the other side of the room is a series of lounge chairs and sofas, enough to house us all comfortably. In amongst it all sits a nice red Turkish style rug covering the cold hard floor.

Actually, quite a lot of thought has gone into this. If it wasn't for the flickering prison lights and the dank grey room, it would be pretty nice. Nikolas steps forward across the invisible line no one else dares to cross. He moves slowly circling the room and inspecting the ceiling to the floor. I don't know what he's looking for but I'm happy to let him take the fall if anything is booby trapped. He tried the first door on the outer wall as he passes but it seems to be locked. I can only assume since there of ten of them they will be our individual rooms, possibly with a bed. It's too much of a coincidence that there is door for each of us.

Happy that he has seen whatever he needs to Nikolas moves to the fridge and opens it. Its full of food and drinks, he helps himself to a can of diet soda and takes a seat at the table.

No one else is yet to move, paralyzed by uncertainty of what comes next. They can't just leave us in here and say nothing after what we have just been through. Surely there will be another announcement? The seconds stretch into minutes as the silence becomes insufferable. My palm in Alice's begins to sweat. Then Ash steps forward without a word and makes his way to one of the chairs. Obviously happy that there is no booby traps Drea is the third to move.

"Well, I don't know about you all, but I'm exhausted." She follows suit and grabs herself not only a drink but a protein bar from the fridge before joining the two boys at the table. This is the sign everyone apparently needs as one by one people grab themselves something and take a seat. I wait until last and lead Alice to the fridge. She doesn't need any to prompting as she grabs a full wrapped packet of sandwich cookies and a bottle of Sunny D. I can't help but laugh. The traumatic night hasn't affected her appetite.

I on the other hand feel sick to my stomach, though I know I should eat something, so I copy Drea and get myself a bland vanilla protein bar to keep me going. It's been at least a full day and night since I've had anything and I don't want to be left lightheaded and weak if they spring another trial on us.

"So, everyone let's go round the table and tell us your name and one interesting thing about yourself!"

Everyone stares at Drea as if she has grown two heads which solicits a pleased smirk from her lips. I pull Alice and me into the two spare seats at the top of the table, much to my dismay the furthest away from Drea. With us all sat round like this it feels like a messed-up AA meeting.

"It's what we call an ice breaker guys, it helps you know, break the ice?" She wiggles her eyebrows trying to entice someone in, but no one is biting.

"I think we are familiar with the concept." Ash laughs, He crossed his legs and folds his joined hands around his knee. He looks like the group leader, with his easy confidence and natural presence.

“I don’t think there’s anything to be gained by getting to know each other.” Nikolas says matter of factly without raising his eyes from the bottle that he twists absent mindedly in his hands.

“Well, I completely disagree, we may all die tomorrow but I don’t see why we should suffer in the meantime. My names Andromeda, I’m a Sagittarius.” Drea looks at me with a twinkle in her eye and I can’t help but jump in to back her up.

“I didn’t imagine you being into star signs.” I laugh despite the situation. “But I’m a Virgo if you’re interested.” I don’t take note of anyone’s reaction to my words, my focus solely on the woman across the table and the way she is looking at me.

“My name is Ash and I think astrology is fabricated by those who have nothing higher to believe in.” His words are light and meant to poke fun but hold no malice. Snorting Drea throws him a wink and I can’t help but release a small giggle myself.

“And do you have something higher to believe in?” I wonder out loud.

“You’re all fucking lunatics!” A shrill voice disrupts the newly found peace before Ash has his chance to answer me. It’s one of the other women, she shakes slightly as though she's so highly strung it's taking everything, she has to keep her body still and seated. "Were going to die and your discussing star signs." She shakes her head in disbelief, face still streaked with blood.

"What's your name?" I smile gently at her. This situation could devolve into madness pretty quickly and if I can I want to move us back to gentle conversation. Drea is right, we don't know what's coming tomorrow, but I would like to spend today in blissful ignorance if it can be accomplished.

"Michelle." She looks down at her hands, they're in a similar state to her face, stained red with the evidence of todays crimes.

"Michelle, I don't know what happened out there but you're going to be okay." I know it's a lie, I don't even know why I say it really. But her eyes brim with tears and I don't want to tip her over the edge.

"No, I'm not!" She screams. "I almost died, some guy came at me with an axe, and I almost died. He … he fell … on a branch" Her lip trembles. "I couldn't let him get back up … he dropped the axe and I … I …" She hides her face in her hands and begins to sob.

I feel bile rise in my throat as I realize she's probably talking about the man who I came across with the dismembered arm and mushed up face. My words fail me at that point, the state she had left that body in had made me feel nauseous. All I had thought of was the unadulterated cruelty the person who did it must have had. To now know it was done in self-defense, by a desperate woman. Well, I don't know how to feel, and so my mouth remains firmly shut. Her broken face displays everything I would feel had I been forced to take someone's life so violently; I'm honestly surprised she is holding it together as well as she is.

"Hey, love, look at me." The older man in the plaid shirt speaks. Her face continues to be firmly planted looking at her hands, but he continues anyway. "Michelle, I'm David and I killed someone tonight too okay. Don't be so upset love. You did what you had to do." Quietly I wonder who it was he killed, and if it was self-defense like Michelle. His face displays a complete lack of guilt or remorse. Whatever happened out there to him, he won't be losing any sleep over it tonight. Which to me means, regardless of why he took a life tonight, he has probably taken one before now. I cant imagine any other reason someone would be so unfeeling in the face of death.

"You did?" Michelle sniffles, as if the blood on other people's hands somehow lessons that on her own.

"Of course, what did you think was going to happen when you were brought to these trials? Did you think you would fill out an exam with a HB pencil and they'd select a winner based on that? They rule us out by the weakest being killed off." I'm intrigued by his words. It suggests he has maybe been told more about the trials than the rest of us. Certainly, more than me, though I knew we wouldn't all be winners I never suspected that failure meant death.

Having this conversation in front of Alice was less than ideal, I'm not totally sure if she was aware that deaths had occurred tonight, but she certainly does now. My eyes slide to her discretely and I see she is listening with quiet fascination, half a cookie sandwich shoved in her mouth. Clearly this wasn't that traumatic for her to listen to if she was still managing to eat.

"Do you know, how this all works?" I ask. "My Master, he never told me either, I just knew there were trials, and the winner would be changed." I look pleadingly to David. If he can fill in any of my blanks, I need it.

"Of course, I know, I said I wasn't coming in here if I didn't know what it was about." His voice was gruff but pleasant. "Twenty come in, one for each family." He starts with something I did already know, though only due to an overheard conversation directly before the trial. Master hadn't openly shared the information with me prior. "Then we do three trials, all designed for kill or be killed. The toughest who survive to the last trial and prove themselves will be changed." He sits back clearly done. Other than the kill or be killed part it isn't exactly anything new, I don't see why he looks so proud of himself.

"Okay so not much further forward then." I can't help but snip, He immediately looks annoyed and the man to his right guffaws.

"Did you know that they already have a replacement lined up?" The man adds. All eyes are on him immediately, the first real bit of unknown information we're getting, and it's a juicy one. "Neal." He raises his hand in introduction but doesn't seem to feel the need to elaborate any further on his point.

"What do you mean?" The young man whose name I don't yet know, almost shouts across the table.

"Did you honestly think they would all risk their personal servants and be left with nothing? Even if your picked as bride someone still has to replace you shoveling the shit. They have all squared up a young eager replacement. They're old they replace us constantly." Neal seems completely unbothered by this fact which has me reeling. The thought that I have a replacement lined up at home makes me feel ill. I feel like a teddy that a child loses at the airport, the words running through my mind. *Oh well don't worry we can always get another one.*

After ten years … Am I that easily replaced?

"I think I would know if my Master has been interviewing familiars." The younger man rolls his eyes.

"What's your name kid?" Neal asks.

"Jared." he says slowly, as if he doesn't fully trust this man with his name.

"Jared, you're thick as mince if you think you know all the goings on of your vampire." His words are laced with harshness, as if he is scolding a child who should know better.

"He's right though, I saw mine." The girl with the dark hair interjects. I almost forgot she was here tucked on a corner of the table she seems to have managed to sink into herself and make herself invisible. "Jessica." She makes a small waving notion, greeting the group as we all turn our eyes to her. We wait patiently but she doesn't elaborate further and instead drops her head again as if remembering she was trying to disappear.

"My Master hasn't left our house in as long as I've known him." I offer up. "He plays piano, he reads, he paints. He. Doesn't. leave. Where on earth would he find a replacement to line up. He can't exactly put a post on craigs list. You might know what your Master does, but I know my Master. I w*ould* have noticed if he left the house, I certainly would have noticed another human visiting and leaving alive." As I say the words, I'm not totally sure if I am trying to convince them, or myself. Though what I say certainly rings true, so do Neals. There is no way I know everything my Master thinks and does. Even after ten years our relationship is surface level. Is there a chance he could have been going out while I wouldn't know? No. I put him to bed and wake him up for God's sake, what is he doing sneaking out like a teenager once I go to sleep? If he wanted to find another familiar, I would have known.

"Mine has someone lined up." Drea shrugs. The nonchalant way the words come out of her mouth baffle me. The thought of that doesn't seem to upset her and I can't fathom why, doesn't it make her feel completely devalued as a person? "We discussed the trials quite a lot, I knew I might not come out. But I still wanted to try, it was tough but we had to talk about what would happen if I lost. She can't be without a familiar and she wanted my input on who she thought was worthy to replace me." She looked down at her nails as if this didn't bother her, but I could tell by the tone in her voice it did. I was bothered for a whole other reason. She sounded like her vampire had a lot of respect for her to want her opinion on her replacement. Another reminder of how shallow my relationship with my Master truly is.

"The girl we picked actually looks a lot like me ironically but about five years younger, at least if I do die it's a trade up I guess!" A not quite convincing laugh escapes Drea and I can immediately tell there is a layer of feelings behind those words. But as ever, she continues to try and lighten the mood.

"Trade up, listen to yourselves!" Jared shouts. He stands, sliding his chair back and slamming his palms on the table. "I was told about this trial, this opportunity, but I was never told that if I failed anything would happen other than returning to my post. I wouldn't have come if I had known!" His outburst has everyone tensing, but I can't say I resent him for it. I understand how he feels. Would I have come here if I knew the outcome was likely going to be death? Honestly, we had never even discussed it enough for me to consider it fully. I had always worked off the assumption that I would be deemed worthy. That he wouldn't have put me forward if that wasn't the case. Now that I know he put me in here to gamble my life … I feel … betrayed.

"Me neither." Michelle sniffles, her immense sadness spilling into the words. It fills the room even Jared's shoulders fall with defeat as he again takes his seat.

“And what did you think would happen if you didn’t win crocodile tears? You’d go back to playing maid. Honestly if you’re that naïve it’s your own faults. Working for vampires and expecting mercy …” Nikolas shakes his head at us, as if our incompetence disgusts him.

“You all are being so dramatic.” David rolls his eyes. “You all work for vampires, I’m like 99% sure that if this doesn’t work out you have nowhere else to go anyway. So, suck it up, at least if you don’t win you won’t end up on the street. It’s a mercy to be honest.” His words are brutal but from the faces around the room I can tell it rings true for many people in here, myself included. Master took me in from the streets, and if I were ever to leave him that’s exactly where I would go. I might not be weak, but I’m not tough enough for that.

“So, they really are vampires?” the words barely a whisper.

Crap.

I had forgot about Alice; this conversation really shouldn’t have been observed by her. This poor girl was about to grow up real quick and I have to make the decision on the spot that I won’t be able to shield her from the truth in here. Later I would have to think about what else we need to discuss, and get ahead of the curve. She didn't need any more bombshells dropped on her like this. Nikolas looks to me and I meet his glaring eyes. They relay everything he said in that first talk. *She's too young, too innocent for this. We should have spared her when we had the chance.* But he was wrong, this wasn't going to be easy for her, I wasn't dumb enough to believe that, but I could get her through it.

"Yes." I say slowly pulling my eyes away from Nikolas and settling back on her. "They are vampires, like you have probably read about in story books. But they aren't all bad." A few people snort at this comment. "And we are all here not to marry them Alice but to become … their companion." I don't think she has fully comprehended that if she does get out of here she too will be changed, an eternal child. That conversation is one I will save for later, after the initial shock has worn off.

"Okay." is all she says, no argument, no disagreement about the existence of these eternal mythological beings. I suppose children believe in the supernatural much easier, but I suspect the truth is it hasn't fully sunken in for her yet. "So all we have to do is not hurt each other and we can all make it out, then we go live with our vampires?" Agree to not hurt each other, if only it were that easy. I smile at her and stroke her head as her only answer. My eyes sweeping the room unable to stop assessing who in here would be the one who would attempt her life if given the chance.

I can't imagine many people round this table taking her life maliciously. Certainly not Jared or Michelle. David or Neal perhaps, but even then, only out of necessity. I don't think anyone is going to target her unless they absolutely have to. Especially Nikolas, his words may say one thing, but his actions have spoken much louder. He's already proved to me that his bark is worse than his bite. It was him who led Alice back to the start through the forest when I couldn't find her. If his words of letting her die really had any weight behind them, he would have left her in that forest to fend for herself. Though I may not know his true intentions yet, they certainly aren't malicious.

"With all due respect kid, it's not that simple, no one knows how many winners there will be. This isn't an episode of my little pony where we help each other and beat it with the power of friendship. This is to weed out the weak and provide a few if not one winner." David speaks to her, though his words are unkind the soft look on his face tries to portray that this isn't his intent. He smiles slightly and his skin creases around his eyes and at the corner of his mouth showing his age. I've heard these called laugh lines before, though that would require a happy life so I doubt whether that's what I should call them on

David.

Alice merely sinks into her chair, her eyes which began to brim as he spoke to her allow a single tear to spill over and tumble down her face. It breaks my heart.

"The fact of the matter is, we don't really have any idea how this was designed. There is no telling what's coming next, nor how many of us are going to make it out, so let's not waste any more time talking about it." My hand reaches out to stroke Alices head gently as I speak giving her what comfort I can. I feel the light bob of her head nodding under my hand, the only indicator that she heard what I said.

Silence falls across the group and for the first time I don't feel tense or scared I just feel absolutely deflated. An emptiness settles in me that makes me feel worse than anything else I have felt tonight, and if I was being really honest with myself, I didn't make that little speech just for Alice. If anyone else kept talking about death and failure I might just fall apart, and I really didn't have anything left to put myself back together again. Each face around speaks a thousand words and I know in that moment that the feeling is mutual. Even stone-faced Nikolas can't help but let his mask slip ever so slightly, sadness slipping through the cracks.

All I can hope is that defeat doesn't turn to desperation.

*

Before long everyone has drifted off slightly to find some separation from the oppressive atmosphere created amongst ourselves. Some choose to retire to the few sofas in the room, sprawling in pure exhaustion. Among them Alice crawls into a ball on one armchair and manages to fall asleep. I envy her. The childlike ability to forget about everything and sleep anywhere. Though fatigue gnaws at my bones and pulls at my heavy eyes, I have a suspicion sleep will be eluding me tonight.

Though my mind is racked with images of blood and gore, that isn't what truly bothers me. My whole life I have always deeply respected my Master and what he did for me, he took me in, fed me, put a roof over my head. At only fifteen, when my parents died, I was a true orphan with no where to go. His offer of employment, though transactional, saved my life. I have always been grateful to him for that, and it caused me perhaps to not question things as I should. Immortality was not a common topic of conversation but he had mentioned it enough to make me think it was always his intention to gift it to me.

Yes, the trials were discussed, but never past surface level. Perhaps it was naivety, but the thought never crossed my mind that he would put me in harm's way, I certainly never considered he would risk my life. My whole world view is crashing down around me and I don't have the mental fortitude right now to deal with it. I'm absolutely furious with him, not only has he betrayed me, but he has also completely embarrassed me. Poor stupid Sabine, putting some blind faith into a creature who is so ready to replace her.

I shake my head as if I can dislodge the thoughts. My mind warring with itself, part feeling utter and abstract anger, the other feeling immensely guilty for questioning the man who did so much for me.

In some cruel twist of fate from the universe, as I sit and contemplate how I should be feeling, the subject of my turmoil walks through the doorway.

His presence is felt immediately, intense and demanding of attention. Every head in the room turns, people sit up in their seats or even raise to their feet as the slow and purposely footsteps slide further into the room.

Melchior, my Master.

My breath hitches at seeing him, he looks as

stunningly deadly as always but he has changed since the dinner. His curls are pulled back and held in a small black tie at the nape of his neck. A black shirt, black pants, and a black floor length robe caress him like midnight incarnate. If he didn't look so regal, I could almost laugh. With his robe he looks less like the man I have come to know and more like a true vampire from a horror novel. It sweeps around him and trails on the floor behind. Long tapered arms almost completely hide his hands and the whole thing sways slightly as he glides with all the grace of one who was flying rather than walking.

Not knowing what to expect, I sit frozen, unable to move or speak for fear of a wrong move. Would he acknowledge me? Congratulate me? Perhaps even apologize for the way in which he let me be dumped in here with no real preparation. Even I have to laugh at myself for that final thought, I have a strong suspicion vampires apologize for nothing, especially to their human.

The steps stop a few feet into the room and he takes us all in from a distance, his calculating eyes revealing nothing, not even as they pass over me. My heart drops in my chest and before I know what's happening I am on my feet and have moved a step closer to him. A hand darts out and grasps me firmly by the wrist, stopping me in my tracks and waking me from my trance. Looking down I see Ash's firm but gently grip as he silently shakes his head. *Don't,* he seems to say. He's right. My chin dips in return at him and my feet slide one step back to show I understand. He may be my Master, but here in the trials, we play by their rules.

"Congratulations." The word forms on his lips. It carries little feeling or enthusiasm, but he does match it with a dazzling smile that shows off his elongated canines. "You ten have survived the first trial and will be proceeding to the next round. I hope the area provided is sufficient for your needs"

He sweeps a handout in front of him motioning to our space.

"You also have all been provided with private quarters which will now be accessible." As if on cue we hear a series of metallic clinks which I can only assume is the locks on the surrounding doors opening. Bedrooms. "You will remain here for the remainder of the trial. After one week of recovery, we will introduce the next element. Please try not to kill each other in the meantime." Another flash of his brilliant teeth, a sickening grin as if he just made an extremely funny joke.

No one laughs. No one does anything but stand in solemn silence, staring at one of the men who holds our lives in his hands.

“Thank you for your cooperation.” He dips his head slightly as if bowing to us.

That is it? After what he just put us through … me through … he’s going to leave without even acknowledging me. I don’t know whether to scream or cry but before I can make the decision he subverts my expectation and finally looks directly at me, his eyes burning into my soul.

“You did well Sabine, you will make a good bride. But do not rely on others so heavily, I know you are more capable than you think.” With that he turns and is gone. No door closes behind him. He was clear this is our pen; they aren’t concerned about us trying to escape it. I let out a shaky breath and turn to see all eyes on me.

“That’s my Master.” I laugh shakily, feeling the need to explain myself.

“Yeah, I got that.” Drea says with assessing eyes.

Though I’m not quite sure, I think I see sympathy or maybe even pity in her face as she takes me in.

“Shall we call dibs on rooms then?” She regains her composure quickly and pushes past me, her long legs striding toward a middle room. “I want the one closest to the fridge." She throws over her shoulder with a laugh.

"A full week" Michelle says meekly, "I didn't think we would get so long."

Honestly neither did I, I wouldn't have been surprised if they had marched us from one trial to the next. But apparently, they are going to enjoy watching our slow spiral in madness while we wait for our deaths. All I can hope is that Master is right, and no one tries to kill each other in the meantime. The assessing and guarded looks around the room tell me everyone is thinking the same thing. Though people may be friendly enough, we are not a team, and I'm going to be sleeping with one eye open.

Not wanting to stand here a second longer I follow closely behind Drea deciding immediately I want to be housed as close as possible to the one person I trust the most to not murder me in my sleep.

"You going to bunk with me Alice?" I call over me should as I lay claim to the door next to Drea's.

"I'll bunk next door, I'm ten you know." She says as if that alone is enough to explain she is a big girl who doesn't need to share a bed.

I laugh but feel inwardly uncomfortable, would anyone in here eliminate her in her sleep? I don't think they would out of cruelty but maybe out of perceived kindness. I look to Nikolas and as if reading my mind, he takes the door next to Alice. She's sandwiched between us now.

"Make sure you lock your door then Alice at least." He drawls in that thick Russian voice as he passes inside the room. I peak my head into my room immediately to confirm he is right, there are inner locks. That makes me feel slightly more comfortable at least.

The room is simple and small, enough to hold a well-made single bed with white sheets. There's a single toilet and sink in the other corner like a prison cell and a wooden chest on the floor at the foot of the bed. The light is like the main area and is a flickering white light that comes from a single bulb hanging from the ceiling with a string pull on and off.

Curiosity winning over, the first thing I do is peer inside the chest at the foot of the bed, its hinges creaking in protests as I lift the heavy lid. It's filled with clothes. Thank God. There isn't a whole lot to choose from but it's certainly better than what I have on. I start pulling things out and realize there's no way any of this is going to fit me. It's made for a man for a start, and one much larger than me. I sigh, I will just have to roll everything up and hope there is a belt or something.

"Wanna swap?" A voice behind my has me twirling around to see Jared in my doorway.

"Sorry!" He holds up his palms at my likely terrified face. "Didn't mean to frighten you, it's been a rough day, I know. I just checked my trunk and unless I lose like a foot of height and forty pounds this aint gunna fit me." He holds up a set of leather pants that look slightly long but a much better fit than whatever I have.

"Thanks," I say. "Shall we just slide the whole trunk probable easier"

I grasp the black metal handle on one side of the wooden trunk and stand to steady myself. As I step back and tug it actually slides with little resistance.

"Good thinking, there's about five outfit changes and a pair of boots in mine." He steps forward and motions for the handle and I let him take it. "I'll be right back" He smiles.

Dragging a chest is something I was more than capable of doing, but exhaustion seeps into my soul right now and I'm not going to argue with his chivalry. I hear the scraping of wood on the concrete floor in fits and starts, suggesting it's a little heavier than Jared thought. A little laugh escapes my lips and I go to see if he does need help after all.

Looking into the main room, Jared clocks me and suddenly finds a second wind. He grits his teeth and slides the chest with more gusto in one fluid motion the rest of the way, not wanting to take the hit to his ego of having to ask me for help.

Drea sticks her head out of her door to see what the ruckus is about.

"Playing swapsies already?" She shouts. "Whose got clothes to fit a tall and sexy lady such as myself? I think I've got sprouts stuff." She holds up a tiny pair of black leather pants that probably wouldn't reach past her knees. I never thought I would see fighting leathers for a child.

"Well, I don't think she's going to wear them but let's get them swapped." I suggest, laughing inwardly at the thought of Alice decked out like a little spy.

The next twenty minutes are spent figuring out who's trunk is in who's room. Everyone in the end has pretty much a perfect match including interestingly enough a set for a child. Any hopes of them not knowing a child ended up here clearly dashed. I tried not to think about this too much as I sit on the floor of my room going through my options. We know we have a week worth of rest, so I don't need to be battle ready but I am pleased though to see a good variety of tight and stretchy options that I will make sure I'm wearing by the next trial.

Right now, I opt for a matching set of cream sweatpants and sweatshirt. The only other shoe option is boots so boots it is. Dress and broken heels discarded in the corner, I stand to stretch and test my clothes. My feet drag slightly with the weight of the boots, not perfect for speed, I'll have to remember that.

The clothes however are soft against my skin and the added warmth is a welcome gift after a night outdoors in a mini dress. My hands stroke up and down the buttery fabric on my skin, I don't think I ever had things this nice back at the house.

Happy with my fit I decide I better check on my new ward, but as I pop my head into Alices room I find her unconscious on the bed, drool down the left side of her face. Poor thing, today has probably been the most traumatic day of her life … so far anyway.

I don't want to wake her up, but I also really want her to lock her door. Leaning back out into the rec room I see everyone else seems to have set up shop, all equally drained from today's events. I'm not surprised, I have never felt this tired in my life. So, I slide the door to Alices room shut and lock myself into my own room. Though I feared I would lay awake fighting with the day as soon as my head hits the

pillow I lose consciousness, my mind and body have nothing left to give.

CHAPTER SEVEN

Disorientated is the only way to describe my feeling upon waking.

How absolutely starving I am, is one of my first thoughts unbelievably enough, followed closely by where the hell am I? I don't feel panicked just mildly dazed as I force myself to sit up and look around.

A bed, a toilet, a trunk, a closed door. The memories of the past few days flood back to me and all I can feel is numb. Images of murdered bodies and that poor familiar on his knees fly through my mind in a demented slide show causing my heart to patter in beat.

My current reality seems so wrong when others have suffered and lost so much. My cashmere like clothes, downy bed and thick blanket just feel wrong and out of place.

If I could I would cocoon myself in this room, bathing in denial whilst I wait for the next week to pass. I could raid the fridge and hole up in here like a raccoon for the next few days, not being forced to interact with all of the people who could end up being my demise.

But I can't just think about myself, and I can't be selfish. The little girl next door will be up soon too, if she isn't already, and she needs me. A reluctant after thought niggles in the back of my mind letting me know I would quite like to get to know Drea a bit more too if the time allows, but I try and squash that as it rises.

I groan dramatically as I pull myself from the haven that is this bed, pulling on my walking boots that have been provided and running my fingers over my hair. I left it in a rough braid last night and its feeling worse for wear after an evening running through the forest and a night on a pillow. There's no mirror in here, I'm guessing they didn't view that as a necessity, so I remove the hair tie from the bottom of the braid and start unwinding the mess. I tug and pull at the areas where the hair has knotted and doesn't want to break free. By the time I make it to the bottom I'm decide that whatever I have at the moment will have to do. My stomach growls in agreement and I slide my door open. It looks like I'm the last one awake.

I feel slightly embarrassed as I see everyone sitting in the living area in various states of dishevelment. Alice is at the table with a bowl of cereal, swinging her legs over her chair. She's wearing a pair of dinosaur pajamas highlighting her age even more and I can't help but think about the vampire who must have had to sit and pack those.

Everyone else looks a variety of grey and black, a mirage of sweatpants, leggings, and T shirts. Dressed for comfort compliments of their Masters.

No one murdered in their sleep then, I snip to myself making a mental count of everyone around the table. I'll take that as a successful first night. I make a mental note of how well sound proofed those doors must be for everyone to be awake and talking and for me to not have heard a whisper of it. Immediately I make the decision that though it isn't ideal to have it unlocked, I'll be sleeping with my door ajar from now on. Being caught unawares isn't a viable option in here.

I pad over and take a seat next to Alice, no one greets me, and I can't help but notice the atmosphere seems even more dower than yesterday. Drea sits by herself on an Armchair, focusing intently on picking the dirt from her nails with a butter knife. She's wearing an oversized black hoodie and black yoga pants. She hasn't bothered with shoes but instead has a pair of surprisingly fluffy slipper socks on. Nikolas is pacing circles round the room looking from floor to ceiling. He already made a point of doing this yesterday, so I don't know why he's repeating himself.

Michelle looks just as depressed as yesterday if not more so, sitting with a cup of coffee at the table in a similar get up to Drea but minus the slipper socks. Her knees are pulled up to her chest and she has one arm wrapped around them. Her chin rests atop her legs and she has the blank look on her face that says whatever her eyes are seeing it's probably a replay of something dreadful. Jessica is the only one not present, the quiet girl from yesterday, she must still be in her room, the door pulled completely closed.

Jared and Ash at least seem to have somewhat made friends and thought they sit in silence they do so together playing cards. I inwardly laugh to myself wondering if one of them brought a deck with them or if the vampire's thought were thoughtful enough to provide us entertainment to pass the time. Ash looks the most different, gone is his pressed linen suit and he now wears a black T shirt showing the lithe body underneath. He is well built and like all the other men looks like he could snap me like a twig. He no longer has his hair pulled in a bun and instead it falls in loose waves to his shoulders.

Alice grins at me with a face full of rainbow-colored cereal as I approach her.

"I quite like it here." She mumbles over her food.

"I can see that." I laugh and take a seat next to her.

"You know I've never had my own room before, I always ended up sleeping with mama wherever we went." Her eyes glazed over slightly at the mention of her mother and her words trail off quietly. As though the afterthought just hit her that she likely wouldn't be seeing her again.

"Well, you have one here. Were you not afraid on your own?" I reach out and brush some of the hair out of her face before it ends up in the shoveling line and in her mouth.

"Of course, not." She puffs up her chest "Though I was so tired I don't think I had the energy to be afraid." She laughs and drops her eyes.

"Well, we've got a week so you have plenty of time to catch up on sleep."

This was clearly not the right thing to say as the air temperature seems to drop in the room at the mention of our time limit.

I clear my throat and look to Ash to change the subject.

"Where did you find the cards?"

He doesn't raise his eyes from his hand but motions his head towards his bunk.

“They were in the bottom of my trunk.”

“Oh, I didn’t know we got presents as well as clothes! Maybe I have something extra too.” Alice forgets the rest of her soggy cereal and runs off to her bunk to see what else is hidden in her trunk, though I’m confident the answer is nothing. The cards likely a shared joke or token of friendship from his Master specifically.

“Do you think our trunks were packed by our Masters?” I ask.

“Probably.” Jared shrugs. “I had nothing but clothes in mine and a hunting knife, but everything fits perfectly.”

“You got a weapon?” I ask him incredulously.

“I wouldn’t disclose if you were given an extra weapons boy.” Nikolas rolls his eyes and stops his march.

“Why, you going to keep yours hidden to stab people in the back?” I mock him.

“I think any leg up you can get is important.” He shrugs.

I take note. Again, this man can’t help but baffle me, someone hiding a weapon for an advantage is not the same person I would have pegged to save a child’s life. Twice. He is a walking contradiction.

"I do not need an advantage, and I'm not a *boy.*" Jared bristles. "I don't plan on using this on any of you, it's for protection if anything."

I believe him, he has sincere eyes and a matter-of-fact tone. Thought the longer I'm here the more I am reminded of the fact my actual human interaction the past ten years has been minimal. My naivety has already shown once or twice. Is it showing now with my faith in Jared?

"Well, you all know Jared's and my secret." Ash waves his cards around.

"Did you used to play cards with your Master?" I ask curious.

He smiles but the smile doesn't quite reach his eyes.

"No, I served my Master, I did not play games with him. The servant's however, we play cards with each other often."

"Oh, I just thought, because of the gift?" I feel like I've touched a nerve and I don't know how to walk it back. His mention of other servants has me itching to grill him, does he work with other familiars?

"A little joke more likely, he thinks he is very clever."

His eyes darken a little more.

“You don’t like him?” I ask.

“I think this conversation ends here.” Nikolas butts in forcefully.

“Who asked you?” I throw back, if he thinks he is going to strut around here like the self-appointed leader he has another thing coming.

“I suggest whatever you say in here, is something you’d be comfortable with your *Master* hearing.” He says pointedly, looking around the room as he speaks. What is he trying to insinuate? I can’t see any microphones or camera lenses but he has been staring at every crevice for the past two days, so maybe her sees more than me. Or maybe he’s just a paranoid asshole.

“My Master is a complicated man, I’m sure we will have a much-changed relationship once I am no longer mortal. Servants of the household, butlers, cleaners … familiars, we are not seen as equals.” Ash interrupts diplomatically.

A big household then, and with all those people helping that likely means …

“Do you live with more than one vampire?” I can only hope my prying isn’t seen as rude but if the trials are anything to go by, I have not been asking enough questions. That stops now.

“A whole family of them.” Is all Ash offers back.

“Mine does, too” David says over his coffee. “He’s got a woman who he changed before I came on. I serve them both really, but I only call him Master.”

“And are they like together, together?” I nudge.

“They are,” he takes a sip from his mug “not all brides are like that, I don’t plan on being part of a menage a trois.” He laughs.

I return his laugh, my face flushing crimson. I don’t know what kind of relationship mine and my Masters would be. Another question I stupidly never asked. I’m not totally opposed to it, but he keeps me at such a distance it seems a wild concept he would want any sort of intimacy. I always thought I would maybe be more like a young protégé or friend. Or honestly maybe no different to what I am now, an eternal servant who would at least always have a roof over her head and money for whatever she needed. I didn’t get paid perse but I had an AMEX that I could use for clothes and food as and when I needed.

“I have a whole family too,” Michelle chips in. She stays curled up on her chair but lifts her chin to join the conversation. “My Master is the head of the household, but he has a brother and a sister. I have no idea if they're related but that's how they refer to each other. We will all have the same last name as our Master once we're turned of course."

"I'm surprised your Master wants another bride then if there's already three mouths to hunt for in the house. You must have to bring back a lot of humans for them." Jared looks at her with a suspicious look on his face and I wonder if he is thinking what I'm thinking. For a woman who is responsible for feeding three vampires she was awfully upset about killing someone yesterday.

"They all hunt for themselves; they go out separately every couple of weeks. I'm there to tend to the house and look over them during the night but I'm not responsible for feeding them. I think they like that part themselves." She shivers slightly at the thought and draws further into herself, as if she had never truly considered what that meant until now. Had she lived in quiet ignorance? How was she going to fair when it was her turn to hunt?

"If you're so squeamish about it, what are you going to do when you have to hunt for yourself?" Neal laughs from his seat at the table, voicing my thoughts.

I may not kill my victims myself, but I am at least used to hunting and luring people to their death. I'm used to cleaning up the bodies. Though it will be an adjustment killing them myself it isn't really much of a step further, though being faced with the reality of it would likely be different I suppose. Seeing that body in the forest yesterday… it was … harder than I thought.

"Honestly, I hadn't thought about that part too much. The idea of living forever, of not aging, that's the part I've been focused on. My sister died of stage four breast cancer when I was twenty-two. I watched it tear her apart year upon year until she finally gave in." Her eyes start to shine with that far off look and I can tell she's not focused on Neal as she speaks. "I was taking her for a walk round the hospital one night when my Master appeared. I was so frightened I thought he was going to kill us both."

I see her hands start to shake slightly and her bottom lip trembles. This isn't easy for her and I don't know why but it's clear she feels the need to justify herself to us.

"It was dark, and we were out alone in the community garden. He said he could put her out of her misery, and he could make sure I never suffered the same way." Her eyes close and a single tear slides down her cheek. "She was in so much pain … but … she wasn't frightened like me. She … She … Begged me to let her go." Her voice breaks at this point and I see Ash rise from his chair to comfort her. He stands behind her and rests a hand on her shoulder.

"He made it quick for her at least." Michelle finally continues after a few long deep breaths. "I honestly can't say why I went with him that night, I was so full of grief. But working for him was a welcome distraction in the coming months. I kept the house clean. I helped them during the nights. They became my purpose. I got so used to looking after my sister Nicky that I felt right looking after someone else. That was about eight years ago now, and finally I thought I would be a proper part of their family. I'd never have to worry about getting sick and suffering like Nicky did. But this…" She lifts her hands in the air gesturing to nothing in particular.

"I don't think I'm cut out for this." She shakes her head and drops it, nothing else to say.

"It honestly doesn't bother me." Neal shrugs.

I throw him a dirty look along with Jared and Drea. This guy wins the gold medal in not being able to read a room.

"What?!" He responds to our silencing stares with genuine confusion. "You wouldn't all be here if most of you weren't okay with death. I've been a hunter my whole life before I came here. Deer mostly but big birds and such too. We all eat prey to survive it's the natural cycle of things." He sits taller in his chair trying to display that he isn't ashamed.

"My Master uses the mountains where we're from to pick off hunters in the season. Easy to explain when they go missing. He saw my talents and thought I'd be useful. He's by himself so adding me will just make us a lethal hunting team."

A hunter, I roll my eyes inwardly. I'm not a vegetarian so it's a little hypocritical of me but I can't help but judge him. It's one thing to eat animals but another to enjoy their demise. I sense that is a shared feeling around the room because no one speaks up to agree with him.

"I make sure I only take bad people." I offer up, not only to break the silence, but to let Neal know what I think of and his hunting antics.

Michelle perks up slightly at my words giving me the confidence to keep going. "It's not ideal, and I know I shouldn't be playing judge, jury and executioner. But it helps me sleep at night." I shrug. It's the truth, I feel little to no remorse over those who I have helped kill. I know how many, I give them that small respect. But I don't feel its eating away at my soul.

"Same here." David says. He strokes his beard

thoughtfully but doesn't make eye contact with me. "I'm a regular at the local courthouse. Make a note of anyone who gets off where they shouldn't. Or any names of suspected helpers. I like to think I've actually cleaned up the streets and getting to watch the life drain from their eyes, well, that's just a bonus." His eyes have a sparkle to them as he voices the last part that sends a shiver down my spine, does he watch his Master drain the people he brings back? And he enjoys it?

This is good, though they may not realize it, people are showing us who can and can't be trusted. Drea jumps out of her seat at this point and makes her way over to me a sway of her hips that must be purposeful. She leans over from behind and wraps her arms around my shoulders. Her hair brushes the side of my face ever so gently.

"Well look at us, just a bunch of guardian angels doing the lord's work. Well, except Neal." She sticks her tongue out at him in jest and have to try my best to not focus on the proximity of her mouth to my face. Neal rolls his eyes and flips her off.

"Hey none of that when Alice comes back out of her room." I scold him.

"We're discussing murder I think the middle finger is the least of her worries." He rolls his eyes. I guess he's right.

"It's a joke isn't it." Michelle laughs without humor.

Drea unwraps her arms and stands straight, she rests a hand on the back of my chair and a small part of me immediately misses her warmth.

"Not a very funny one by the miserable look on your face." She snorts as she stands. I want to chastise her for her cruel words but I know she means to lighten the mood, even if it isn't working.

"We're a bunch of assistants to vampires and none of us have the heart to murder." Michelle clarifies.

"Well, I do." Neal laughs, again completely lacking the ability to read the room yet again.

"I rather enjoy it, if I'm being honest." David laughs along with him.

"We're all murders in here in one way or another." Nikolas stands at the head of the table. His voice silencing. Man, this guy is a buzzkill, his words do stir something in me though. He is right of course, but hearing it from someone else is something I haven't experienced in all my time doing this. Having someone call me a murderer, it makes it a little more real than it was before.

"Everyone here is responsible directly, or indirectly for quite a few deaths." He continues. "The only thing that makes us different is we rationalize it to ourselves. Our twisted moral compass is probably what drew our Masters to us in the first place. Vampires wouldn't want completely immoral psychopaths as familiars would they. Part of our purpose is to guard them they have to be able to trust us to have some kind of moral compass and loyalty."

He leans forward, and both his palms are pressed flat against the table. From this angle I can see the flex in his broad shoulders. He has changed since last night into a grey muscle T and sweatpants and right now it's not leaving much to the imagination. His hair is pulled into a somewhat smooth bun on top of his head but a few stray strands fall over his face. He looks absolutely beautiful, and absolutely lethal.

I really should have tried to make some time to date I think to myself, shaking the mental image of Nikolas rippling muscles from my mind. It's absolutely embarrassing that we are in a life-or-death situation and all I keep thinking about it how hot my opponents are. I'm twenty-five but I feel like a schoolgirl. I need to get a grip.

"I got a present too!" Alices shriek breaks the tension followed by the sound of her little feet.

She leans out of her room waving a teddy bear around by its leg. Poor bear. She immediately disappears after showing off her prize back into her room. Probably to dress it up or have make believe tea with it. God this is so messed up.

“I still say she shouldn’t be here.” Ash speaks softly.

“Well, I agree with you but what can we do.” I whisper back. “They know she’s here now; my Master saw her yesterday when he came in. They’ve even packed her a trunk.” I throw my arm out in the direction of her room. “If they were going to give her a free pass out of here, she would be gone already.” I feel awful for being so pessimistic but it’s true. Whatever we think, Alice is here to stay.

“You don’t think they’ll change her do you?” Drea sounds serious for a change. “Have they never watched interview with a vampire? She stays in a ten-year old’s body, but she’ll get old and bitter and burn their house down.” She laughs, that comment was more like her. I roll my eyes.

“Changing children is against their rules, I know this from my Master. There was … an incident in Mumbai.” Ash pauses, unsure as to whether he wants to share this or not. The stares of eight people burning into him lets him know we probably won’t give him a choice so with a deep breath he continues.

"One of my Masters brides had changed a child without permission, their lack of self-control and inability to follow the rules led to the slaughter of thirty-six people in two days."

My breath hitches at his words. Thirty-six people. Thirty-six innocent people from the sounds of things. Could Alice truly be capable of something like that? Would that little girl with her teddy bear and pajamas end up a serial killer?

"If its against the rules then what will they do with her?" I manage to ask.

"Perhaps she will live with them and continue as a familiar until she matures." Ash shrugs. "I do not deem to know their mind; I would have thought she would have been removed already."

"We are all here at their mercy." Nikolas mumbles.

Well, that's my appetite super ruined. I push my chair back, forgetting Drea is still standing behind me. She harrumphs and takes a step back as I knock the chair into her.

"Sorry." I mumble, taking myself back to my room without another word. I'm done with this conversation, and I can't be bothered for everyone's moral posturing right now. Alice is here and there is nothing we can do about it. Frankly I'm worried someone's going to suggest offing her again. After hearing Neal talk about his hunting and seeing the sparkle in his eye, I'm not so convinced its unrealistic someone isn't going to hurt her. The truth is I don't really know any of these people. They could all be putting on a good show.

I get back into my room and don't realize I'm being followed until I hear my door slide shut behind me. I turn to see Nikolas, his figure dominating the room and it seems so much smaller with him in it towering over me. The look in his eyes of sheer anger.

"What are you doing here." He demands.

"This is my room." I snark, pretending to be much braver than I feel.

"You know what I mean, you show up here, adopt the only child in the room and talk about how you only kill bad people. You're not exactly the stuff vampires are made of, so what's your deal."

"My deal?" Is he joking right now, who the hell does he think he is to march in here and ask me what my deal is.

He takes a step toward me, and I can't help but take a step back. I'm annoyed at myself for showing I'm afraid of him, but my survival instincts override any sense I might have.

"Michelle is vain and doesn't want to die, Neal is a sociopath who likes the hunt. What are you going to get out of being a vampire, adopt all the needy children?" He sneers at me, my fear and anger swirling imperceivably together.

"It's none of your fucking business why I'm here and don't act like I'm some weak pathetic girl because I don't want that child to die." I throw my hand out and point at the wall that joins to Alices. "You have done just as much to save her despite your words, so I could ask you what the hell you're doing." I try to square myself up to him but he snarls back at me and I immediately take another step back like the total wimp I am. His feet move forward confidently not allowing us any space.

I've lured plenty of men, but It's rarely ever ended in a struggle. I usually manage to knock them out with a pill in their drink or a needle in their neck long before they suspect anything from me. Now facing down the brute strength of this furious stranger I am absolutely terrified, and I have no idea what to do. For what feels like the millionth time this week, adrenaline sours in my body and makes my heart race. As if he senses my fear, he takes another step and take a step back which puts me flat against the wall. Nowhere to run.

"I wanted to put her out of her misery in her sleep. I wanted to show her kindness but I'm not blind to the reality. You're prolonging her suffering because you can't do what needs to be done. What are you going to do the first time you need to drain someone huh?" He inches closer, eliminating the last space between us. I can feel the heat from his body now.

"Are you going to be able to do it or are you going to let them run?" He reaches out and grabs me by the throat, pushing me firmly in place against the wall. I grasp his wrist with both hands, but he is immovable. He doesn't press down so hard that I can't breathe, but I certainly can't escape.

Something in his eyes changes and he looks less furious and more entertained. He leans his head in toward me and I can feel his breath on my face. His free hand he places flat on the wall alongside my head.

"If you had your prey, like this, at your total mercy, would you be able to take a bite?" He leans down and sinks his teeth into my flesh at the base of my neck where it meets my shoulder. I yelp in surprise, the pain itself not fully kicking in due to shock.

He pulls back slightly almost immediately and runs his tongue over where he has just bitten me. I can feel my heart beating like a rabbit in headlights. I wonder if he can feel it against my neck.

"Would you taste their blood and like it?" He whispers

against my skin.

Heat pools in my stomach and my fear quickly turns to something else. I've never been touched like this. I've never had someone's body pressed against me like this and my own body doesn't know how to react. His tongue against my neck sets off a chain reaction that I can't ignore. I release a whimpering breath and a small growl escapes Nikolas in return.

He pulls back fully and releases my neck. I almost fall to the floor without the sudden support from him holding me in place. He seems to have moved instantaneously now a foot away from me in the room. His eyes glisten with a mischief I haven't seen from him before.

"Maybe I'm wrong little rabbit." He smirks. "Maybe you'll enjoy it more than I thought." He looks me up and down like a predator. I've been looked at many times by men. When I'm in bars and clubs trying to pick up prey. I've always hated it. But now as Nikolas devours me with his eyes, I can feel the heat rise to my cheeks again. He turns to leave, and I am completely stunned. I can't speak or move. I just stand there, against the wall completely dazed and confused. He slides my door open and slams it shut behind him.

I lift a hand to my throat and feel for where he bit me. I pull my fingers away and stare at the red liquid smeared across them. I can't believe he just did that. Even more worryingly, I can't believe I liked it. This place is going to be the death of me, in multiple senses of the word.

*

I stay in my room for at least an hour. Pacing at first, unsure what to do with myself. Unsettled is the only way I can think to describe how I feel. I certainly don't feel less afraid of Nikolas, but I also feel a little drawn to him. This man who has threatened to end then saved Alices life. I lift my hand to my throat more than once and place it where he had his. What was his goal? Did he just want to intimidate me? Somehow, I think not. There are many ways to intimidate me that would not have resulted with me being pressed against the wall.

I replay the look in his eyes and the noises escaping his mouth over and over. He enjoyed doing that to me, I'm just not sure why.

The way he looked at me like he would eat me alive if he had the chance. And bearing in mind I have sweatpants on right now that's saying something. He didn't look at me like that in my skintight velvet dress.

What's wrong with this guy?

No matter how my body might be reacting to him one thing is for sure, I don't like the guy. Whatever his motives are here they aren't good, and I can let myself be put in a position like that again. This weak stuff ends now. I need to step up my game. The door must be closed and locked behind me at all times. If Nikolas had wanted to, he could have closed his hand tighter there and drained the life out of me, and there would be nothing I could have done about it.

But he didn't, I think to myself.

I shake my head as if I can make the thought fall out. Don't be stupid, just because he didn't kill me this time doesn't mean he doesn't want to. Maybe he was just testing the water to see how easy I could be eliminated. Pretty damn easy is the answer. I resolve myself to take a knife next time I'm in the kitchen.

I already know some people here have weapons after Jared disclosed his Master's gift. I can't be caught unarmed again. At least if there's a next time, I can jab my secret butter knife into his neck before he decides to squeeze the life out of me.

Do I want there to be a next time? I immediately scold myself for the thought, but it comes anyway. Before I know it, I'm thinking about not Nikolas but Drea holding me against the wall like that, her soft hand around my throat, her blue eyes full of fun looking down at me as she pressed me into the wall.

I need to get a grip.

I stop pacing and look around the room for something to distract myself. My eyes come to my trunk, and I scold myself for being so stupid. I had a rifle around in it last night but I was so exhausted I barely noticed what was in there. Maybe my Master thought to pack me a present too. One by one I take every item of clothing out of the trunk and shake it before throwing it on the bed, hoping something is going to fall out. Unfortunately, nothing like an AK-47 could be hiding in here which is probably what I need to defend myself, but anything would help at this point. I get to the last T shirt and shake it frantically still holding out hope but there's nothing. I throw it furiously across the room before sinking to me knees.

I can't believe he didn't give me anything. It obviously wasn't against the rules because other people had things so why would he leave me vulnerable? Does he want me to be his bride or not? This trial is not doing good things for our relationship.

Before I can through myself a full-blown pity party I notice a small silver tab at the bottom of the inside of the trunk. I reach down thinking maybe it's a tiny loose blade but as my hand meets it, I'm disappointed to feel its fabric. Still, I pull at it to have a closer look and as I do the full bottom of the trunk lifts slightly with it.

I close my eyes; I shouldn't get my hopes up.

I slide my fingers around the edge of the false bottom and work it free. I pull it out and place it on the floor next to me.

Holy fuck.

The entire bottom of the trunk is lined with weapons. There are large hunting knives, small switch blades, there's even ninja stars. They are all slid into leather holders keeping them separate and organized. In the top corner there is a series of leather straps folded over that I reach over and lift out.

It has a series of buckles and after some tinkering, I realize it's a strap to go around my thigh I'm guessing is to hold a weapon. I'm both relieved that my Master thought to help me, and gob smacked he thinks I'm qualified to be wielding any of this. I pick up a throwing star and turn it over holding it up to the light. I can see how sharp the edges are from here, this would be absolutely lethal. I very slowly and gently put it down. It would be just my luck to slice myself open with it and I wouldn't be able to explain it away to anyone. I don't want to give away I have these. Mostly because I want to feel like I have even a tiny bit of an edge but also because I have a feeling it might make me a target for break ins and robberies.

I might not be able to wield a throwing star but that doesn't mean I want them in the hands of anyone else. I stand up and strip of my sweatpants. I pick the leather holder up and try to figure out which way it goes on. After an embarrassing number of attempts I realize it goes all the up to my waist. One strap runs around the smallest part of my waist and buckles on the right side. The two straps run all the way down my hips to each thigh where they buckle again. There is a knife holder on each side that runs down my thigh and a strap and buckle again just above my knee. Once in place I select a small but robust serrated knife and slide it into the right-hand side. I don't need to double up and I'm right-handed anyway.

I replace the false bottom, careful to ensure the tab of fabric doesn't get tucked in and is still accessible. I stand and look at the mountain of clothes on my bed to fold back in. I might have to change to make sure You can't see my new accessory. I try pulling my sweatpants back on but as I turn you can clearly see I'm carrying something on the right side. I try pulling on some yoga pants which flattens out the knife, but the outline is clearly there. I opt finally for a combo with the sweatpants on top of the yoga pants which I'm happy conceals it enough. I'll be sweating when I'm walking around but it will have to do. I won't sleep in layers at least, I decide and will just keep the knife under my pillow.

I'm about to rejoin the group when I suddenly remember the bite mark on my neck. My hand slaps over it instinctually even though there is no one to see it. I don't want to have to explain that to people. Turning back to my trunk I begin to sift through the clothes again. There's a tight black turtleneck T shirt which I can use. But the material is thin, and you'll be able to see my waist strap through it.

I groan as I realize my only option is more layering. I curse Nikolas under my breath as I pull my sweatshirt off to add the shirt in.

I'm definitely going to be sweating now. At least if the next trial is outside again, I will be better prepared than I was in my stupid dress.

I pull at the neckline once everything is in place to ensure it covers the mark, which it does and more. As I do I can't help but feel like a teenager covering a hickey. I laugh to myself, I never had that. A hickey, or a family to hide one from. But I saw plenty of it on TV, plenty angsty teens with "love bites" from their boyfriends. Furious dads when they find them, audience laughter as he chases off their unsuspecting boyfriend.

My laughter disappears as I remind myself of the reality. Stood here alone, in a cell, with no one to care I have a hickey but me. And the boy who gave me it, not a boyfriend, not in a moment of lust. But a strange man who wanted to make me afraid. I don't often mourn the life I missed becoming a vampire familiar in my teens. But now, as I stand here feeling vulnerable and sad, I can't help but contemplate all the things I've missed.

I only allow myself a minute to throw myself a pity part then I straighten myself out, hold my head high and head back out. I'm here like it or not, and if I want to win this then I need to play the game. To do that, I need to size up my competition. I'm not going to win on brute strength, so I need to be smarter. Time to get serious and learn what I'm up against, so I can learn to beat them.

CHAPTER EIGHT

I slide my door open and walk out as nonchalantly as I can manage. Everyone is sitting or standing in little groups, the idle chatter of small talk filling the small room. The atmosphere doesn't feel as oppressive as earlier and I can only hope everyone has decided to at least play at being friends.

My eyes find Nikolas first and I wonder how or if he will react to me. He sits on the sofas shuffling the deck of cards Ash had earlier. Even though he clearly hears me come outside he doesn't look up or make any attempt to meet my eyes. It annoys me that he doesn't even deem me worthy to look at after the stunt he pulled.

I feel my chin raise slightly in defiance and instead look for Alice. She's standing with Drea making ridiculous looking Kung Fu poses. Drea stands, almost twice her height, looking down on her with appraising eyes. Her silvery blonde hair has been detangled and braided away from her face and she's wearing a black tight matching sweatsuit. On her feet she has nothing but black socks. Her arms are crossed as she watches

Alice as if she's her Mr. Miyagi.

"Wax on?" I say as I make my way over to them.

Alice, who was busy trying to stand with one leg raised and her palms held in front of her, immediately loses her balance as she hears me approach.

"Oh man! I almost had it." She scrambles back up and stamps her foot in a little temper tantrum.

Ash who is busy making a cup of tea nearby laughs at her in a lighthearted way.

"She isn't very patient." He adds when I join him with a giggle.

"I'm teaching her some moves." Drea says and stands in a crane kick pose which actually looks rather elegant and threatening when she does it. Her right leg is raised surprisingly high, and she bends her left slightly to balance herself. She looks solid and I have a feeling I wouldn't be able to tip her over if I tried.

"You make it look so easy." Alice pouts.

"Well, I had ten years of ballet and genuine taekwondo, so it is easy for me now. You'll get there." She remains on one foot but extends a hand to pat Alice on the head which elicits a giggle.

“Ballet?” I’m surprised, though I suppose she is built for it being tall and lithe I picture her more being part of a junior Harley Davidson gang than in a pink tutu.

On cue she twists and extends the leg that’s in front of her so that its points out behind her. She raises her arms out to the sides and curves her upper body. She immediately looks like a swan, her body long and pointed but also soft and fluid. She must be extremely flexible because the leg extended behind her is lifted so high her toes come in line with the top of her head. In the get up she currently has on she looks like the black swan, beautiful but deadly.

Just to show off for extra measure she bounces slightly, and I notice the foot planted on the floor is now balanced on the tip of her toes on point. It makes her look even taller and like something absolutely ethereal.

“Now you’re just showing off.” I say, my words coming out almost breathless.

Her head which was tipped slightly back, tilts forward to meet my eyes. She winks at me and relaxes her body back to standing as slowly and gracefully as she can manage.

“The ballet surprises you but not the taekwondo?” She asks.

"I wouldn't be surprised to know you learned how to fight but you don't seem like a dancer." I regret the words as soon as I've said them, she has always held herself with a grace that I couldn't quite place. I hope I don't offend her. Luckily, she just shrugs.

"Learning to fight and learning to dance are part of the same breath. To fight you must know balance and fluidity, to dance you must have strength and fortitude."

I simply nod. wondering who taught her that phrase, the way she said it was practiced. As if someone repeated it to her until she could recite it by wrote. Her Master? Her parents? I want to know, but also don't want to pry.

"So is Alice learning the crane kick and the nutcracker?" I jest with her a smile tugging at my lips. Choosing to not pry into her private life.

"I was thinking more the hand jive for her level of skill." She winks at me.

"What's the hand jive?" Alice asks.

I groan feeling old, she's probably too young to have seen Greece or heard the song. I look at her curious little face and feel a sad twang again, she probably never will be old enough for a lot of experience if things go badly in a few days' time.

“Don’t worry about it.” I say, gently patting her head. She bats me off immediately.

“That’s enough for today anyway we’ve been at it for an hour, and I’m exhausted from expelling such deep and profound knowledge. Being a teacher in draining.” Drea theatrically flings the back of her hand against her forehead in mock exhaustion eliciting a laugh from both me and Alice. Without another word or a thank you Alice takes herself off to the fridge, gets out a bag of chocolate candies and disappears back to her room.

“Well, I didn’t have to tell her twice did I. You’re welcome little brat.” Drea laughs, though the sparkle in her eyes shows me she doesn’t mind.

“What exactly are you teaching her then?” I say as I follow Alices lead and grab myself some food.

Drea follows me over the fridge and leans in over the top of me grabbing an apple from the highest shelf. I grab a premade sandwich from the bottom.

“I said I would teach her some basic self-defense and fighting moves.” She takes a seat at the table.

I take a seat next to her, we’re at the far end with Michelle, David and Neal all gathered at the other. They seem in intense conversation which surprises me, they didn’t seem the type to all make friends. I try not to overthink it but make a mental note to keep an eye on them, perhaps alliances are forming. They speak in hushed tones, and I could hear what they're saying if I wanted to but not without making it obvious I'm listening. Espionage will have to wait for another time. I turn back to Drea and smile trying my best not to worry about it, unwrapping what looks to be a cold chicken salad sandwich.

"That's nice of you." The words taste empty on my tongue.

She raises an eyebrow at me.

"You sure about that?" She laughs.

"No, I do mean it! It's just, honestly how much good do you think it'll really do if you know…"

"What? if someone in here tries to take her down? It'll do diddly squat, but it killed an hour and I think maybe it'll make her less frightened." She shrugs and bites into her apple. Fresh juice running down the side of her face. She takes the back of her sleeve and wipes it off.

In that case, it really is nice of her. But my heart does sink as she admits she also thinks what I do. It won't help her, but at least it can lessen some of the fear she has of not being able to protect herself. If I'm being honest with myself, I have the same fear. I wonder not for the first time whether I should give one of my smaller knives to Alice. It's certainly made me feel less vulnerable, maybe it'll work for her too.

"It was a good idea." I say honestly, not knowing how to put anything else I feel into words.

Drea looks at me sympathetically.

"Listen I know this is awful, none of us thought we were going to be in here against a kid. But there's no rule that says we need to eliminate each other, just that the strongest will make it out the other side. Have some faith in her she might surprise you."

Her words are a kind lie rather than the harsh truth, I know, but I am grateful for them regardless.

"She's just so young, and so small. I don't know what the next trial is going to be, and I don't know how I'm going to get myself through it never mind her." It's a small admission but it hints at something else I'm afraid of. I want to help her, I do, but I don't even know if I can help myself.

How am I supposed to look after Alice and get myself through this. What happens if it comes down to helping her or saving myself. I already know the truth. I showed myself the truth in the last trial, when I couldn't find her, and I let Drea turn me around. Sure, Alice was already safe, but I didn't know that. I was going to go back there to safety and leave Alice in that cave because I couldn't find her, and I couldn't save us both. Put in the same situation I know deep down that survival instincts will kick in and I would save myself. But would I be able to live with myself afterwards?

"If it comes down to it Alice will get herself through this. Trust me from someone who went through hell as a kid, a little girl against the world is tougher than you think." I stop avoiding her eyes and lift mine from my uneaten but picked apart sandwich. Her eyes seem to be holding an invitation as if she wants me to ask her more.

"Not a picket fence childhood then?" I press gently.

She snorts.

"Yeah, you could say that." She doesn't offer more than that and I wonder if I've read her wrong for a moment. "My mom died when I was really little, and my dad was kind of an asshole. Well, a giant asshole. He used to knock me around some when I did something he didn't like. Which was often."

My hand reaches out instinctively and I place it on her knee. I think of a little Drea, it's hard to imagine her not as a super confident kick ass woman but instead a little frightened girl with a monster for a dad. My mom and dad might have been complicated but one thing I can say is they were kind and loving with me. I can't imagine what it would have been like to grow up feeling unsafe in your own home.

Drea looks down at my hand on her knee and smiles.

"If I had been particularly bad, he would make me sleep out on the front porch of our trailer, I used to sit there all night watching the stars. I thought maybe if I saw a shooting one, I could wish that he would drop down dead." She laughs an empty laugh. "I was only nine, a year younger than Alice, when my Master found me. I was out on the back porch watching the stars and she came out of nowhere. I still remember thinking she looked more like a guardian angel than a demon in the night. She cocked her head at me and asked me what I was doing outside at that hour. I told her about the mean man in my trailer who wouldn't let me in."

Nine, only nine years old. I have a feeling I know where this is going, and I don't like it. Though from what Drea says I don't know what would be worse, staying with her abusive father or going with the vampire.

"She asked me if I wanted her to get rid of the bad man for me and she would take me with her. I remember thinking I was so lucky. I hadn't even seen a shooting star and here was a guardian angel answering my wish." She drops her head and shakes it slowly as if scolding herself for her own naivety.

"I don't remember saying yes but I must have because she walked straight past me and into my trailer. Whether she made any noise or not I have no idea I must have blocked it out. But she came out not long after, took my hand and I've been with her ever since." She shrugged. "She's the one who put me through ballet and fight lessons. She worked me like a drill sergeant but I had everything I ever needed. Then once I was old enough, I started serving her. She saved my life."

"It sounds like she groomed you." I say before I can think it through.

She looks at me and for the first time I see her eyes flash with anger.

"She kept me safe, more than my family ever could. And she made it so no one could ever hurt me again. I think helping her with the odd blood bag is the least I can do."

"I didn't mean to speak ill of her." I flail "I just mean, did you ever think you might grow up to do something else, don't you see a life for yourself outside of this. You were so young when you were taken." My words soften her and as quickly as the anger appeared, it is gone.

“It’s all I’ve ever known princess, and my Master and me do have a genuine relationship. She’s my mentor, my family. Where else would I go huh? What else would I do? I can’t list trained by a vampire to be a killing machine on my resume for Harvard.” She leans back and crosses her legs as she speaks, knocking my hand off of her. She’s done being vulnerable. She opened up and I ruined it.

“When you were little and you were wishing on stars, what would you have wished to be when you grew up?” I try again. I like Drea, I feel a connection to her. We may have had different beginnings but were the same in a lot of ways. When she talks about not having a choice, about being in this life since she was so young, I can’t help but see myself reflected back in her words. This little girl who never had a chance, what would she do if it had all been different? I want to know because I want to know her better, but I also want to know because if someone asked me the same questions I honestly don’t know what I would say.

Her face softens slightly but she doesn’t relax her posture and maintains a distance between us that seems to be widening by the second.

“Honestly princess I have no idea, I never got those

choices. I did the best with what I had. Quite frankly it didn't turn out that bad, it could have been worse, I could have been left with my dad."

The admission is hard for her I can tell, but there's something comforting in hearing her say answer with that honesty. I have thought in the past what my life would have been like if I was normal. I would drive down the street or to the store and watch the world go by. I would see young couples holding hands, in so much love that they couldn't be separated. I would see families with little kids running around and throwing tantrums. I would look at them and wonder what it felt like. To have someone love you, to have someone to come home to who asked about your day or was excited to see you. But ultimately, I never lingered too long on those thoughts because I always knew I would never have it.

But being here has rocked my foundations, this is the most I have talked to another human being in as long as I can remember. I'm not watching my words or making polite small talk; I'm having a genuine real life conversation and it suddenly hits me. I have been immensely lonely.

"You sound like you have found someone really important in your Master." I say wistfully. "You sound like you guys mean a lot to each other, do you ever feel, lonely though?"

She has a puzzled expression for a moment as if the thought had honestly never struck her and at that moment, I know that though we have shared a lot of experiences in some ways we are worlds apart.

"Not really, she brought in trainers for my classes, so I always had a variety of people around. I was expected at dinner with her, and she would educate me on things about vampire way of life, or ask me about my training. As I got older, she would ask me about finding kills for her. It's not like having a BBF, we didn't have sleep overs and talk about our crushes and paint our nails. But she's kind of like … well … my mom. So, no I've never been alone."

I think for a moment before I respond, but finally I decide to push her.

"I didn't ask if you were alone, I asked if you were lonely."

"Is there a difference?" She asks.

"I think so, my Master and me were in the same house but I have felt lonely every minute of every day since I lost my parents." My voice cracks slightly as I admit this not only to her but to myself.

For so many years I have ignored the empty place in my heart, quietly wondering but pushing it down. I think it feels so much more painful now because for the first time I feel like I could have a friend. I feel so pathetic that this girl who I have known for two days is making me feel this way.

“When did they die?” She asks me.

“When I was fifteen. They had been out on a date night and got in a car crash on their way home.” I shudder as I recall opening the front door of our little suburban home. Blue lights flashed in the dark and two police officers towered over me with grimaces.

“Apparently a deer ran out in front of them, the car flipped and landed in a ditch. A quick death they told me” I laughed as if that made any difference to a grieving fifteen-year-old girl.

“We had no family; my parents didn’t really have any friends. I was going to end up in care. I thought I’d be able to stay in the house but apparently, they had debt, and it was seized. I packed a bag and ran, not knowing where I was going but knowing I wasn’t going into the foster system. I’d seen enough true crime documentaries to know the kind of people you could end up with there. So, I packed a bag, and took the hundred bucks I had stashed in my room and I went to the train station. That’s where he found me, told me he knew my dad and he could take care of me. It’s funny I don’t know why I didn’t want to go to a foster home but went home with a stranger from the train station.”

I laugh at my own stupidity, though it worked out alright in the end.

"Well because they can charm us probably." Drea says matter of factly.

"Excuse me?" I say.

"They can charm us, it's not like mind control but they can switch on something that puts humans at ease and makes us more malleable. Makes the prey struggle less when we're dazed." She laughs and makes her eyes go crossed.

"I didn't know that." How did I not know that. Master has always been secretive; he's always said I would learn once I was changed one day. But this? This is pretty important information; how many times has he made me more *malleable* over the years? Would I even know, I don't recall him using any kind of woowoo power on me in the train station that night. Though I wasn't exactly myself. Surely, I would know if I was being manipulated, wouldn't I?

"You didn't? Hey, you okay? I didn't mean to upset you." Drea reaches out and puts her hand on my knee this time but I can't meet her eyes.

"Would we know? If they used it on us?" I ask her.

She draws back unsure and shrugs.

“I don’t know cause my Master’s never used it on me, she says it’s for putting prey out of their misery and that’s all. She doesn’t like to abuse her powers, thinks it’s for vamps with more bravado than control.” She sniffs as if she agrees that it would be completely beneath her.

“How benevolent of her.” I scoff.

“Hey, don’t you get all judgey on me now, we all have prey. You’re going to be draining someone one day. Wouldn’t you rather they feel no pain or suffering while you do?”

I consider this. In general, I pick up scum people who would have hurt someone else had I not intervened with them. So, no, I never particularly have concerns about whether they are in pain or if they suffer. Though I can always tell by the bodies Master leaves he doesn’t play with his food.

Would I use a charm on someone to calm them in their final moments? I think maybe I wouldn’t, I wouldn’t want someone to use it on me. If I’m going to be murdered, then I should at least have the right to be myself and feel genuine emotions in my final moments.

“I don’t know.” Is all I can honestly reply.

“I think you’ve got a lot to think about before this is

over. No offense but I've had a lot of prep on this. I've thought this whole thing through. It sounds like you've been kept essentially in the dark. Are you really sure becoming a vampire is what you want?" She asks me skeptically.

I laugh humorlessly. The honest answer is I have no idea. In the past two days I have found out my Master probably lured me in with coercion, put me in here to die without me knowing, and has given me not only no preparation but no real depth of relationship the past ten years. I'm having an absolute inner crisis.

"Do I have a choice at this point?" I laugh.

Drea's mouth twists as she realizes no matter what she would like to answer me she can't really say that I do. If I don't make it through this I die, If I make it through this I get changed. If there's a safe word that would allow me to go walk the streets, then I don't know it. And anyway, I would have nowhere to go. I have to remind myself of my earlier thought, there is no point moping in here. Regardless of what I want to do after, I have to win.

"Maybe though, you could help me prepare?" I ask.

She raises an eyebrow at me, and her grimace turns into a smirk.

"I think there's lots of things I could teach you

princess, where would you like to start?"

I feel the blood pool in my cheeks and my brain betrays me by thinking of all the things I want Drea to teach me about, not of which are appropriate for discussion in the public room.

"Look at you blushing like a schoolgirl." She laughs at me. "You really do have no experience do you, you're so easy to fluster." She bats her eyelids and I cross my arms in defiance.

"And how much experience do you have, you've been a familiar in training since you were nine!" I accuse.

"I was still allowed to go out, I still had to go to hunt. I've been to bars and parties. I've got experience enough don't you worry." She waggles her eyebrows.

"And how much experience is enough?" I can't help the curiosity.

"Ten" she admits.

"Ten … people?" I say, realizing I almost went with the automatic and said men, but from our interactions its clearly not men. Or not exclusively anyway.

Understanding my blunder Drea laughs again and I of course, blush again.

“Four men and six women if you must have my detailed statistics” She specifies.

I am so out of my depth.

“I think you can just teach me about being a vampire for now.” I have to change the subject because I’m going to spontaneously combust with embarrassment if I don’t.

“For now.” She agrees, a promise lining her words.

“Look at me, teacher to two students and we’re only one day in. Perhaps I should set up a sign-up sheet and post an hourly rate.” Her tone is lighter again as she continues to speak. The moment, whatever it was passing. I’m not sure if I’m relieved or disappointed.

CHAPTER NINE

The afternoon passes more slowly than any other afternoon of my life. Everyone does seem to mingle, and I make it my mission to observe and keep note of who is talking and about what if I can manage it. There are clearly some lines being drawn.

Though everyone rotates slightly and at times we find ourselves all-round the table eating, there are definitely cliques forming.

The main person who sticks out like a sore thumb is Jessica who yet again isn't present. I glance to her door, and it remains closed. I wonder if she has even been out for food or if she intends to sulk alone until the next trial. Perhaps she will find it easier to kill us if she hasn't got to know us.

Ash and Jared seem to be spending most of their time together, chairs pulled closely always playing cards. I suspect the cards are a pretense because they keep their heads bent close and maintain a steady stream of quiet conversation.

They are clever however in ensuring that they

routinely get up and mingle in between so as to not draw too clear of a line. Ash spends some time with both me and Alice, he teaches her go fish and plays a few rounds with her. He talks to me about his Master. They both live in India but travel around the world regularly to visit other vampire families. I'm surprised to hear not only that a vampire can travel but that Ash's Master actually has a small cabal who sometimes join him. His family sounds rather large.

I genuinely enjoy hearing about how they travel by boat and hearing stories of his home country. India sounds beautiful. He offers for me to visit one day if I ever find myself there, as if were too people who've met on vacation and plan to stay in touch. I smile and say I would like that though we both know it will never happen.

Jared takes a turn sparing with Drea and I get to see the full scope of her skills. Though I suspect that she is still somewhat holding back, not wanting to reveal how good she truly is. Which honestly is terrifying because she still absolutely kicks Jared's ass. He takes it on the chin and laughs each time she knocks him to the floor or lands a punch. They last a few rounds before he graciously bows out admitting he is outmatched.

Though the two men clearly gravitate toward each other they are obviously still friendly with the rest of the group and though I understand they will likely have each other's back during the next trial, I don't think they'll be out to stab anyone else in theirs.

The trio of trouble however, as I have so eloquently named them. Sit scheming, isolated, almost the entirety of the day. Neal, David and Michelle have retreated back to Michelle's room and remain there. They have the door slid half closed so you can't make out exactly what is happening, but hushed voices resonate from there all day. Occasionally a raised voice breaks through as they clearly squabble about something.

They worry me the most. Neal can hunt, Michelle seems absolutely unhinged, constantly swinging between crying, or snapping at people. And David is far too quiet to make me feel comfortable. From how he said he selected victims David seemed like a good guy, but he obviously is here to win, regardless of who he must throw his hat in the ring with.

I don't know what they are planning together but what I do know is this, when that next trial starts I want to be as far away as possible from them.

Nikolas goes between pacing the room to sitting brooding in one of the armchairs for most of the afternoon. Ash does manage to pull him into a card game once or twice and he is amicable enough. He doesn't seem rude or threatening. He just seems to want to keep his distance. Especially from me. He hasn't so much as looked at me since he cornered me in my room, and he hasn't engaged in any group chatter.

I don't know if its personal, but I can't help but feel it is. I don't know what I've done to offend him so much, other than being weak apparently. I try to resolve myself to not care but so far, I am failing miserably at that mission. I find him completely unreadable, and it makes me nervous.

Drea however seems to be happy with everyone. When she isn't fighting Jared she sits with me or entertains Alice. It's a bizarre feeling. In a very short amount of time, I've become so comfortable with some of my fellow familiars. We chat and play games as if we are all old friends and not adversaries. I wonder why I never met any of them before. Other than Ash no one mentions that their vampires travel and even Ash seems to have never met and socialized with other familiars. I suppose when you have immortality on your side then fifty years between catch ups doesn't seem like a long time.

And for some they live with more than one vampire so they aren't wanting of company. I think about my Master and wonder how long he has been alone. He was alone when I found him and there's nothing around the house to suggest that someone he once loved is now missing. I may well be the first bride he makes if I make it through these trials. I'm assuming for those who have brides they must have at some point gone through this too. Maybe those with bigger families are just more successful at picking tough familiars.

My Master obviously didn't have that in mind when he picked me. He also didn't seem invested in prepping me for this which the more I talk to Drea and the others, the more I'm offended by. Drea has obviously been trained and prepped within an inch of her life and its clear her Master is invested in her winning this and joining her family. Ash also seems to know more about the vampire way of life than me generally. He is aware of being able to charm people, as is Jared. Both the men are strong and know how to fight, though neither is capable of beating Drea. It's unclear whether they were self-taught or trained but I don't ask.

"What else don't I know; will I be able to turn into a bat after?" I ask Drea after she takes a seat, she's been running drills with Alice and thoroughly tired her out. She smirks at my question, and I immediately feel stupid.

"Don't believe everything you read, or watch." She simply replies not answering the question. When I continue to stare at her in silence she laughs.

“No, you can’t shape shift princess, nor will you sparkle in the sun.”

“I know we don’t sparkle in the sun.” I scoff as if to infer I’m not stupid, though I sure do feel it.

“Do you know what does happen in the sun?” She asks giving me a sidewards glance as she crosses one leg over the other to rub her left foot.

“It burns.” I say simply. I know this, and I always ensure the house is adequately protected. Drea seems to give me a look which suggests she is expecting me to say more and I start to worry. I honestly don’t know the extent of the risk I’ve never asked. But bearing in mind how strict Master has always been about omitting sunlight and not being woken too early I’m assuming its severe.

“Indeed, it does burn.” She laughs. “It burns as if being touched by boiling water, your skin would start to blister and break down almost immediately. The main issue though is that it’s one of the only things a vampire can’t heal from.”

I almost wish I had a notebook and some paper so that I could write down the lessons for later. Hopefully Drea doesn’t have any pop quizzes before the next class.

"What else can't they heal from?" I ask. From the corner of my eye, I notice Nikolas, who was standing leaning against the wall beside his door, perks up. Its ever so slightly and he recovers quickly, but I can tell, he's listening to us.

"Some myths are true, well half true anyway. They can't heal from a wooden steak but it's not through the heart it's through the head. The heart doesn't beat properly once they've turned anyway, but everyone needs a brain to function." Drea knocks on her head with a closed fist.

"Makes sense, but everything else they can heal?" I know my Master can heal quickly, I remember one evening waking him up and he had been clawed by a victim. The left side of his face had three distinct scratches down it, by the morning it was gone.

"Pretty much, wounds close, limbs regrow, major blood loss regenerates. They do heal quicker if they're well fed."

"Limbs regrow?!" part of me starts to think she could just be talking absolute rubbish and seeing how much I will believe.

"Yeah, my Master lost her finger once in a scrape, it was fully regrown two days later."

I try not to show I'm aware, but I try to keep Nikolas

in my peripheral vision to see if he is reacting to anything being said but I can't make out his expressions without looking directly at him.

"Okay, can't be bat, mustn't go in the light, can regrow limbs. Got it." I hold my fingers up one by one counting off my new vampire fun facts which makes Drea snort.

"And they can charm, you know that too." She reaches out and straightens another one of my fingers for me to represent my four whole facts. I laugh and bat her hand away playfully.

"How does the charming work, can they make us do whatever they want?" I wonder again how many times I've been charmed without my knowledge.

"No not exactly, it's kind of just makes us more agreeable. It calms you, your heart rate, your breathing. It releases chemicals in your brain to make you feel relaxed and safe. You wouldn't remember it afterwards either, you'd have a blank space. Like if you got hypnotized, or really drunk." She laughs.

I nod thoughtfully.

"I don't think I'll be using that still." I say.

"Well to be fair you won't be able to at first. It's not an automatic thing, like the speed, that you'll inherit.

Charming someone takes practice and skill. You'll have to work on it to be able to use and control it reliably. Even me, super A* familiar won't be able to charm immediately." She winks at me, and I roll my eyes in response.

"You're insufferable." I laugh.

"Lies, you're smitten with me really." She winks in response.

I'd argue but it's kind of true.

"Well perhaps if we both get changed you can continue to be my teacher." I suggest.

"I don't think so, princess. Families rarely mix." She looks genuinely sad as she says this, and I can't help but feel a little pleased.

"In that case you'll have to make sure I am fully trained before we part." I shrug. "Tell me about the families."

"Well, there's twenty main families I know that much, but you might have found my weak spot because I don't know much more than that. A lot of the main families have one main head of the household, and that's the only person who can turn more brides. But lots of them have vampires who have branched off and just visit for the holidays like human children would."

She tells me.

"Your Master lives alone though, right?" I ask.

"She does but she has brides. She's changed three vampires in total over her two hundred and fifty years, but they don't live with her. They travel or have their own houses. I see them from time to time if they visit." At her words I consider whether my Master has any other brides out there that just don't visit. I doubt he would tell me about them if he did. Perhaps once I'm changed, I'll find out.

"Will you live with her?" I ask her.

"Oh yes of course, all my Masters' brides lived with her for a long time. I imagine lots probably choose to never leave, certainly not while you're settling into the lifestyle. And after all, when you turn a bride, they're family and family should stick together." Her tone shifts and she drops her eyes when she says this. I wonder if she's thinking about her parents. Her Master is like the mother she never had; I can understand why she wouldn't want to leave her.

I ask myself if I feel that connection, but I already know that the answer is I don't. I wish I did; I wish I had what Drea had. Instead, I feel like I have a distant relative who adopted and tolerates me. I amuse him in small doses, but do I ever see myself as thinking of him as family? I don't know the answer to that, perhaps everything will change.

That's what I have always told myself. When I was young and he was so cold and distant, but he would dangle the carrot of being turned and I would follow along like a starved donkey. I always thought that once I was turned he would see me differently but here is Drea, who sounds like she has always been treated as an equal. Always been treated like a protégé and part of the family.

I haven't exactly been neglected. And the knife strapped to my thigh tell me he does care in his own way, but for the first time I don't know if it's enough. For the first time I've seen what it's like to sit with someone and talk like an equal and now the thought of going back to that house and maintaining shallow small talk makes me feel even more lonely than I did before.

"You're really lucky you know." I tell her. "You sound like you're going to be really happy when you get out of here." I try and fail to not sound sorry for myself.

"First of all, IF not when," she tells me. "Second of all, you say that as if you won't be happy?"

I don't know how to respond to her because what

would I say? That I'll be immortal but immortally alone, that I'm scared my Master will never bring me into his confidence or build a real relationship with me. More importantly and more terrifyingly, I don't know if I want to build a relationship with him anymore. For so many years he's been the only person in my life, and I've taken his scraps of attention and kindness. But he's never took my hand, or made me blush, not like Drea does. He's never made me feel important, and now that I have, I don't know if I can go back.

"I guess we'll see." Is all I choose to say.

I put on a brave face and meet her eyes which are brimming with curiosity and concern. I can't give her more than that though. Not when I don't even really know how I feel. What would it accomplish anyway, in a few days one of us will probably be dead. Who are we kidding, I'll probably be dead.

*

Not long after I speak with Drea, I decide to take myself to bed, one of the days of respite has gone by very quickly. I'm glad to be able to strip all of my layers at least including the knife holder. I fold it up and place it at the bottom of the trunk, but not bothering with the false bottom. The knife will go under my pillow tonight.

I've made the decision to not fully close or lock my door. I want to be able to hear if anyone is mooching around or plotting during the night. More importantly I want to keep one ear at least on Alice's door next to mine. She excused herself to go to bed a while before me and firmly locked the room. I suspect after all her fighting lessons today she will sleep well tonight at least. She looked thoroughly exhausted by the time she retreated.

I on the other hand can tell sleep will not come easily. I toss and turn waiting for reprieve that never comes. Every time I feel I could drift off I jolt awake thinking I've heard something. I never actually have. My mind is playing tricks on me. I both hope that the gap between the next trial will be longer and shorter. I can't decide if I want more time in here, talking to and learning from Drea, or less time to stew in the never-ending fear that this waiting is bringing.

It is a new kind of torture that I don't know how to deal with. I think about what the next trial could be at least fifty times as I lie in bed. Will it also be outside? Will there be weapons? Will we be pitted against each other?

If we are pitted against each other, who would end me first.

I must finally fall asleep because I have the worst nightmare I've had since I was a child.

I'm running through the forest at night. The leaves crunch beneath my feet and branches snap in my wake. I can feel my heartbeat like a warning bell beating through my chest. Behind me something follows but I don't know what. All I know is that its fast and if it catches me, I'm dead. My breath quickens as I try frantically to zig zag between rogue trees without slowing down.

The hair on the back of my neck stands up as whatever stalks me closes the distance. I try to run faster but it's like I'm weighed down with lead. Each step becoming harder and harder to fight. Tears begin to fall down my face in frustration, I'm running and running but I'm just not getting anywhere. Something reaches out and grabs me by my hair jolting me to a stop.

I cry out as I'm pulled flat against the body of my captor and a strong arm constricts around my waist.

"What's wrong little rabbit?" Nikolas voice growls in my ear. "I just want another taste." He sinks his teeth into my neck from behind.

With a gasp of air, I'm awake.

I'm not in the forest, I'm alone, in my room.

My hand flies to my neck and I find the bite mark he left on me yesterday, not open but beginning to heal.

I flop back down onto the bed and try to calm my beating heart. The adrenaline courses through my veins urging me to run or fight and I try to suppress it. I don't know what time it is but it's still dark, and no noise comes from outside of the door. I close my eyes and pull my blankets up around myself as far as they will go, cocooning myself. My mom used to do this with me when I was little.

"If you're inside your blanket the monsters can't get you."

She would say as she tucked me in and tickled my feet through the blankets. I would giggle and kick and by the time we had finished whatever nightmare I had was safely left behind, outside of my blanket of safety.

Little did I know the caliber of monster I would be up against.

CHAPTER TEN

I lie there unmoving for what feels like hours before I hear the first door slide open. The now familiar buzzing sound of the bulbs starts as whoever is awake switches the main areas lights on. They flicker once, twice, three times, before finally settling on and light pours in through the small gap in my door.

I sigh, I'm so exhausted. I will take the opportunity to have a nap midday today. This is supposed to be our main rest before the second trial, and I need to make sure I am feeling my best. Throwing the covers off I stretch and swing my legs out of the bed. The clothes I wore yesterday are strewn on the floor and I opt to just go with the same outfit after I secure my knife. As I pull out the strap, I wonder whether it's necessary to wear it at all times. I doubt anyone is going to attack me in the common room, but then the ghost of last night's nightmare creeps across my skin and I immediately reach for the leather holder. Better safe than sorry.

Once I'm layered up, I slide the door fully open and step outside. I immediately regret my decision because the only person in the room is Nikolas.

Our eyes meet and I freeze, I can't just retreat into my room. I'm sick of looking weak in front of this man, I won't allow him to make me afraid a second longer. After a moments delay, I reluctantly step out of my safe haven and into the lion's den. He's stood in the kitchen area filling a kettle. He breaks eye contact with me after what must be no more than a millisecond but feels like an eternity. As if I'm not there he continues on his task placing the kettle on the hob and goes to fetch a mug from one of the freestanding cupboards. He's wearing no shoes, loose grey sweatpants, and a tight black t-shirt, his hair bundled loosely into a bun atop his head.

"Good morning." I say, determined to be polite.

"Morning." He replies gruffly. I'm surprised he deemed me worthy of a response.

I don't need to make any effort for further conversation than that, so I make my way to the fridge to investigate what is left over. I open it and murmur in surprise. It's been restocked. Where the shelves began to look barren yesterday from the hungry mouths of ten people, they now look plentiful. Fully restocked fresh fruit, pre-packed sandwiches, snack bars. Obviously, my plan to keep my door open so I would hear movement was completely useless. Or it was restocked whilst I was dreaming of Nikolas sinking his teeth into my throat.

“What didn’t you think they’d restock?” I jump, not expecting him to be so close to me. His voice comes over my shoulder so close I feel his breath against my hair.

I turn but he makes no move to step back, so I end up pressed closer against him than I intended, almost face to face. His eyes burn into mine with an intensity I can’t place.

“I just didn’t hear anyone come in.” I whisper, my voice sounding weak and almost frightened.

The corner of his lips twitch, I think he’s enjoying that he scares me.

“Well, you wouldn’t, they’re quick and they’re quiet. It’s what makes them such good predators.” Spoken like one, I think to myself.

It takes all the willpower I have but I turn away from him and take half a step forward to put whatever distance between us that I can. I lean forward and grab a banana, all the while feeling his gaze not leave me. My heart quickens, would he hurt me here, none of the other doors are open so no one would hear if he wanted to take the opportunity. Or is hurting me even what he really wants? I remember that look in his eyes yesterday as he had me against the wall, fear isn't the only thing he wants to make me feel.

"Are you scared of me little rabbit?" He laughs.

I freeze. Little rabbit? The two times I have heard him call that me is before he sunk his teeth into me, both in real life and my subconscious. My body cringes at the name though, it shows me exactly what he thinks of me. He sees me as weak and small and scared. Finding a bit of bravado in me, and determined not to let him think he is winning I stare him directly in the eye and say …

"I prefer princess."

The gap I put between us isn't very substantial, He isn't even an arm's length away, he could probably lean forward and take another bite out of me if he really wanted to. He looks down at me with a look on his face that makes me tremble, somewhere between threatening and playful. His eyes gleam and he raises an eyebrow at me.

"Do you really? I see the way you look at her, the girl who calls you princess, she definitely scares you, but in a different way to me I think."

I feel the blood rise in my face as he says this. It's so obvious then that I find Drea attractive, even Nikolas has noticed. That's embarrassing. I try to play it off and side step away from him. He moves closer immediately and I curse myself for playing into his game. He likes it when I try to escape him, it gives him the chance to chase me.

“Scared? Of Drea? Why would I be scared, she didn’t choke me, nor did she sink her teeth into me.” I throw accusingly at him.

“Would you like her to?” He drawls, reaching out a hand to stroke a finger over his mark on my neck. Though I’m fully covered the feel of his touch through my shirt sends a tingle down my spine. Of course he see’s it happen and his lips tug into an insufferable smirk. He’s using me like his plaything and its starting to piss me off.

“I think you would … like her to … but then again, I think you enjoyed it when I did it too. Tell me little rabbit what about if it was both of us?”

I take a small step back and he matches me. Did I enjoy it? I got a thrill out of him being so close to me I can’t ignore that. But I don’t feel the same way about him as I do about Drea. He excites me in a way that makes me feel scared, Drea excites me in a way that’s thrilling sure. But with her I would feel safe.

“I guess I’ll have to ask her to throw me up against the wall and see who did it better.” I poke at his bravado.

I take one more step away from him and my back hits the end of the table. He grins evilly and closes the distance again, I have nowhere to go now.

"Let me know how she measures up; I quite like some healthy competition. Who can turn you a darker shade of red?" He laughs and presses closer against me. I hitch up onto the table now that I have nowhere else to go and he moves to press between my legs. "Who can get your heart beating faster? I do wonder." His voice drops an octave, and he bends down slightly, looking over me.

There are so many things I want to say. I want him to get off me, and I want him to press closer. My mouth is unable to translate any of my whirring thoughts and I can do nothing but look up at him and wait for him to make the decision for me.

He reaches out a hand and hooks his finger in the top of my turtleneck. I shudder as his skin touches mine but don't move away from it. I feel him start the pull and expose my neck, the side he let his mark on yesterday. His mouth twists into a smug grin as he admires his work, and he strokes a thumb over the bite mark. It's still a little tender from yesterday and I wince as his warm skin drags along the area.

I notice the moment he registers my pain, and his eyes instantly glaze over, they move from glistening with mischief to cold and void of feeling in a split second. His mouth drops from his grin and straightens into a flat line. Before I know what's happening, he removes his hand from my neck and pulls back about two paces.

I feel my face scrunch in confusion. What the hell just happened, one second ago I was about to be this man's breakfast right here on the table, now he looks as if I've mortally wounded him.

"You should put some ice on that, *princess.*" he throws at me as he turns away and walks back to the kettle. I'm left half-sitting, half-leaning on the table, feeling decidedly embarrassed again.

How is it that every time I interact with this man I feel absolutely humiliated. He might be hot but one things for sure, he's an absolute ass and I'm done being drawn into whatever stupid little game he's playing with me.

I stand myself up and straighten myself before going to collect my banana from the floor. I don't even remember dropping it but clearly my brain had an absolute blank the minute he laid his hands on me. I drop down retrieving it and go plonk myself in one of the armchairs. I won't let him make me feel small or embarrassed anymore. Even if that means I have to sit here alone with him until someone comes to break the tension.

“For the record, Drea would win hands down every time.” I decide to try and deal some emotional damage myself in return before I let the matter drop. I watch him from the corner of my eye as he pours his tea and I swear for just a split second I see him tense up. He recovers quickly and takes a seat at the table to continue his usual routine of absolutely ignoring me.

It’s a ridiculous thing to say, I don’t even know if Drea would care that I would choose her. But I would, if there was someone in here who I would want to come make my heart race it’s her. I might not be able to control how my body reacts to Nikolas but I’m starting to think that’s not really my fault. I’m twenty-five years old and I’ve never even been kissed before. Of course, if someone gives me that kind of attention, I’m not going to know what to do with myself. He doesn’t necessarily know this, but I can’t help but feel in hindsight he’s taking advantage of my naivety. There’s a difference between lust and a genuine attraction. If I’m being honest, I don’t think I truly know what that is yet, I’m learning a lot of lessons later than I should be. But I am learning.

I know how I feel after Drea talks to me, it isn’t embarrassment or confusion. It’s warmth, and happiness and sometimes loneliness when I think about all the days to come when I won’t be talking to her. I'm not stupid enough to think we're going to fall in love and run away together, I've known her a handful of days and Drea sounds like she has had some genuine experience with relationships. I'm probably a girl she just finds cute and wants to flirt with which is absolutely fine. But for me it's different, she's part of me figuring out who I am, or who I would be if I was normal and though it's hard, its important. Nikolas is just an alpha asshole who enjoys getting me flustered.

"I bet your Master is pleased he picked someone who plays for the wrong team." I hear Nikolas murmur into his mug.

I wasn't expecting him to speak so it takes me far longer than it should to register and process what he's said. Once I do, I'm absolutely furious. No more weak little Sabine, I'm going to have his ass for that.

"Excuse me." I hiss as I turn to fully face him from my chair.

He isn't even looking at me, keeping his eyes in his mug and I wonder if he realizes he might have just made enough of a mistake to push me over the edge.

"If you're trying to insinuate, I'm gay for one then I'm pleased to inform you that I'm attracted to people, not just a gender. I like *kind* people, *funny* people, people who don't make me want to break their nose. Now that might be hard for your puny brain to comprehend that someone could not want you, and so you're trying to logic it's because I'm gay but news flash I like men just as much as women. You are just insufferable, and I would rather be alone than have you pressed up against me again." I've absolutely lost it now; I worry I've overcommitted but honestly, I want this guy to know I'm not a pushover. I still don't know what his loyalties are but I'm about to make it very clear that he should twice before crossing me.

I rise out of my chair, slowly and probably far too dramatically, then stalk over to him. He looks up to meet my gaze now and for a split second I think he might be just a tad frightened of me.

Before I can second guess whether this is the stupidest option in the world, I slide my hands into the left side of my leggings and grip the hilt of my knife. I pull it out just as I reach him and manage to get the blade to his throat before he has the chance to understand what I'm doing. If his eyes held fear before, now they are absolutely terrified. I'm shaking as I hold the blade against his skin, not hard enough to draw blood, but almost. I stand there for a moment letting it sink into him that he is completely at my mercy before I lean in and growl at him.

"So, if you ever touch me again, I'll slit your fucking

throat."

It's too much, I know it's too much. If I was watching me do this, I would laugh. Little barely five foot me, holding a knife to this giant man's throat. If he wanted to, he could snap my neck probably with minimal effort. I doubt I'm actually intimidating him, but hopefully worst comes to worse he thinks I'm an absolute psychopath and stays away from me. I've been meek and quiet for too long, and he is the straw that just broke the camels back. And damn, it feels good to be on this side of the exchange for once.

"Let's take this down a peg shall we?"

I whirl around and see Ash standing with his palms raised walking slowly towards me. My hands begin to shake even more violently, and I stand pulling away from Nikolas dropping my knife in the process. It lands between us, and I begin to panic. Should I dive for it? Stupid, stupid woman I am! He's going to get to it before me and I'm going to die. Gutted right here by this man. Nikolas reaches down and has his hand on the knife hilt before I can force my body to move, and I silently resign myself to death. All because I flipped my lid, that feeling of pride managed to dissolve real quick when I wasn't the one with the weapon in my hand.

I'm barely able to register what's happening when he

flips the knife in his hand so that he's holding the blade, hilt extended towards me.

"Take it." He says.

I continue to stare at him in silent confusion, this is a trick. I'll go to take the hilt and he will stab me anyway. I know this guy is a walking contradiction but surely he wasn't going to give the knife back to the woman who just used it against him.

He bobs the hilt toward me and hold up his other palm in a sign of peace.

"I'm not going to hurt you Sabine, take it." His eyes look frightened but in a different way than when I had the blade to his throat. They now look full of trepidation, as though he's frightened. *Who's the scared little rabbit now? I think.*

His face is soft, and his eyebrows are scrunched together. I slowly reach out a trembling hand and wrap my fingers around the hilt. As soon as I do so, he releases the blade on his side and I can feel the weight of it in my hands like lead.

I don't thank him, nor do I acknowledge Ash, I merely return to my seat. I slide the knife back into my holder before I sit and pull my knees to my chest. I brave a look at Nikolas, and he still stares at me, as if he moves he will spook me and I'll take flight. One thing

I'm pretty sure of is, he won't underestimate me again. I'm yet to decide whether that's a good thing.

*

The three of us sit in awkward silence for what feels like a life time before others start emerging. The incident with the knife isn't brought up but as others start to make small talk and make themselves some breakfast the air lightens and I'm able to relax slightly. My shoulders finally sink down and I realize I've had them tensed around myself unintentionally. I have to do a few discreet shoulder circles to work them out as the muscle cramp sets in.

I distract myself by noticing Jessica has finally been brave enough to emerge from her room, she doesn't speak with anyone but she does nod a good morning to anyone she makes eye contact with. She makes herself some cereal and sits in a sofa alone, her head dipped discouraging conversation. If I have time today, I will try and talk to her. I'm unsure still if she is painfully shy or a painful threat. At this point she is the only person I don't know anything about and that makes me nervous.

I slowly stop shaking and eventually get myself up to

make myself a cup of tea too. I can't sit like an outcast all day. Nikolas doesn't make eye contact with me again, but I swear I can feel him watching me when I'm not looking. I instantly feel a little guilty, maybe it was a bit far to threaten the man's life but he was intimidating me in his own way and I think I've successfully put a permanent stop to that. And if I'm being totally honest, it did give me a rush to finally be the one in control.

Alice is in good spirits this morning after a good night's sleep, and she begins to bother Drea the minute she steps out of her room. I almost choke on my tea as she emergences dressed in low hanging grey sweatpants and a cream cropped, sleeveless top that shows the taught, pale expanse of her midriff. Her pale hair falls loose around her shoulders and over her chest.

"Are we going to do more fighting today?" Alice circles her as she approaches the kitchen, Drea does a fantastic job of managing to keep moving forward without tripping over her. She laughs as she moves.

"After I've eaten yes." She submits. Everyone here was hesitant about Alice but quickly they have all become to like having her around. I can tell. Most of the others watch the display with small smiles or the odd soft laugh. Except Michelle who sits sullenly, glaring at everyone like usual.

Drea makes herself a cup of coffee and grabs a protein bar and heads straight over to me, perching herself on the arm of my chair. She smiles good morning and starts devouring her breakfast. I grin to myself and hide my face with a sip of coffee, I can't ignore the small bit of satisfaction I feel that her automatic response is to place herself next to me now.

"I will warm you up little one if you're raring to go." Ash offers Alice and raises his fists in mock threat.

Alice laughs and moves to bat at him with her tiny hands. He dips and dives around her making her chase him. Alice is still in the little printed pajamas she sleeps in which makes her look even younger than she is, matched with the ecstatic giggling noises she is making as she flails to land a hit on Ash. He is far too fast for her, but I see him purposely slow down or make a wrong turn at a few points so that she can land a slap on him. There's no force behind her attacks but there isn't meant to be.

Sitting here with Drea beside me watching her play it feels like an easy Sunday morning with a super dysfunctional family. I turn from the scene to look at Drea and see the most beautiful and genuine smile ever on her face. I think to myself that this is the first time I have really seen her with no mask on. Rather than seeing a confident, playful, dangerous woman, I just see, well a girl. A girl who at this moment is enjoying a moment of pure untainted bliss. I don't even realize how long I've been staring until I see her eyes flick to me momentarily.

"Can I help you?" She laughs, but she doesn't seem annoyed and thankfully her perfectly happy and relaxed face doesn't tighten up as she speaks.

"Sorry." I say. "You're just really pretty when you smile like that."

In this moment I hope she doesn't take this as me trying to flirt. It isn't like that. I just want her to know that I see her and that I really like this version of her.

She doesn't turn her head fully to look at me but keeps watching her little protégé try and fail to catch Ash. Her smile does widen though, and I see a flash of her perfectly white teeth.

"It doesn't happen often princess, so you admire me all you want."

I laugh, a hearty genuine laugh that I don't even recognize myself. If I had one wish, I would wish to pause in this moment for as long as I could. I reach out and put my hand over Drea's which is resting on the arm of the chair. I rest it gently on top hoping to communicate some of what I'm feeling. That whether she's my friend, or a little bit more, I'm really grateful to get to share this moment with her. She gently tucks her thumb on top of my hand and makes gentle stroking motions back and forth.

We sit there like that until Alice is eventually exhausted, which takes longer than anyone would think. Luckily Ash is patient and has good stamina because he hasn't even broken a sweat before Alice finally collapses exhausted into a chair at the table. As she does, she elicits a round of applause from Neal which David joins into. This makes her grin ear to ear feeling proud of her performance.

"I think you did more than warm up her Ash, you've exhausted her." Drea laughs.

"I'll be ready to go again soon, I just need some loops first to refuel!" Alice assures her, she jumps up and goes to make herself a bowl of sugar and milk to regenerate some energy for round two.

As quickly as our moment of bliss was created it is destroyed.

A familiar sounding alarm rings out making everyone stop in their tracks. I feel my head spin and my heart race at the noise. We're getting an announcement.

"Hello familiars, apologies for the change of plans but your rest period is now over. The next trial will begin in ten minutes. Please ready yourself with anything you need. We will retrieve you soon and you

will receive a full set of instructions shortly."

I can't breathe. My chest feels like it's being crushed and my ears ring. It's too soon, we were supposed to have a week, what the hell happened?! I haven't prepared properly, neither has Alice. My brain races through all time I've wasted these past days, wasted on stupid Nikolas and his games, wasted in my room. Wasted time that could have been spent with more time observing others and planning.

I feel a hand making circles on my back. I'm barely aware of it. All I can hear is my heart pounding in my ears, my vision has gone blurred, I'm aware I'm breathing too fast but there's nothing I can do to stop it. I hear mumbling but I can't make out the words, can't even concentrate on them. All I can think about is Alice. The last trial. I think about standing in the middle of the dark forest in front of Drea, watching her tell me we had to leave Alice behind. Agreeing and leaving her to die in the forest. Will the same happen this time, will I have to leave Alice to die, will I be able to live with myself if I do? What if I have to choose between helping Alice or Drea, who would I pick? Would I even be able to choose?

I feel a cold hard slap across my face bringing me back to reality. Instead of focusing on my rapid breaths or the ringing in my ears, I now focus on the stinging across my face.

"Sorry." Drea says whilst cringing.

Her face comes into focus in front of me, she has just bitch slapped me … at least she looks guilty about it.

"You were kind of freaking out and you need to get ready, like now Sabine."

Now, yeah, I need to get ready. I don't even thank her as I scramble upwards and run toward my room. I need weapons first thing first. I throw open my trunk and clothes go flying as I try to reach the false bottom. I don't know how many weapons I can carry but I'll take as many as I can, I take a huge, serrated knife and add it to the other side of my holder. I don't have time to take off the layers that I've used to conceal everything, so I slide the weapons under the yoga pants and sweats, at least if were outside again I'll be warm. I pull on my boots and lace them up before I pack more knives, if I'm being completely honest I'm probably going to have a better chance running than fighting so the correct footwear might be more useful.

The boots are also another place to store more blades so I pick through to find something that will be small and compact enough to shove into my boot without stabbing myself. Luckily there's a small blade that's already in a little sheath for me to slide into my right side. The hilt sticks out the top, but I don't worry too much about it. I've already showed my hand with the stunt this morning. If Nikolas and Ash both know I'm armed, then everyone might as well know.

I consider taking something to arm Alice with but decide against it. She barely knows how to defend herself. There's no point in adding a knife into that she's probably just as likely to hurt herself than someone else. She will have to rely on me being there to protect her. Now that I'm sorted however, I need to make sure she is.

The last thing I do is quickly redo my braid pulling it taught behind me and out of my face before I run next door to Alice's room. She's busy getting ready as I enter, she's already wearing little leather pants and is in the process of pulling a black hoodie over the top. I'm surprised to see she's rather calm as she does so. I feel a lot more panicked than she looks. As she tugs her head through the top of the hoodie, she spots me and smiles.

"I'm almost ready, just got to get my shoes." She says happily, as if were getting ready for a day at the beach. She picks up her shoes and plonks herself on the bed to put them on. They are the same tie up hiking style boots I have. She must be in denial, or not fully processing what's happening at least. Though why would she be worried? The last trial was a walk in the park for her, we found her flag and she hid until the end. She saw no death, spilled no blood, she has no reason to think this will be any different.

“Whatever happens we’ll stick together okay.” I say my voice shaking. “I’ve got some weapons this time so if it comes to fighting let me take care of it, I’ll make sure we get through this.” I go to her and kneel down so our faces meet. She continues looking down at her shoes as she ties them, doing nothing but nodding her head to let me know she’s acknowledging what I say.

“Do you hear me Alice, this is serious.” I grab her face between my hands forcing her to look at me.

“I hear you.” She wrestles out of my grip and pushes past me to stand up. “I’m just as scared as you Sabine but freaking out isn’t going to help!” She yells at me.

I feel immediately awful. She’s right, here I am thinking somethings wrong with her but really, she’s being the more mature out of the two of us. I’m supposed to be the adult looking out for her, I should be trying to reassure her not get her even more frightened.

“I’m sorry, you’re right.” I reach my hand out to her and try my best to soften my face into a picture of serene confidence.

“We did just fine last time, we’ll do just fine this time too.” She steps forward hesitantly and takes my hand giving it a light squeeze.

We smile at each other, and I let myself for just one moment feel like everything will be okay.

"Let's do this then." I nod, and we walk back out into the main area.

Ash and Jared are both ready in black sweat suits and boots. Ash with his hair secured firmly back. They stand together which doesn't surprise me. I had already suspected they would make an alliance. Ash smiles at us though as we emerge and nods to me. They might be a team, but they certainly don't wish us ill, I know this. As long as me and Alice stay out of their way, they won't be a problem.

The same can't be said for tweedled dee, tweedled dumb and their pet lunatic. Neal and David both wear camo gear and are clearly packing to the nines. They haven't bothered to try and conceal their weapons, instead they have knives visible on the outside of the clothing for easy reach. Michelle wears a grey sweat suit showing her for the black sheep of their little team that she really is. She has only one knife that I can see but she clutches it in her hands as if she could go mental and start slashing someone at any moment. The three of them stand closer to the doorway clearly thinking to get a head start so I move towards the back, standing behind Ash and Jared.

Nikolas hasn't changed from this morning but has added shoes and secured his hair. He does his usual trick of stalking in circles round the room and makes no eye contact with anyone. Drea is the only one missing and I look to her room to see what she's doing. Her door is slid half shut but I can hear her moving around. If she isn't out soon, I'll go and get her. I'm unclear whether she will want to stick with us or go off on her own for the next trial, I won't hold it against her either way. But I want her to know she has a place with us if she wants it.

"Two minutes." I say to Alice squeezing her hand and make my way to her door. I slide it open slowly. Drea is in high waisted leather pants, knee high leather boots and a black hoodie. Her hair is in the process of being tamed into a long braid, her hands are extended behind her head trying to pull it in tightly as she turns to me and smiles.

"Calmed down now princess?" She laughs. I grimace at her and move behind her taking her hair in my hands.

"Let me it'll be quicker." I say and start to braid her hair tightly. She says nothing but removes her hands and instead lifts her hoodie adjusting the corset ties on the pack of her pants.

"Do you need any weapons? I have spare." I can't see

any knives on her, and I feel terrible that I didn't think of Drea when I considered Alice earlier.

"I'm good they're in my boots thanks princess." I see the corner of her mouth rise into a smile. "We're all going to get through this you know." She says to me.

"I hope you're right." My voice trembles slightly and I try to remind myself I am supposed to be being brave.

"I am, you might not realize this yet but I'm always right." She turns and winks as I finish of her braid with a hair tie.

I smile back and turn to lead her back into the room when she suddenly slides a hand around the back of my neck and pulls me towards her. Before I can react, she leans down and presses her lips against mine. It isn't a soft kiss, but one filled with urgency. My head is tilted back and I extend up onto my tiptoes and lean back into her. As we sink together and she understands I'm returning the kiss her spare hand snakes round my waist and pulls me even closer. Her lips part slightly, and I feel her breath mix with mine. I reach my hands up and grip her face on both sides kissing her fervently, this is my first and possibly my last kiss and I'm determined to make the most of it. This is how it's supposed to feel, I understand as I lose myself in Drea, I feel excited and safe all at once. I feel like I could exist in this moment forever, our lips touching, our breaths becoming one. Her warm body caresses mine and all I can think is that I want her closer, I want more.

But unfortunately, there isn't time for more.

She pulls her lips away from mine but doesn't let me go from her embrace. I realize I must have closed my eyes as they fly open when she breaks the kiss. I look up at her with a dazed face and she smiles down at me gently, her eyes alive with what I can only imagine is the same as what I'm feeling.

"One for good luck princess." She winks at me and slides out of my grip, her hands dropping from my neck and waist.

I'm left feeling cold and emptier than I have ever felt. I thought I had known true loneliness before, but I was wrong. Now that I have felt what it is to be held in the arms of someone you truly care for, it makes being left alone even more painful. Drea is clearly not having the existential crisis I am as she smacks my ass and laughs before striding to the entrance of the room.

"Come on, let's go kick this trials ass then there'll be plenty more where that came from." She waggles her eyebrows at me playfully lightening to mood and I can't help but laugh. I honestly think with the adrenaline running through my veins after that I could take on the world. She seems to have passed me some of her confidence through her lips and now I'm ready, as she suggests, to go kick some ass.

I stride past her back out into the main room to join Alice and I don't even need to look back to check that Drea is with me. The unspoken words that were in that kiss can be felt between us like an unbreakable tether. We are a team now and we will be until one of us isn't standing anymore. Perhaps even then.

Everyone now stands facing the doorway in silence. The air feels thick with apprehension but for the first time I feel strong, with Alice to my left and Drea to my right I know that whatever comes we will face it together.

A few moments which stretch into infinity pass before the lights suddenly cut out. There are a few gasps and muffled words, but no one moves until they see green floor lighting switch on in the entry way leading down the corridor. I'm not the only one who takes that as an instruction, as Neal and his rag tag crew bolt straight out of the door following the green luminescent road. Jessica pushes confidently behind them keeping pace which surprises me, for someone so shy she seems confident in her place near the front of the pack.

Ash and Jared are close behind them but at a much more cautious pace. Ash looks behind and nods at us as if to tell us to follow and the three of us fall in line closely behind the pair. I can hear Nikolas footsteps behind us though it feels he is keeping his distance slightly. I hope turning our backs to him isn't a mistake, but we aren't left with much choice.

We take a right turn outside of the door and go deeper into the building rather than heading back past our original holding cell, I quickly make the assumption then that we must not be heading outside. I can't decide whether I feel better or worse with that knowledge. Only a short way down I see the three leading the pack turn right again into a doorway that leads to a clearly lit room. As we catch up and pile in, the view of the room is obstructed by the six bodies in front of me, what I do know is that there is a small, barred area keeping us from fully entering just yet.

I feel the heat of a body behind me as Nikolas pushes into the small space that is left from the room and the noise of an automated door indicates we have just been locked in.

I try to get on my tiptoes to see what is happening inside the room but there's no way, I'm a foot smaller than most of the people in front of me and no one is making an effort to clear a space. What surprises me is that there's no murmurings or discussion. Either the room is too boring to comment on or they're all shocked into silence. I can only hope it is the former and not the latter.

"Hello familiars, and welcome to your second trial. Today's trial will deduce your understanding of the importance of blood."

I blanche, whatever that means it can't be good.

"A vampire needs approximately five liters of blood every two weeks to survive. Today you will show us your ability to harvest said amount of blood. There will be some blood bags in the room but perhaps not enough for all of you. So please, be as ... inventive ... as you like. Blood is a necessity. Show us what you are willing to do for it."

Blood bags, when the voice says blood bags, I can only imagine what it means. I highly doubt there is a fridge of plastic medical grade blood bags in the room. I don't have time to fully worry about this however because the bars around us begin to raise and pull into the ceiling. As soon as they reach about four feet tall I see Neal, David and Jessica duck and roll underneath. I have to wait until everyone in front of me is cleared and the bars fully raised by the time I can move forward. I clutch Alices hand to ensure we aren't separated and move forwards.

The first thing I notice is how clinical the room is. The walls are white, the floor is white, the lights are bright, unrelenting. It reminds me of a how a surgery room would look on a horror show.

The second thing I notice are the hostages. Four people are bound and gagged on the floor. Their hands are tied behind their backs and their feet roped together. They aren't blindfolded which makes it even worse. We may have to kill them, but we will have to see the fear in their eyes as we do so.

The third thing I notice is ten clear cylinders lining the left side of the room, each able to hold at least five liters of fluid and each with a rotating saw at the bottom. The mechanical noise of them spinning in unison grates me to the bone. I don't want to consider why there is ten, with only four possible victims. Inventive. That's what they said, meaning if anyone wanted to, they could make the other familiars fair game.

My vision blurs and I feel sick to my stomach. I know exactly how much five liters is, and it's not enough to make one body last for two of us. I look to Drea, but she is already moving, she grabs my arm and drags me forward. My grip on Alice being vice like she is almost dragged along off her feet too.

Everyone is a blur of motion around us. Two of the victims have already been seized. Neal is dragging a bound woman by her hair across the floor to one of the cylinders. She tries to scream beneath her gag creating a sickening and strangled noise. Jessica surprisingly has the second, she has grabbed a bound man by his feet and drags him face down across the floor. She's certainly a dark horse.

I don't remember clocking anyone else before we reach the final two "blood bags" By that point it has become an all-out struggle. I'm dragged into a gaggle of thrashing panicked bodies and noise. I can hear shouting and huffing from voices that I recognize but can't differentiate.

There's no way that were getting out of this, not without some of us dying. There are four bodies meaning four familiars have a free pass. After that there's six of us left meaning only three are leaving alive. Which three is going to depend on who comes out strongest.

I wish that we had some preparation for these trials. If we were able to strategize beforehand, I probably would have been able to make some sort of deal with Jared and Ash to off Neal and his friends first things first. I could have played this smart and guaranteed who could get out of here.

But they don't want to see how smart we are, they want to see how vicious we are. How cutthroat we are. How desperate we are.

They want to see who wants this the most and who's willing to kill for it. I hate it but I know I'm willing to kill for it at this point. For the first time since I've been here, I feel not only that I'm trying to survive but that I have something to lose. I can feel how the level of desperation has changed in me. I'm not just thinking about getting out of this. I'm thinking about getting us a*ll* out of this. It changes things. I might not be willing or wanting to kill an innocent person for myself, but I certainly will for the woman and child by my side.

Wanting to and being able to, unfortunately, are two different things. I feel pulled around like a mosh pit unable to see which way is up or which way is out for what feels like a lifetime. Finally, everyone parts and I fall in a heap on top of Alice. When I orientate myself and look up, I see our victors. Drea thank God has hold of a young woman and is dragging her to a tube. Ash and Jared work together to pull the other.

I can't process my next steps because I hear a blood curdling shriek and the sound of metal struggling against flesh. I flail and clamp my hand down over Alices eyes so she can't see whatever is happening.

I'm glad I do as I look over and see David shoving Michelle's neck onto a circular saw. Well, that alliance lasted long. Michelle fights like a stray cat against David's grip but she just doesn't have the strength to match his. One arm is around her middle like a vice and his spare hand is tangled in her hair shoving her neck down onto the blade. Blood fills her mouth quickly and she gurgles one last noise of protest before going completely limp. He grabs her body by the middle with two arms and lifts her upside down above the saw, which is clearly beginning to fill his cylinder, draining her like a pig for the slaughter. The air is filled suddenly with the tangy smell of iron.

His tube fills quickly but it isn't the only one. Neal also has his victim already draining into his cylinder as does Jessica. Jessica is struggling to drain hers. Though she has managed to slit the neck on the saw she doesn't have the height or the strength to lift her victim and so she can't get an efficient drain out of him. I wonder if someone will help her, a strangled unhinged laugh escapes my lips at the thought. Imagining the scenario as if you were watching someone struggle to load their car at the grocery store.

Oh hey I notice you're struggling to empty your human victim of blood, can I give you a hand with that?

Jared and Ash have managed to drain their victim cleanly and efficiently and they have filled their cylinder together. I'm assuming there's no sharing so they're going to have to find another blood bag soon. But so are we.

I look to Drea and see she has mercifully snapped her victim's neck before draining them. She has them lifted but I can see she's struggling to keep them upright. She picked one of the larger ones and her strength isn't quite holding up.

"Okay Alice I need you to keep your eyes closed but follow me okay don't let go of my hand."

She squeezes my free hand in agreement and I uncover her eyes which are thankfully closed. I pull her to her feet and across the floor to where Drea is struggling. I slip slightly as I let go of Alices hand and move in to help her. I don't look down; I know what I'm slipping on. I reach up and grab the person around their waist helping to hoist them fully upside down.

"Thank princess." Drea's voice is strained and I can tell how much this is taking out of her.

I don't answer her. I don't trust myself to be able to. I think if I opened my mouth no sound would come out. Or perhaps a sob. There wasn't even any deliberation, from anyone, about whether we should kill these people. No one hesitated to end their lives and only Drea thought enough to give them a quick and painless death before they strung them up for slaughter. A silent tear slides down my cheek. I hope whoever this is they don't have a family at home. I pray to anyone who will listen that these are bad people who won't be missed. I know in my heart it isn't true, but if I admit it to myself my heart might just break.

I don't have time to be weak right now, a broken heart won't help Alice. All I can hope is that no one will target Alice because she's likely too small to hold five liters of blood. It would be a pointless endeavor draining her. Hey maybe I'll escape too because of my tiny stature. There's one plus side to being short that I had never considered.

I begin to hear winners being announced through the intercom which is the only reason I know it's okay to let go.

"Familiar Neal pass and proceed."

"Familiar David pass and proceed."

"Familiar Jared pass and proceed."

"Familiar Andromeda pass and proceed."

I let the body slump to the floor, and it makes a sickening sound, at least one bone must break as it hits the white ceramic floor from the multiple bone chilling cracks I hear. It also makes a squelching noise by landing in its own blood. Blood that I'm sure is now splattered all over me if I were to look.

I won't look however, I need to hold it together, for just a little longer. I step forward and grab Alices hand again, doing my best not to slip in the lethal combination of shiny floor and hot liquid human remains.

I turn to the noise of grunting and see Jessica still struggling with her victim. She's only managed to drain about three liters at this point and she looks ready to collapse. Nikolas steps up behind her and for a spilt second, I think he's going to help her. He reaches both his hands out and I expect to see him grip the victim's body she struggles with. But he doesn't. He grips either side of her head at the base, and in one fluid motion, snaps her neck.

My free hand flies to cover my mouth as I gasp. Just like that Jessica is dead. I'm frozen in place until he turns to me and looks me directly in the eye.

"Take her." he says to me.

I stare blankly at him, not having the mental capacity to process what he is saying.

"Take her!" He shouts, "Before someone else does."

And with that he turns around, takes Jessica's half drained victim by the middle and lifts it to finish the drain.

It is Drea who full me forward and Alice with us. After only one or two steps my feet catch up and I'm full on sprinting the few feet down to where Nikolas has left us our prize. Like a cat who drops a dead bird on your lap.

This man continues to baffle me. This morning I could have killed him and slept blissfully. Now I could cry I am so grateful to him. I don't know why he did what he did, he continues to save us again and again. Yet everything else he does insinuates he hates us, well me at least. His psychological profile will have to wait for later, however. I don't care why he has helped us but he has and I'll be damned if I let it go to waste.

Our feet all slip and slide as we move down the tubes. We have to dodge around Ash and Jared who are frantically looking around and assessing their next move. They both saw Jessica go down and Nikolas shout, but neither of them make a move for her thank God. I was right that they are good people, I was right that they would get in our way. If we all make it out of this, I will thank them for their kindness, I'm sure I wouldn't be offered the same from others.

We make it to Jessica who luckily lies in front of an unoccupied tube. Nikolas doesn't turn around as he is focused on draining the last needed drops. He shakes the body, almost jumping up and down as it slowly continues to trickle from the neck. Finally at his limit he dips down and forces the neck against the circular saw again creating a stronger blood stream. I close my eyes and focus on my breathing. Trying my best to ignore the sound of metal on flesh. It's a wet sound that drills into my head no matter how hard I try to ignore it. The compounding smell of blood is becoming absolutely oppressive as well and its taking everything I have to stay on my feet.

"Focus princess we still need one more after this." Drea's voice is sharp and authoritative and snaps me back into motion. I look to Alice her eyes are still closed; they're squeezed so tight it must be almost painful. I let go of her hand and steel myself for the task ahead.

Meeting Drea's eyes I nod and bend over grasping Jessica under her arms and lifting her. As I do Drea grabs her legs and begins to lift her bottom half higher, so she is tilted at an angle. I try not to focus on the noise of the rotating saw but its proving impossible. So, before I lose my nerve I plunge the neck of the woman I barely know down against the metal. It hits with more resistance than I thought, and I have to step one foot back to stop myself falling off balance. The blood splatters all up my front and across my face. I don't have time to lose my composure, so I press harder, splitting the flesh irreparably before I pull back up and let the steady stream of her life force drain into the cylinder.

It fills quickly, faster than I anticipated and within what feels like minutes the tube meets its fill capacity. As soon as it does, I drop my half of Jessica without warning and she falls to floor with a heart wrenching thump.

"Familiar Nikolas pass and proceed."

"Familiar Sabine pass and proceed."

I didn't consider that the kill would automatically go to me, I would have given this guaranteed kill to Alice if I could and made the next one for me. I don't linger on this point though, I can't, the next kill with be Alices. It must be. I look to her as I think this and am immediately horrified by what I see. Her eyes are open, and she is absolutely covered in blood. She looks like Carrie at the end of prom night. It's up her clothes in splatters made from the motion of the saw. It covering her face and in her hair sticking it down in wet matts. Her eyes are fixed open and unblinking, a blank look on her face as she stares back at me.

"I know I wasn't supposed to open my eyes, but then I got wet." She says flatly, she lifts her arms and looks down left and right at herself.

"Oh Alice." I start.

"Familiars, Neal, David, Jared, Drea, Sabine and Nikolas are all currently pass and proceed. Familiars Jessica and Michelle have been eliminated. Familiars Ash and Alice are yet undetermined. Undetermined familiars will now have ten minutes to either fill a cylinder accordingly or be forcefully eliminated."

The announcement is like a bomb dropped on all of us. Ten minutes. We have ten minutes to kill two familiars to get Ash and Alice out of here, and I think we all know who is on the hit list.

I turn to look at Ash to find his eyes already on me. I raise an eyebrow at him in a quiet question and he responds with the gentlest of nods.

My head turns slowly and I set my gaze lethally on Neal and David stood together. Smug looks painted on their faces and arms crossed. In their matching camo gear now covered in blood they think they are the ultimate pair. Let's see how well they fair against the rest of us. I lean down and pull a knife out from my left side holster. My decision has been made instantaneously. I may not have the stomach to commit murder against innocent people but what I can do is take out the trash. I've been doing it for years. How many men have I lead to their death without a second thought. These two monsters will be another tick to put in my little notebook back home. If it's us or them, then I will fight with every breath I have left in me to ensure its them.

I'll peel the skin from their bones, steal the breath from their lungs, watch the life drain from their eyes. If they think they're going to takeaway someone I love so their miserable existence can continue, then they have made a grave mistake.

I remove the knife fully from my pants and hold it in front of me. My hand doesn't tremble now. There is nothing but certainty left.

Neal laughs at me.

I take a step toward him. The smugness from David face falters slightly, he isn't as sure of himself.

I take another step forward.

David pulls his knife and holds it forward.

"Don't even think about it you little brat, that kid of yours isn't going to make it through anyway. You're not wasting one of our lives to prolong her suffering."

One. More. Step.

I'm closing the distance now, he's only about eight feet away. I could lunge for them but I'm not so sure I could take one of them down before the other one got a few deadly blows in.

I hesitate on the next step. I know I want to do this, but I'm not so sure I can. As if reading my mind, I feel Ash fall into step to my left. He has a large hunting knife drawn himself. To his left Jared steps into place. My confidence replenished; I might not be able to do this alone. But I can do this with them.

I take another step forward.

Neal starts to panic. They're backed against a wall and when animals are backed against a wall they panic. They both have their knives out now, their eyes are frantic. They both try to back up to create some distance but there is nowhere for them to go.

"Don't you fucking dare." Neal screams waving his knife back and forward along our line.

"I think we fucking will." Drea growls as she steps to my right.

Four strong now, we might take some damage, but they certainly won't be able to pick us off. They are scared which makes them sloppy. Along our line there is nothing but a deadly calm. An absolute decisiveness that can be felt between us, it connects us in a way that makes me feel stronger than I ever have. I'm not just doing this for Alice, I'm doing this for Ash too. For the man who has shown kindness and morality. He deserves to get through here just as much as any of us.

Perhaps if the next generation of immortals were more like the people here then it wouldn't be so bad.

We take a step forward in unison, our synchronized footprints making a solemn sound against the ceramic floor in an otherwise silent room. Just two more victims, for two more cylinders.

Our line has become a small semi-circle, there will be no escape. The irony of the two men being corned in their hunter's gear does not escape me. I wonder how many people Neal cornered like this when he hunted victims for his Master. I wonder how much enjoyment he got from watching them quiver and shake like he does now.

We stay in that final moment for what seems like eternity. I don't notice who moves first. It could be them; it could be us. All I know is one moment I am still and the next I am a flurry of movement. I slash and stab with every morsel of energy I have in my body. I know who I am hitting, I look only for the greens and browns of their clothing. Clothing they thought would keep them hidden and safe no doubt is now what I use to aim my knife at. It lasts no longer than a minute the struggle before they both slump to the ground.

I drop my knife almost instantly. My hands are covered in blood, though I admit some of that could have come from earlier draining related activities, perhaps I just hadn't noticed yet. Yet some of the stickiness on my hands is definitely fresh, it is wet and warm and has drenched into the sleeves of my sweat shirt. I am dotted in the evidence of my crimes from head to toe.

"Quick we need to get them to the cylinders." Ash. The voice of reason as always.

Him and Jared Pick up Neal, though he is hardly recognizable he has been mauled so severely. This was no clean or careful kill. This wasn't done with kindness; this was a murder of pure desperation and ferocity. They carry him across the room with efficacy and slit his already dead throat before hauling him upwards to fill Ash's tickets to freedom.

"Our turn." Drea nudges me and leans down grabbing David's feet. I give myself only one moment before moving behind him to hook my arms under his armpits and lifting my half. We struggle over to an unfilled cylinder and drop him like a ton of bricks.

I stand and take a moment before we have to move onto the next unpleasantness. I realize at this point I had dropped my knife so I'll have to retrieve my other to slit his throat, it will be cleaner than the saw and waste less blood. I cringe at the hands, covered in thick and fresh blood, that's not going to feel nice sliding down my leg to grab the other knife.

“Don’t worry I got it.”

I’m unsure who’s spoken until I look down to see Alice standing over David, she holds the knife I dropped. She must have picked it up when we moved the bodies. Her tiny body is hunched down and she looks over the body in front of her with a type or morbid curiosity.

Gone is the blank traumatized look I saw in her before. Now she looks fascinated by what she’s seeing. She looks Neal up and down like a piece of meat before landing back at his throat. Then, slowly, she raises the knife, brings it to his throat and makes a strong single cut across his neck. She is thorough, the cut goes ear to ear.

Drea and I look at each other over the top of her with the same look of perplexing worry. This might be the most unsettling thing I’ve seen all day. It’s like watching Winnie the pooh commit murder. This little girl has seen far too much, she’s been absolutely traumatized. I don’t believe she fully understands what she’s doing. Though at least he is already dead, she hasn’t taken someone’s life. But for her to want to do this, with so little emotion. I’m worried we’ve broken something in her that can’t be fixed. Perhaps I should have told her to close her eyes again before we attacked the two men. I didn't even consider that until now, she just witnessed her new parental figures slaughter two people mercilessly.

Is this her way of trying to imitate us, is she just trying to help? Whatever it is, it isn't right. I'll try and talk to her about it when we get back to the rest area.

She stays staring at the pooling blood for a moment before she releases a shaky breath, her only sign that she understands the emotional impact of what she has just done.

"This one is for me to win right? I'm guessing I have to contribute in some way." Alice shrugs without looking at either of us. Instead, she just stares at the floor next to David.

"It's okay." I say unconvincingly "We got the rest of this Alice don't worry."

She can leave the worrying for me. I have plenty for the both of us. Drea and I lean down and prepare to lift our ex-roommate for draining. Tonight, is going to feel very empty back in the rest area.

As we are in the process of filling the tube, we hear the familiar announcement voice.

"Familiar Aashutosh, pass and proceed."

Only moments later do I hear the words that finally allow me to drop my body out of fight or flight.

"Familiar Alice, pass and proceed."

"Congratulations familiars, Alice, Aashutosh, Nikolas, Andromeda, Sabine, Jared. You have all passed the second trial and will proceed to trial number three. You will have two rest days between now and the commencement of your final trial. Please follow the green lights to use the shower facilities before returning to the rest area. Thank you."

We all stand, the six familiars left, staring at each other. A mess of blood and gore and newfound trauma.

"At least we get to shower." Drea says loudly and elbows me.

CHAPTER ELEVEN

I stand in the group shower completely naked. I don't care that we are all in the same block, I don't see anyone else around me. I'm aware that there are bodies everywhere, but no one speaks. We were directed here in silence to a wet room with a wall of running water. Wordlessly we all stripped and stood under the steady stream to try and wash away the past hour.

It is bizarre to think all that transpired occurred within only sixty minutes or so, it feels like a lifetime away that I was sat with my new found friends laughing and drinking my morning coffee. That Sabine is a different person to the Sabine standing here in a pool of blood. The blood mixes with water and swirls in a never-ending mirage down the drain beneath my feet. I don't try to wash it off me, I don't need to. There is enough that it carries easily away with the water. I let my head fall under the water and run down my face closing my eyes. It scalds me but I'm pleased for the feeling, it distracts me from thinking too deeply about what just happened.

I knew the next trial would be tough, but I never imagined that we would be exposed to that horror show. It was like something out of a saw movie. A disturbed trap meant to test which one of us would break first. Who could deal with the most gore and guts without completely mentally giving up. I can only imagine how Alice is feeling, thought I can't bring myself to look at her right now. Images of her tiny frame covered in blood crouched over the corpse of David, knife in hand replay in my head over and over on a sick repeat. In between the blood circling the drain my eyes flash between past and present, seeing the knife being dragged slowly, with precision and intent.

I wonder what Alice sees now as she washes the blood from her face, does she even process what she just saw. I can't help but feel like I've failed again. Perhaps in a more significant way than the last trial. Before this started, I told her I would look after her this time round. It was my responsibility to make sure she was kept shielded; I should have ensured she kept her eyes closed. I shouldn't have let her put herself in the position where she could draw blood, or see it being drawn in the first place.

Delusion had settled in the past few days in here. I had thought that we could get through this as a team, I had certainly thought that we could get through this whilst not losing ourselves. That was wrong, a piece of me is gone, I can feel the gaping hole where it should be. The moment I decided to gut those men like a fish something fundamental inside me broke and I will never be able to put those pieces back together. Tears mixed with water and blood down my face. I can't even say I regret what I did. That would be a lie.

Perhaps I wish I didn't have to do it, that's about all I can honestly tell myself. If there had been a way to get us all out of there would I have taken it? Again, I can't answer that because I'm unsure whether I know how to. I never trusted Neal or David, they were the main reasons I worried about sleeping soundly and Michelle made my skin crawl just with her presence. It didn't mean I wanted them dead, did it?

If I really allow myself to think about it, I know I don't actually care that they're dead. I don't care that when we go back to the rest area they will be missing. What I do care about is what their empty spaces represent. The empty seats around the table at breakfast will be reminder of the first victim I ever really killed myself. It's a weak excuse, I know I've killed before. The one hundred and twenty-two victims I lured to their death would all probably point the finger at me in court just as much as they would point it at my Master. It doesn't matter I didn't pull the trigger; I still loaded the gun. So why does this feel so different?

Perhaps it's the absolute ferocity of it all, the brutality. The first trial was brutal, but it could be avoided if need be. I had hidden Alice and myself well enough to get through without being directly involved in any violence. My naivety was obviously rearing its head when I assumed all the trials would be like that. The vampires don't want someone weak who wins through running and hiding. They want someone who will strengthen their families, not be a burden to them. But I had always gotten by with my Master in my own way, if this was what the trials really involved what on earth had he seen in me that made him think I was up to this?

Unless he was sick of me and wanted to off me for a new familiar. Surely this wouldn't be the easiest way, I guess it would be the most entertaining for him.

No. I don't really believe that. He said he was proud of me; he gave me a cache of weapons. For some delusional reason he thinks I am capable of this. I lift my hands and stare at my palms, still not clean even after the minutes of boiling water. I guess he would be right. I am capable of this. I might not like it, but I killed tonight. I killed for the people around me, and I killed for myself. Now that I have killed, I don't think it will be for the last time.

My breaths quicken and my heart races. I can feel myself beginning to panic. I must get this blood off me. Grabbing a bar of soap suspended from a rope on the wall I start frantically scrubbing myself from top to bottom. The foam being created is tinged with the vibrant color of freshly dried blood. It flakes in places where it was thin enough to fully dry out. I scrub so hard and for so long that I'm not sure some of this isn't my blood. No matter how long I wash, I'll never feel clean again. I know rationally that probably isn't true, but I don't want to be rationale right now. I want to cry and scream and claw at my skin so I can feel something other than overwhelming nausea at the day's events.

At some point they shut the water off and we're forced to shuffle back to the rest area half dried with only one towel each to wrap around ourselves. We all march in silence back down the corridor, leaving a trail of soapy footsteps behind us. My wet hair cools quickly and drips down my back making me shiver. As we file into the big room of our makeshift home everyone seems to silently agree to go back to their rooms without further discussion.

I look to Alice, she may not have had the hardest day, but she is only ten years old. Her brain isn't mature enough to process this kind of trauma. I see her little feet padding towards her door, the wet outlines she leaves behind her look so small. With her wet hair and hunched over shoulders she's like a drowned puppy. Before I can call out to her, she disappears into her room and slides the door shut. Perhaps that's for the best. Processing time could be good for her and honestly, I don't have a clue what I would say to her right now.

Being careful not to slip I follow everyone's lead and pad quietly into my room. I slide the door behind me but don't bother to lock it. I think we're past that worry now. For a moment I stand there in the dark, not knowing what to do. It isn't until I feel myself begin to shiver that I realize how cold I am. If nothing else, I need to get myself somewhat dried and dressed.

After I towel my body off, I wrap my hair inside the already damp towel and grab some black sweat pants and a black hoodie out of the chest. At this point I remember I left my holster and knives in a discarded pile of bloody clothes in the shower room. I would chastise myself but I'm pretty sure everyone else did the same as I didn't see anyone digging through the bloody mess before we came back. It's not like I don't have other weapons, and honestly, I couldn't give a shit if I never held another knife again anyway.

Having done the best I can manage; I drop into my bed and create a tent with my blankets. Cocooned inside my blankets thinking again of my mother. It's been years really, since I thought about my mom and dad. But now all I can think about is how she would ensure there was no air or light in my blanket cocoon and then tickle me from head to toe showing me that the monsters couldn't get through blankets even if they wanted to. More tears slide down my face and for the first time since I've been here, I finally let myself sob. A loud, messy, snot filled sob that takes my breath away.

I cry for the unjustness of Alice being brought in here, I cry for the loss of my comfortable routine life back in Alaska, I cry for the piece of my soul that I've carved away today. I cry until I can't cry any more. The tears dry up and my voice hollows out, I don't bother drying my face I just allow myself to slowly drift off and find what solace I can in my sleep.

*

My eyes open and I'm immediately blinded by a white light. I groan and roll on my side disorientated. My right hands hit the floor palm down to stabilize myself. I try to push myself up, but I feel so weak.

"Poor little rabbit." a voice rings in my ear.

My head pounds and I try to blink my eyes open again. I'm back in the room from the trial but it's been cleaned. Gone is the myriad of blood, mixing so you can't tell which pool comes from which victim. Now the floor is pristine white, as are the walls. Its what's making the light above so bright, reflecting against every surface it hits. Head reeling, I manage to sit myself upwards, bend over slightly.

"I knew you didn't have the stomach for it little rabbit, when it comes down to it, you just don't have the metal."

I twist my head around looking for the source of the voice but there's no one else in the room. It's just me and four walls.

"Poor little princess, always needing someone to save her." The voice morphs into something different, less masculine.

"Little princess, little damsel in distress. What a waste of a familiar you are."

That's not true*. I think in response, but my mouth doesn't seem able to form the words.*

"You can't even protect a child, how are you supposed to protect yourself?" The voice melds again, sounding younger. It sounds familiar, doesn't it? I can't quite figure it out. Its familiar but not quite

right. Like a song played on two times speed or raised an octave.

I can protect myself just fine. I struggle to my feet, swaying unendingly. There are shadows around me now. Figures I can't quite make out. Like Peter Pan's shadow there's familiarity to their outlines but my brain can't quite link up who they are to me.

"I say she's the weak link." Another masculine voice appears as a shadow starts to accumulate. They surround me now.

"We need to shave down the numbers, we can't all get out." The little shadow says.

No, no I'm not the weak link. I'm not weak.

I try to stand up tall and raise my chin in defiance, but my legs are shaking, and I feel an invisible force pulling me back to the floor.

"It's us or her." They chant in unison a blend of voices tainted with wrongness. They step closer to me and raise their smokey hands. I feel a sudden and unshakable chill as their fingers run over my skin.

Don't. I beg silently, unable to speak. I would fight if I could, but my muscles are weighed down with led.

"It the hard decision but you understand Sabine." The

shadows whisper, their voices mixing and melding into one.

Do I understand? Would I make the same decision? I don't know, a memory claws at the back of my mind. Did I make this decision before? The confusion creates a crushing headache and I cry out and clutch my head. I finally stop fighting and fall to my knees. My skin tingles and shivers all over as shadows fingers run over me.

Unsure why I feel a strong sense of injustice. All I have been through, and this is what finished me off. It isn't fair.

What have you been through?

A voice pokes at me. I don't know, I can't remember. My head protests again with a sharp jolt of pain from trying to push through the confusion. Between that and the overwhelming cold making me shake violently I don't know how much longer I can keep fighting this.

Just as I'm about to burst into tears or scream out in pain I take a sudden and shocking deep breath.

I'm no longer in the room but in the dark. It takes longer than I'd like to admit reorientating myself. My breath comes thick and fast as I try to understand my sudden change in circumstances. I am cold, and I still shiver violently. My head does hurt. As I reach up, I find the culprit. A sopping wet and now freezing cold towel has twisted tightly around my hair in my sleep.

I'm in my room, and clearly my mother's trick of cocooning me did nothing to keep the nightmares at bay.

I violently wrestle the towel off my head and scramble to my feet. My hair is still damp and now falls down my back soaking water through my hoodie all the way down to my pants. Quickly as I can manage before I lose my backbone, I strip off the wet top and frantically dig through my chest. I pull on a fresh T shirt and a grey hoodie to create some heat through layers. I then take the small grey throw blanket at the bottom of my bed and gently wrap it around my head, careful to not wrap so tightly that it will exacerbate my headache.

Now that I'm not so uncomfortable I trawl back through the chest adding anything I think will help; thick socks made for walking boots, there's a thin bodywarmer I hadn't notice previously and a thin pair of cotton gloves.

I feel layered like the Michelin man at this point, but I don't care, at least I'm feeling somewhat human. Mental note made to never fall asleep with wet hair again. Not like this five-star resort has a hair dryer.

At least the traumatic nightmare and borderline hypothermia has seemingly knocked me out of my previous apathy. I suppose I should really go check on Alice at this point. I might not be the only one plagued by nightmares and at her age she should still be in a my little pony bed with at least one parent to tuck her in, stroke her hair and tell her everything's going to be okay.

I can't do the last part without lying to her, but I can certainly do the first two. I take a deep breath to steel myself and step forward to open the door. Whatever happens next, I know one thing for sure. There's no way in hell I'm going to let myself end up being the weak link.

CHAPTER TWELVE

Stepping out into the main hall it almost feels as though nothing has changed. This could be de ja vu from yesterday morning if there were not certain members already missing.

I take a few tentative steps and see Drea and Alice sitting together. Alice eats what must be her sixth bowl of cereal in so many days, I should probably try and make sure she eats something borderline nutritious while she's here. Drea sits quietly but apparently content beside her, her arms crossed lazily across her stomach as she lounges back. For one of the first times the thought of Alices mother crosses my mind, would she be the kind of mother to cook her meals? Watch her sugar content? All we know if that her mother gave her up to be here so that she saved her own skin, and if that's what I have to go off I can't assume she was anything less than a monster.

Though it's been mere days since I met Alice but already, I've put my life on the line for her more than once. If it came down to saving me or her, I wasn't originally sure, but now I am. Nothing could make me save my own skin while selling her down the river. The girl is slim but not malnourished so her mother must have at least kept her fed. I wonder how she managed to balance being a familiar and having a child.

Surely Alice didn't live in the house with her and the vampires, yet I can't imagine a familiar clocking out for the day and heading home to her own house and kids. This job is for people who have no one and nowhere else to go. So why on earth did Alices mother end up tied up in this?

More importantly, where is she now? If she swapped Alice for her freedom that means she's still out there. Looking at Alice now in her little pajamas again, with wild bushels of hair scattering in every direction, I wonder if she looks like her mother. Is he mother out there building a new life not thinking twice about her? Or has it torn her up inside every day since she left her here? If she could see what her little girl had gone through in the past few days, would she make the same decision again? I would hope the answer is no, but I don't fully believe it.

Alice certainly doesn't seem bothered by her mother, after that first day she has never mentioned again how she came to be here or what it really means. We've done our upmost to shield her so far, but it isn't doing her any favors. And after today's antics it's obvious whatever childhood innocence she had will be completely and forever tainted.

We have two days left before the final trial that decides all of our fates, and by the time that trial begins I decide I will have had a conversation with Alice to discuss what that is going to mean. She might know our captives are vampires but until that last trial I suspect that she didn't know what that truly meant.

For a change I am not one of the last up and other than Drea and Alice only Jared is not in his room. He stands at the kitchen counter drinking a cup of coffee with a blank look on his face. I try my best to meet his eyes and smile, it takes him a little longer than it should to notice me but as soon as it does the ghostly look he has lifts slightly and he does his best to return a small grin.

Neither Drea nor Alice speaks as I sit down with them, I suspect perhaps no one can find the words.

"How are you, Alice?" I start. My words come out rather harsher than I intended, and I see her flinch slightly before dropping her spoon into her bowl.

"I'm fine." She replies not looking up.

"Alice." I close my eyes and take a deep breath. "What you just went through was extremely traumatic, I think you should talk about it. Do you understand why you're here?"

"Because the vampires are looking to make new vampires?" She phrases it like a question. It reminds me of watching a lesson with small children. She answers me as if she was answering a times table question that she isn't sure the answer to.

"Well yes. Did you know, before you came here that the bad men were vampires?" She flinches again, more severely at the mention of her mother. Without meeting my eyes, she nods slowly.

"My mama said they were, I didn't really believe her. I do now." She regrips her spoon to continue eating but her hand doesn't move. Her little knuckles turn white as she grips it with all the strength she has. Images of her gripping a knife like that over David's throat flash through my mind and I have to steel myself for a moment before I press onward.

"Had you ever seen someone … die? Before today?" the words come out through gritted teeth. I can tell I'm upsetting her, and I hate it, but I don't want her to bottle this up and have a total breakdown later and the worst possible moment. Maybe when she's presented with another dead body.

"Is this really necessary?" Drea's voice is scolding. She can sense how upset this is making her too, but she needs to suck it up, we all do. We can't keep tip toeing around her. If this trial taught us anything it's that we are completely unprepared for what could be coming next. Alice needs to be able to be a member of this team, it will be her best chance of surviving.

Turning to look at her I see her eyes glisten slightly with moisture. This isn't just hard for Alice it's hard for all of us.

"I've seen a dead body; I've seen lots of dead bodies." I start. Alice's grip loosens slightly.

"But I've never killed anyone before." I admit. "Not really, I bring them back for others to kill. Today was the first time I … I" My voice breaks slightly, and I curse myself silently for being so weak about this. If I turn into a blubbering mess about this, how can I expect Alice to be strong.

"It's the first time I've killed someone like that." Drea joins. Her hand comes to rest over mine and she winds our fingers together. Her eyes closed she takes a slow shaky breath and continues.

"I usually am very clean, very calm. I find people suitable and I do something like snap their neck or poison their drink. Today is the first time I've ever had to fight someone kicking and screaming. It's the first time I have had to drain someone like an animal." I focus on the meaning of each of her words slowly.

Most importantly I wonder what *suitable* means. Does suitable mean someone morally deserving like I've always thought, or does it just mean someone easy to kill. This key piece of information about how Drea hunts has never been discussed but I make a mental note to ask more about it later.

"I've never seen someone die before." Alices voice is less than a whisper. "There was so much blood." Her grip fully drops from her spoon, and she lifts her hands to inspect her palms. As if, if she looks hard enough the blood will reappear. "I don't want to see anyone else die either. When I'm a vampire I'll buy my blood or get it in those bags you see at the hospital. And I'll drink it out of a mug so I can't see it" She nods her little head as if that is the matter settled.

She is avoiding the topic, but Drea squeezes my hand in a way that lets me know not to push her. Alice is sat staring straight down into her now soggy bowl of cereal and I get the sense it is taking everything she has not to completely fall apart. Her plan isn't going to work, I doubt her Master is going to feed her from mugs, he will expect her to contribute. Though if I'm being honest, I don't know her Master perhaps he will enjoy have a child to dote on. For all eternity.

A shiver runs through me. A topic for another day, but a topic I will be bringing back up. Now might not be the right time, but Alice needs to face this reality. Whether I think it's important to discuss or not, Alice isn't ready for what the reality of being a vampire is. Unfortunately, as the days go on it is becoming blindingly obvious, neither am I.

A moments silence passes and Drea's grip on my hand loosens, happy I'm not going to cause a full mental breakdown over the table.

"I didn't mean to upset everyone." I say. "I just thought maybe we should talk about it."

Drea gives me a sympathetic lopsided smile before hopping out of her seat. She makes her way to the fridge and selects a few different muffins and croissants before gliding back over and plinking them on the table in front of me. She sits and starts demolishing a chocolate chip muffin.

"We don't talk about our feelings, we eat them." She winks.

"You're ridiculous." I say but pick up a banana muffin to show I appreciate her effort to lighten the mood. In a much lower tone, she leans in toward me and whispers in my ear her nose gently caressing the hair falling free from my braid.

"Me and you can talk later princess, let her live in ignorance." Her voice is kind and not meant to chastise me, but I still feel it. Nodding I drop my eyes and focus really hard on my muffin and nothing else.

"Yes, let's just pretend nothing happened!" I forgot Jared was even here until he spoke. Standing sulking by the sink with a look of rage on his face, I suspect Drea will have a harder time shutting him up than she did me.

"Alice why don't you go get dressed and pull a brush through that bird's nest of yours." I suggest.

She feigns mock offense by patting her hair, but gets up and makes her way to her door. She takes in Jared from the corner of her eye on the way.

Talking about this is the last thing Alice wants to do and I suspect she's quite pleased for the out I just gave her. I may have wanted Alice to open up, but whatever is about to spew from Jared won't be helpful for her. Each pad of her little bare feet across the floor seem to echo in the whole room while we sit, tensely, for her to shut the door behind her. As she turns and slides it she shoots me a small and worried smile, but I dip my head into a nod, hopefully communicating it will all be okay. When we hear the final click of her door, I open the floodgates.

"What's up Jared?" I lean back, both into my chair and into Drea. Feeling her next to me gives me some confidence I wouldn't otherwise have.

"We turned on each other quicker than an alligator in the everglades." His head is dipped now and he doesn't say the words with malice. More disappointment. Perhaps he thought we would be morally superior; I don't think we had the choice.

"To be completely fair, they weren't good people Jared, they killed Michelle." Drea offers.

"I know they weren't good people." He sighs. "And I can't lie and say I'm sorry they were the ones to go. But what if it was the other way round, would you have killed me or Ash if that was the only alternative?" He isn't accusatory, more genuinely curious. His eyes look to us, and I can tell there would be no point in lying to him. He isn't looking for kind lies right now he wants the hard truth.

"I don't know." I say. "Maybe I would have to save Alice, I can't promise you I wouldn't. But I do know one thing it would have been much harder to make the decision. I wouldn't have just jumped you like I did with Neal and David. I don't know if I could have brought myself to do it at all."

It's the truth. Jared and Ash both seem like kind

people. The last few days has given me the pleasure of getting to know them slightly. I don't have the bond with them that I do with Alice and Drea, but I would consider them friends. I've enjoyed listening to Ash's stories of travelling. Watching Jared play and spar with Alice has brought me moments of joy that helped me forget where we were.

If I had to swap one of their lives for Alices I would have been hard pressed to justify it. And I certainly don't know if I could have actually brought myself to do it.

Jared nods at my words as if he understands, he probably can't say he wouldn't have taken one of us out if it meant his life.

"Look there's a reason we turned on them together. Technically we could have taken you out Jared, you had a spot already. But we didn't, I knew immediately that if there was someone else, I could save and get out of there other than Alice it was going to be Ash. I did what I did just as much for him as I did for Alice." The words taste wrong because I know they aren't quite true. I did want Ash to get his spot, and I absolutely wanted to save him, but I can't pretend that it was the same feeling as wanting to save Alice.

"I feel the same." He admits. "When faced with it, I wanted it to be us who got out of there. I just feel a little bad that I don't, well, feel bad." He winces as he says it as if it pains him.

"I don't feel bad." Drea snorts. "They were both assholes and they won't be missed. We deserved to get through and we did what we had to do. Two less oxygen thieves left in the world now."

"Honestly Drea." I say with an awkward laugh. She's not wrong but my gosh she isn't one for mincing words

"Don't pretend you don't both feel the same! We all would get out of this together if we could. I'd happily see all of you turned. But going out into another trial with those guys would have been a recipe for disaster, they killed their own teammate! They are a piece of this game I am happy is no longer in play." She nods her head as she says the last word indicating what's what.

I know she's right; I feel the same. I'm honestly relieved that they aren't in play anymore. But do I worry like Jared? I have a flash of my previously forgotten nightmare. Being turned on and taken down by everyone around me. Is that what my subconscious truly thinks? Would Drea, or Jared or Ash turn on me if I was being the weak link. No. I know in my heart that isn't true. I probably had that dream thinking about Nikolas.

"Did Nikolas help us?" The words are out of my mouth before I process them. Jared and Drea turn their attention to me questioningly.

"Did he help? He killed Jessica, for me, for us to have another win. But I don't remember the … um … incident with Neal and David very well. Did Nikolas help us?"

"I honestly have no idea. But that is, unexpected, that he took out Jessica" Jared's words are careful. I wonder if that bothers him more than us killing the men. Jessica hadn't involved herself or spoken hardly at all, so we don't really know if she was a good person or not. Nikolas killing her was pretty cold hearted.

"He was killing her to steal her kill." Drea huffed. "Let's not pretend he did anything heroic princess; he gave you her body because he didn't need it."

I have no doubt that's true. If he needed Jessica to finish off filling his cylinder, he wouldn't have given her to us. Still, I was a total lunatic with him right before the trial, he could have given Jessica to someone else. This man's intentions are more layered than an onion and its starting to really get under my skin.

"It isn't the first time he's helped." I remind her. "He

held everyone back for us to get a head start in the first trial, and he brought Alice back."

"He's trying to help a child." Drea shrugs, "most of us would." I decide not to bring up that Drea didn't exactly step up to help Alice initially but that would be unfair, she has been helping me since trial one. I can't blame her for inaction before she got the chance to fully get to know us.

"It sounds as though he was quick to kill indiscriminately though." Jared points out, looking around to check it is still only us three. "Something to keep in mind I would suggest."

On the list of people, I would trust Nikolas would come in bottom anyway so I don't really dwell on it. Instead, I change the subject.

"Two more days of rest and relaxation then." I say heartily. Drea laughs and slings her arm around the back of my chair. Her hand just barely grazes my shoulder where it rests, and I lean back slightly trying to increase the points at which her skin touches mine.

"Let's hope it's two *full* days this time. I wasn't expecting to move so soon this morning." she says. Jared moves to take a seat at the table with us.

"I think we have to be prepared for every reality, think the worst and you can only be pleasantly surprised."

He says.

“That’s depressing and inspiring at the same time, well done!” Drea lifts her mug towards him in a cheers and I laugh.

“I just mean, if there’s anything you wish to do, don’t put it off. More training for the girl perhaps. Though I’m not sure what good it will do her.” He offers.

Alices training is the last thing I’m thinking about for the next two days. If this trial showed us anything it’s that in the end it really won’t matter if she can throw or block a punch. Alice will be reliant on us regardless of what comes next. Let her enjoy the next two days as much as she can, and we will take on what comes next together. Together. A foreign concept for me. Most of my life, all my adult life, I’ve done everything alone. I’ve eaten alone, I’ve hunted alone, even when my Master was present, I realize now that I still always felt alone. But in here I don’t feel that way anymore. And the main reason for that currently has her arm draped over my shoulder.

“I say let’s just enjoy the next two days.” I turn to smile at Drea and find she is already looking down at me. Her snowy hair falling loose around her face, I have the sudden urge to reach up and gently tuck it behind her ear. If Jared wasn’t sitting right across from us maybe I would, but my lack of experience and confidence shows, keeping my hands held tightly together in my lap.

“Enjoy?” He asks incredulously.

“Yes, enjoy.” I repeat “I don’t know about you, but I’ve found aspects of the past few days rather nice. Two days of preparing or training isn’t going to turn anyone in here into the next Dracula. After the next trial we’re going to be dead, or undead, so let’s enjoy our last two days of life.” I hadn’t really thought of it that way until I say it but it is true. Come the last trial we will no longer be alive as humans, this is my final days of human life whether I pass this test or not.

“Here, here!” Drea laughs and raises her mug again but towards me this time. “A lot will change you know.”

“What do you mean?” I ask her.

“Well, when we aren’t human anymore, I know it sounds obvious but a lot of things about you will change.”

“Has your Master told you about the transition?” Jared leans over the table slightly toward Drea unable to hide his intrigue. I’m guessing he has been kept in the dark about this part too.

“Of course, she has prepared me for everything.” Her

chin lifts slightly as she says this, and I'm reminded of the reverence Drea has for her Master. If she didn't view her as a mother figure, I would almost think I felt jealous. Almost.

"First of all, do you know how we actually change?" She opens to us.

"Yes, blood exchange." Jared fires back quickly. I did know that at least, my Master had briefly mentioned it when he had discussed creating brides. He said it was an extremely intimate act, one of the many reasons we don't just change anyone.

"Yes, our Master must drink our blood first almost to the point of draining. Our blood being in their system creates temporary antibodies that they then absorb into their blood stream. They're specific only to the person's blood they have digested and last for a day or two. Once these are present in the blood they can feed us, a small amount will do. When the blood mixed with the vampiric antibodies enters our system it starts the change. Snapping our necks is the final step" I blanche at her last words, I've seen a neck being snapped, if I could pick a way to die, I don't know that I would choose that.

"It heals over the course of a few days as you change. Your body rewrites itself. You'll become faster, stronger, more agile. But also colder, more inhuman.

Your sense of smell, sight and taste will all be enhanced. You will see the world in a whole new color."

As she talks, I watch Drea's eyes, they cloud over with an almost dreamy look. She seems to be enamored with the whole idea but again here I am left sitting on the fence. Parts of the change sound amazing, but becoming more inhuman? Perhaps I'm naive but I had fully intended to keep a hold of my humanity. Killing people should never become easy, especially not people who are good.

What does one who is inhuman feel anyway? Do they feel love, joy, attraction? I guess if they don't, at least they won't feel the other side, no more pain, sadness or loneliness. I may never feel the blood rushing through my veins when someone who I'm attracted to touches me, but I will also never feel lonely again. I can't quite put my finger on it, but that sounds like a form of purgatory to me.

"Many physical changes then." Jared summarizes in the biggest oversimplification I've ever heard.

"I would say becoming inhuman is a rather deeper change than physical." I say, the bravest I am able to be about expressing my displeasure at that prospect.

"Oh no don't misunderstand I don't mean you'll

become a monster I just mean you'll feel … different. You won't feel human anymore, my Master described it like waking up with a primal part of you finally switched on. Like you are a predator, operating on a different, a higher, level." Drea beams as if this is so much better, I'm not sure it is.

"A predator who can control minds." I say.

"Mind control?" Jared asks. I feel slightly less inept that at least one other person didn't know about vampires being able to charm us.

"She means charming." Drea says sidewards to him without turning her head.

"Oh right." He nods confirming, I am indeed inept, and he actually knew about charming already. "It isn't really mind control you know, more like … gentle but forceful coercion."

"Thanks for the lesson in dubious consent." I say bitterly, feeling rather sorry for myself. Drea clearly had a more dedicated Master than most. Teaching her everything she knew, but there's things that are clearly common knowledge amongst others that I was blind on. It hurts deeply every time I realize how little my Master trusted or cared for me to keep so many secrets.

"Don't be down about it princess, a lot of Masters

don’t tell their familiars about these things until they’re turned. You’ll get the manual in initiation.” She winks at me, and I wonder how stupid I would look if I asked if there was actually a manual.

“I was aware of some of the physical changes through observing my Master, but it has never been expressly discussed. Not for lack of trying, I have also been told many times I will find out if and when I am deemed worthy” Jared offers sympathetically.

It does make sense for us not to know all their secrets, what if a vampire hunter infiltrated their mist as a familiar. Can’t give away too many secrets. Still though I appreciate Jared’s words I know I have been kept particularly in the dark, though I am unsure why. Does my Master even want a bride or does he just do this to get rid of his old familiar’s every so often and replace us?

“Well, I guess it doesn’t matter whether Drea tell us now.” I say rather petulantly. “We’ll be one dead one way or another in a few days.”

“Don’t be a buzzkill or I won’t tell you any more secrets.” Drea says playfully and pats my head like a child. “You’re not as cute when you sulk.”

Despite myself I smile. Being called cute usually annoys me, being so short I get it a lot from men in bars when I go hunting. The way it rolls off of Drea's tongue though pulls my face into a grin and I decide I would let her call me cute whenever she likes.

"Better." She nods.

"You two are insufferable." Jared laughs heartily and I flush unaware of how obvious I was with my swooning.

"What do you wish Ash would call you cute?" Drea laughs back. I hadn't sensed that between the two men, but what do I know I've spent most of my time either staring at the woman to my side or trying not to stare at the broody man who bit my neck.

"Alas no, though he is a lovely man, I'm not on the market." He says kindly.

"Not on the market as in someone already has your heart?" Drea asks pushing him further.

"My Master has stipulated that if I were to be romantic with someone, they would become my familiar and be expected to join the family through the proper process." He doesn't seem annoyed by this, but rather proud as he says it. As though he is looking forward to choosing his familiar one day.

"Oh, how very proper of you." Drea puts on a fake posh English accent and laughs "I don't know how it would work with my Master she's never mentioned it and I've never really thought about keeping anyone around that long."

My heart sinks a little as she says that, I know we have only known each other a short while, but with the close proximity it feels like a lifetime already. It isn't possible but it would be nice to think that she had considered, even just a little, what it might be like for this to continue outside this room.

"Do vampires from different families ever date?" I ask, it was meant to sound casual but the moment I hear the words they sound anything but. Though I keep my head down as I ask the question I feel Drea's eyes burn into me and I can't help but raise mine to meet them.

"That would be a no princess, your family is your family. You can branch out and spend some time away. But in the end, you always come home to your Master. Two vampire families meeting would technically make a new family. Like with human marriages. That doesn't happen." It surprises me how crushing the devastation I feel is at her words. I thought at much, there's a reason no one has talked about staying friends after this is over. But to hear it from her mouth, that there is no chance me and her could meet together, outside of here, it breaks my heart. What I feel for her is real, I would have liked a chance to prove that outside these walls.

"In another life princess." Drea says wistfully, the only inclination that she feels this thing between us just like I do.

Sensing he is in the middle of what has become a very private moment, Jared quietly slides his chair out and busies himself inside the fridge.

"You know if I could pick a family Drea, I would have picked you I think." the words come out quietly, as if I'm not sure whether to say them or not. But they are true and part of me wants her to know that. Whatever happens next if I could pick to leave here with her I would. I would leave my Master in an instant, the man who has taken me in and put a roof over my head these past ten years. Because he has never given me in those ten years what Drea has in a few days. A feeling of belonging, a feeling of being loved.

"If I could put you in my pocket and take you with me I would." She whispers back.

Our first true admission to each other. It feels far more intimate than our kiss was. I feel far more exposed. A small part of me almost wished that she didn't feel the same, it might make it easier. If I thought she wouldn't want to see me after this, it might have been a tiny bit less painful to walk away.

I highly doubt that asking if her Master wants to adopt me would be an option but it's something I'm genuinely considering at this point. That thought sends somewhat of a crushing panic over me. If I'm that happy to leave my Master, do I really want him to turn me. Do I really want to be the eternal bride to someone who I feel no genuine connection to at all other than perhaps a sense of gratefulness and a debt owed.

I guess the hard truth is, it doesn't matter. My feelings in this equation won't have any impact on the outcome. My Masters wishes and will are the true and only important factors. So, if I don't die and I make it out the other side, I will spend the rest of my eternal life in a purgatory. Maybe I can build something with him, once I'm no longer the human help, but I honestly don't think I want to anymore. It would feel a slap in the face and disingenuous at this point, if I wasn't good enough for him as a human, he doesn't deserve me as a vampire.

Sensing the inner meltdown I am having, Drea places one palm flat against my face, with the other around my shoulder I almost feel embraced by her.

"Don't worry about things you can't change princess, we got two whole days to have some fun." Then she sticks out her tongue, leans forward and licks the tip of my nose.

After a few seconds of stunned silence, I burst into laughter. The absolute absurdity of it. There was nothing sexual about what she just did, and by the please smirk on her face I suspect that her objective was to just baffle me into calming down. It worked.

I dramatically wipe my nose with the arm of my hoodie and feign disgust.

“Is that vampire for calm down?” I laugh.

“No, that’s Drea for lighten the fuck up.” She winks and jumps up from her seat. She places one arm behind her back and extends the other to me as if she were a gentleman at a ball about to ask me to dance.

“Shall we get something to eat?” She asks.

“We shall.” I say and take her hand in mine. I try not to focus too hard on how well they fit together and lace my fingers through hers.

“Jared what sweet stuff we got in there, I may have eaten all the muffins already.” She winks at me and swings our hands between us.

Jared pulls out of the fridge, releasing a breath that he can rejoin the conversation now. I don’t know how long he's had his face stuck in the fridge exactly, but I bet its longer than was necessary to find the yoghurt he now holds in his hand.

"There's some donuts actually." He offers.

"Donuts?!" Drea mock gasps. "How did I miss those; I will take them all."

Jared slides out a small box which must be holding half a dozen and hands them our way. Drea pulls her hand away from mine so she can place the box in them, and I miss the warmth instantaneously.

"You. Sit down with these I'll make the three of us some fresh coffee." And with that she swishes over the fill the kettle.

Me and Jared take our seats just as Ash emerges from his room. He looks extremely well groomed and put together. His face is rather serene, and he doesn't seem as affected as me or Jared by today's events. Taking a seat opposite me he slides himself the box of donuts and takes one.

"I want at least two mind Ash." Drea calls over her shoulder.

"Be quick then woman." Is all he calls back giving Jared a playful wink.

Drea is right, why spoil the next two days of this worrying about something I can't change. For now, I will live blissfully in ignorance with my little group of murderous friends.

CHAPTER THIRTEEN

The next day passes in a pleasant blur of small talk and relaxation. There is no more talk of the trial, and everyone makes a concerted effort to keep the discussions on lighter topics. Jared tells us more of his plans for his immortality, he sounds as though he is thoroughly looking forward to it. Talking about the vampiric life he makes, it sound almost fun.

Him and his Master stay in the penthouse of a high-end apartment complex in New York. They have a few vampires from their family who come and go and spend their nights out on the town seeing the city that never sleeps by night.

His Master hunts for himself while they are out so Jared is a glorified butler really, like Michelle was, attending them at home and everywhere they go. Ensuring they are back by sunrise and that everything is sealed.

It sounds like an exciting life, and I can imagine enjoying the concept of living forever with so much fun at your fingertips. I wonder the last time my Master was out in the real world. He has never left the house so long as I have known him, preferring to spend his time reminiscing in old books or playing himself at chess. Content is a word I would have always used to describe him, as though he has done everything in life he wanted to and now he is enjoying a leisurely retirement.

Imagining him dressed in one of his eccentric velvet suits and hitting the town with Jared and his vampiric family is a difficult thing to do. I'm unsure he would even know how to react when he was out in the modern world. How long he has actually been a recluse, I don't know, however even the last ten years I have been with him has showed massive changes to the world.

I remember when the computer in our house was dial up when I was a child. The security systems in the house certainly weren't what they are now when I first arrived, that technology alone should give him an idea of how much has changed. Other than having that system regularly updated though he has massively resisted any change. Using a smart phone isn't on his radar, nor does our house have a television. Though he looks young my Master is outdated, I imagine him being handed an iPhone and asked to complete a task, like an old person who grew up in the war he would likely poke and prod at it until he gave up in frustration and handed it to me.

When my parents died, I had a flip phone that I could send texts, make calls and play snake on but that was about it. Over the years I updated it a few times, getting a smartphone when one was first available. I had enough of an allowance to do so and it was my only real connection to the outside world, using it to watch vloggers on YouTube, or telenovelas and reality shows on demand. A more important reason though was safety, going out to bars and prowling for men put me in positions where I wanted to be able to call for help if I needed.

Like a teenager I stashed it under my bed during the nights when I was up with Master, I don't think he would approve. He did communicate often with who I assume now were members of other families but always via written letter. Beautiful, expensive, letter headed paper than he would use a quill and ink to write on. He would even go so far as sealing it with a wax stamp before giving it to me to post.

I would always add another layer of a traditional envelope, on which I rewrote the address. I certainly never read any of the letters, whether that's why they were wax sealed shut I'm not sure, but he never offered me the contents of the letters as conversation, so I respected his boundary.

Jared's Master had his own smartphone so is clearly a more modern thinking vampire, but he did communicate some by letter. We discover through conversation that Jared, who scribed the letters for his Master, had written responses to my address in Alaska on multiple occasions. Fighting the urge to ask about myself I don't bring it up immediately, but eventually I cave and query whether I was ever mentioned in his letters, I wasn't.

The disappointment must be clear on my face as Jared assures me his Master never wrote about him either, they had much more important topics to talk about.

Each new tid bid of information though just solidifies my new understanding of reality. My Master doesn't care about me. He doesn't spend time with me the way the others do, he never involved me in his life or discussed plans for the future. Even those here who know limited, if any, information on the secrets of the vampires, still have had discussions about what will mean for them after the trial.

Drea will be like a daughter, becoming a true part of the family. Jared will become a brother, another male to join the fun in going clubbing and picking up women and victims, before taking his own familiar. Ash is somewhat more subdued about his future; this familiar gig has been a family affair for him. The men in his family have served for generations this way, allowed to enjoy freedom and retirement through the stipulation their son take their place.

It's a good insurance policy for letting you familiars go. You won't divulge secrets if your son is in the house with the man who's secrets they are. His Master's family sounds much like a hierarchy rather than a genuine family. They have businesses that they run in India, apparently this is part of the reason they travel so much. Ash will become a partner in said business, though he doesn't discuss what the business is. I assume it's not perhaps on the straight and narrow. His face twists when he tells us how proud his family will be if he is successful in the trials. His grandfather was given a chance to take part but chose to retire just before, now he wants to see Ash take up the dream he perhaps always regrets not taking.

The unspoken words let me know that this isn't what Ash necessarily wants, I suspect if he had another option, he would be gladly taking it. Vampirism is his families dream not his, but when I suggest this, he assures me that his greatest dream is making his family proud and he leaves the conversation at that.

Even if Ash isn't getting his perfectly happy ending he knows where he stands. When I'm asked what my plans are I have no idea what to say to people. My Master told me that if I continued to serve well, he would turn me, that's all I have to offer. I have no deeper relationship with him than a ward or a well looked after servant. No expectations have been discussed regarding how that dynamic will change once I'm changed, and I will likely spend the rest of my pathetic existence in a big house with a distant vampire and maybe another familiar. Hopefully the new familiar is kind and will be my friend because that's my best bet at having any kind of meaningful relationship after this. Though it's what I think, I don't say this. I merely tell people I'm not really sure and that I would be told more information after I was turned.

They try and hide it, but my response elicits side glances of sympathy and confusion. I can just imagine what they are all thinking about me. Poor pathetic Sabine, so alone and desperate that she is going to become a vampire based on not only empty but absent promises and misguided hopes. I will be an easy vampiric bride to manipulate, that's probably what they are thinking, probably what my Master thinks too. Last week I would have agreed with them, but the Sabine here and now is not the same Sabine who entered this trial and I'm no longer so thoroughly convinced I will be able to return to a life of quiet and isolated servitude.

Nikolas in particular gives me a really strange and intense look as I speak, as if, if he looks hard enough he might be able to see through some lies and into my soul. But there are no lies on my tongue, no deeper reason to why I am here, I'm just a girl with nowhere else to go.

He is the only one who hasn't spoken much, he listens and nods along but unlike everyone else he offers no little pieces of information on his life. I have met his Master, he seemed an interesting and even kind vampire, in the way he treats Nikolas. Part of me is dying to ask him about his life, I want to know everything, how he became a familiar, what he thinks of his Master, what his plans for immortality are.

Perhaps if I knew more about where he came from, I would have some sliver of hope of figuring out who he is now. A lech, I know that much from his repeated attempts to get me hot and bothered. Ruthless, he has made that clear with each life I have seen him take, he snapped the neck of that man in the first trial like he has snapped a hundred before. He didn't think twice about ending Jessica's life. Yet he is also kind, I cannot deny that he has helped Alice on many occasions when he didn't need to.

It would have been so simple to not help us in the blood trial and let us fight our own way out, but he didn't. Heartless isn't something I could call him in good conscious it wouldn't be fair. Secretive however I certainly can.

Though I'm determined to not pry into his life, he

does get a few questions from others around the room. Jared pries as to whether he has been with his familiar for a long time to which he receives the taught and unhelpful reply of "yes". Ash tries his luck and asks him whether he would take a familiar of his own, this question tells me a little more about him at least as Nikolas looks absolutely disgusted by the suggestion and brushes it off. So he is happy to be a familiar, but not to take one, interesting.

He does well to keep his cards close to his chest but listens intently to everyone else. I can see from his eyes that he is logging everything that is said, Nikolas still has a game to play yet. I just don't know what it is.

*

After an afternoon of sharing people slowly drift off into their smaller groups. Ash and Jared go back to their usual past time of playing a quiet game of cards, Alice sits crossed legged on the floor next to them watching the table and quietly trying to understand the rules of the game they are playing. Nikolas, happy he has gathered all the information he needs from us, slides away to his room for some privacy, the door closing firmly behind him.

Drea and I are laid on the sofa, she stretches out and I throw my legs over her. We both are turned watching the boys play cards, close enough to see the strained look of concentration on their faces.

"Once he is a vampire Ash can simply charm people into letting him win." I muse quietly.

"Where would the fun in that be though." Drea runs a finger up and down the leg that is resting on her over my sweatpants.

"I bet it is fun sometimes, you could go to Vegas and wipe the casino out. Never have to work again." I imagine rolling up to a twinkling casino and taking them for all they have, people thinking in the new bite sized female rain man. Perhaps Drea has the same mental image because she laughs heartedly at me.

"Sure, maybe that how your Master made his millions." She suggests.

"Do you not plan on using your charm much?" I ask, barely able to focus on anything other than the small touch she offers me. Tracing gently up and down my leg, stealing all rationale thought.

"Oh, I do, I'll use it for lots of things, but not robbing casinos." She rolls her eyes.

"Like what then?" I ask genuinely curious.

She looks at me skeptically, as if she almost wants to preface the next part with asking me not to laugh at her.

"We're from New Orleans." I realize I never knew where she lived before now, I really should have asked. "There's a lot of crime, but also a lot of really good people. The community there is really beautiful. My Master uses charm to find kingpins, mob bosses who are causing issues in the community. Particularly bothering kids or local families in the area. Then she charms them into finding their morality." A small secretive smile creeps over her face as she says this.

"They tend to have an overnight epiphany and find more morally acceptable business ideas that don't affect the locals and they give us lists of men who would make a good snack."

I didn't think it was possible, but I like this woman even more. Her and her Master … fight crime together?

"Let me guess, you hunt down the men from the list." I put the pieces together.

"They make suitable meals." She grins.

"And no one in the town has clicked on to your little

justice league?" I ask incredulously.

"There's a group of long-time locals who know there's something supernatural about us. In New Orleans there are a lot of people who are in touch with nature, spirits, and their ancestors in a way that I've never seen anywhere else." Her eyes hold reverence and I know from the weight of her words that she holds a lot of respect for the people she lives with.

"They have connected the dots that whatever we are, we help the community not harm it. They actually have a lot of respect for us. I go out myself a lot, but my Master comes out on occasion too, she meets with people, hears stories of those who are struggling. She has been in New Orleans a long time; her soul is connected to the place and I think people can feel that."

The way she described it sounds beautiful, like a pair of vampiric guardian angels. Is this what Drea will be doing when she goes back as a vampire? It's no wonder she doesn't think about leaving, why would she. She has a figure in her life who loves her, a town who she serves and protects, she has … well … a purpose.

"Soul." I muse out loud. Drea looks at me curiously. "You said her soul is connected to New Orleans, most people probably wouldn't consider vampires as having a soul. Is that another piece of vampire lore you can educate me on." I tease her playfully.

"I think everyone has a soul, how much you taint that soul is up to the individual," there's no playfulness in her eyes, she has thought about this before I can tell.

"My Master is the kind of person who has chosen to spend her immortality putting down roots in a community that she feels she can help. She might have taken a lot of lives, but she's saved a lot during the process, including mine. If anyone would deserve a soul, it's her."

The reverence in which she speaks about her sparks a violent flare of jealously in me that I'm not proud of. It isn't only that I want Drea to feel so passionately about me as she does about this other woman, no, If I'm being honest with myself, it's that I am jealous I don't have that for myself. Drea was saved, like I was, but in being saved she found someone who she can look up to. She found a family and one she can be proud of. I feel like a puppy who got picked up from the pound only to find I'm destined to be a street dog. Drea is lady and I'm the tramp.

Any words I might have escape me and all I manage is a pathetic nod to show I understand her. For the first time I notice her hand has stopped moving and instead she grips the top of my leg with slightly more pressure than necessary.

"What is it?" Something is wrong.

"I just …" She notices her hand and loosens her grip. "She worries about that too you know, that if she died, she wouldn't have a soul to pass on. She doesn't talk about it, but she had a family a long time ago, before she was turned. I think deep down her greatest wish is to see them again one day. Honestly, I think if she didn't question her soul then she would have maybe … passed … already to see them."

I reach down and place my hand on top of hers, stroking my thumb in soft soothing circles. The hard part of immortality I had always thought would be the endless stretch of time in front of you and how you would fill it. Never had it crossed my mine about the people who would be left behind, because … well … I had no one to leave behind.

"Well, she's found a new family now, in you. And I for one think she's very lucky." I mean the words wholeheartedly. Drea's father didn't deserve her, and this vampire sounds like a woman to be respected and even loved. They are lucky they found each other, and I know without even meeting her that these two will be very happy in their new family once Drea is immortal alongside her.

“I’m the lucky one.” Drea snorts.

“Can’t you both be lucky?” I voice the thoughts I’ve already had.

“I guess we are.” She smiles gently and turns her hand over, palm up so that she can’t twine her fingers through mine. “I think she would like you. She would like how much you’ve risked for the safety of Alice” She tilts her head slightly toward the little girl, sitting engrossed in watching what is now a game of poker.

“Maybe I’ll get to meet her one day.” I offer even though we know its empty. “I would very much like to, she sounds amazing.”

“If you’re ever in New Orleans we would love to have you for dinner.” Drea smiles.

A tear comes rolling down my cheek, a part of my sadness that is so overwhelming it has to find a way to spill outward. The thought of going to a new city, seeing Drea again with my new eyes, taking in her smell with my new nose. I would embrace her like old friends who have been parted too long. She would take me back to meet her amazing Master, who wouldn’t be her Master anymore. I would be welcomed with open arms into what I imagine is their cooky little apartment with a glass of blood from some evil man Drea had hunted down specially for me.

The tears fall faster now, no sound accompanies them. This isn't a desperate and gasping sadness. It isn't the kind of tears that fell when I first arrived. These tears are a silent mourning. I see what Drea has and I want it, I want it so badly it hurts, I don't just want her life though I want to be part of it. I want to have a purpose and a place. I want a family.

The smile on Drea's face carries the sadness that I feel, her free hand reaches out and she places her hand flat against my face. She cradles my face in her hand and I close my eyes and lean slightly into it. I feel her thumb swipe gently across the stream of tears making an attempt to clear them.

Without me having to say the words I know she understands how I feel. Whatever connection is between us, its stronger than I ever remember feeling with anyone. Sitting here with her, feeling our bodies touch and our hearts reach for each other, I wonder how it will feel to never see her again.

Will my body remember the feel of her smooth skin, will I lie in bed at home and think about what it was like to feel her touch me? Would her touch even feel the same when I'm changed? Would it feel even better against my new more sensitive skin? I want to find out. Experiencing everything new as a vampire sounds so much more exciting if it was Drea, I would be experiencing it with.

"You said two vampires couldn't start a new family, but what if one vampire just joined the existing family?" My voice breaks slightly as I ask my impossible question. I don't know if I want the truth from her, but I think that I would always regret not taking the chance and asking.

My eyes don't dare reopen to see how her face reacts to what I just asked. I don't know if my already breaking heart could take that.

"I have never heard it done. If both families agreed I suppose it would be okay, but Sabine, the chances of that … the chances of a vampire letting one of his brides go … I …" She doesn't need to finish; my Master isn't going to hand me over to a different family.

Or would he? Knowing his actions and reactions isn't exactly something I can attest to. My observation of him over the years has been extensive but shallow. He doesn't seem to care for me that much on a personal level, he may already have another familiar lined up. In terms of taking a bride I see no evidence he has done so in a long time if never, so why not wait another couple of decades for a new candidate?

"So, I could ask?" The words come hesitantly, my eyes daring to look up and meet hers. What they find is reluctance and resistance. The hope I was brewing dies on the spot. “Unless you don’t want me to.”

Of course, she doesn’t want me to, am I crazy. I’ve barely known the woman two minutes and I’m asking to spend eternity with her. But it isn’t just her, I want to be part of her family. The purpose, the belonging, the possibility of a me and Drea becoming more. That’s all I’m asking for, a chance. And if over time … it became more … well that would just be a bonus.

“I’m not saying that.” she says firmly gripping my face with both hands now not just one. “You would make a great fit with us, you would, and I would love the chance to get to know you more but Sabine … It might not just be as simple as your Master or mine saying no. What if he gets mad, would he be vindictive? Would he hurt you for wanting to leave?” She’s just concerned for me; I might have only known this woman for two minutes, but I love her. I almost laugh before I truly consider her words.

She’s right. I don’t really know his intentions at all, he may well be furious. He could view it as a snub, a blemish to his ego. What if he decides to just off me instead of turning me for the insolence of asking to leave after he’s put a roof over my head and food in my mouth the past decade. Is it a risk I would be willing to take? Would I give up my life for a chance at eternal happiness? I think I would. I take a slow shaky breath before considering how I want to phrase this to her.

"Before I came here, I was just existing. A pretty pathetic excuse for existence too. When I thought about becoming a bride to a vampire it was for no other reason than I was living in a state of suspended reality, a coma of comfortability with nowhere else to go. Those first few days I didn't want to *die*, but now … now I want to *live*. What you have Drea, it's a life, it's a future. I want that, I don't want to put pressure on you, and there would be no expectations. But if you would have me, as a friend, I can't explain how happy that would make me." I can feel myself getting louder as I speak, and I know that the men and Alice are probably listening to this all, but I don't care. Spending the last day talking about ourselves and our lives they are under no false assumptions that I'm happy where I am.

Drea can't make me any promises and I'm not looking for any, but she can promise to a*sk.* If the opportunity presents itself, she can offer to take me with her.

"I would enjoy teaching you how to be a badass vampire little princess, if I can, I will." No promises, no specifics, but she's given me everything I wanted. If she can take me with her after this she will.

"Get a room already!" Alice shouts at us in mock horror and it breaks us both from our moment. We both turn to look at her and she's holding her stomach as if we nauseate her. A hearty laugh erupts from both of us, the tension well and truly broken. Even Ash and Jared smile or giggle to themselves respectively.

"First chance I get don't you worry." Drea waggles her eyebrows at me and leans round to squeeze my ass. The motion takes me totally off guard and the look of shock on my face is genuine.

This sparks another bought of laughter from everyone in the room, and renewed horror from Alice who throws her hands up in exacerbation.

"Sorry princess." Drea says, her hand still firmly grasping me and pulling me slightly toward her. "Did I offend your honor?"

I can feel the crimson rising in my cheeks, from the embarrassment of everyone watching but also from something else. Having her pull me toward her like this, grasping me like she doesn't want to let me go. If we had the option of getting a room right now, I think I would take her up on it. Her fingertips dig slightly into my flesh in a way that feels deeply possessive and my mind drifts to all the other places I want to feel her hands on me.

Realizing the silence is stretching between us I try to kickstart my brain to find some words.

"You can offend my honor any time you like." Its far more daring than anything I would usually say but I'm running on adrenaline from our heartfelt conversation. I want her to know that though I might not have lived a daring life like she has, I'm certainly willing to try it if she is the one taking me alone for the ride.

My intended affect doesn't quite play out however, as instead of the eliciting some kind of flirty response or excitement Drea's laughter renews even more heartily than before. She tilts her head back and the hair falls from her face. Unadulterated joy is the only way I can describe her expression, she has little crinkles around her eyes, and they shine with something that is only present in moments like this.

"You are just full of surprises; I'll make a heathen out of you yet." She promises, and all I can think of is how very much I would like that.

*

When dinner comes around, we all sit around the table like a big dysfunctional family. Even Nikolas joins us, though he keeps his distance in every sense of the word. Ash has used some ingredients out of the fridge to make a tomato-based pasta dish and after days of cold sandwiches and protein bars I am absolutely salivating as the smells come through the air.

Aromas of garlic and a variety of spices fill the room and Alice dips around Ash trying to get a good view of what he's doing. He lifts the spoon out the sauce that he's stirring on the hob top and blows on it before letting her have little tastes. She smacks her lips like a little food critic and tells him that he needs more salt or less spice.

Deciding to contribute I set the table for everyone handing out plates and cutlery and putting down place mats for Ash to place the food onto. Nikolas even thanks me quietly as I pass him his plate, to which I return a small smile. Whether or not I trust him is still up in the air, but I certainly don't want to do anything that would put me in his bad books.

Sitting in our little makeshift home its strange how quickly it became normal, even comfortable. Harsh flickering lighting, something that make me cringe when we first came in, has become almost unnoticeable. Our little family dining room has become so familiar that we even have our own spots now, with Drea, me and Alice always sitting down the side facing the fridge. Ash always seems to take the place at the head of the table which I don't mind, his calm and decisive presence does make me feel like he would be a good head of the family. Even the rugged sofa and armchair set is something I have grown fond of, curling up, usually with Drea, I can imagine being somewhere long enough with someone to form an indent. A little Sabine shaped divet to mark that I had been here.

We make room as Ash brings over a big bowl of sieved and dried noodles and the family saucepan with oven mitts on. Alice has the good sense to stay out of his way while he moves so that she isn't accidently cooked alive under a spilled boiling pot. A picture of super weird family bliss. Dysfunctionality is a pre-requisite in every family anyway, right?

"If I could eat, I would ask to join you." An unidentified voice with a distinct Cajun English accent pierces through our conversation bringing absolute silence.

We all turn in a synchronized motion toward the sound of the voice at the door. A short middle-aged black woman stands there. She looks around forty in years, but her face doesn't show any hint of creasing. Her midsized figure is beautifully dressed in a loose and floating dress which holds all the colors of the rainbow. Large, hooped earring hang from the lobes of her ears which are fully exposed as her hair is up and tucked under a vibrant pink scarf matching the colors of her dress.

"Master." Drea breaths.

Master. This is Drea's Master. She looks like an absolute work of art. A force of nature. Though she is dressed brightly it isn't that alone that draws me in, it's the confidence she exudes. As though she could take on the world and win, yet she still looks kind. Her face doesn't seem soft exactly, but open. At first, I was absolutely baffled at the idea that the people of New Orleans, in their community, knew what they were and didn't fear them.

Now I understand, though I have no doubt she could end me in an instant if she wanted to, she doesn't have the same deadly and threatening energy of the other male vampires I've experienced. Overcompensation isn't something this woman needs, she exudes confidence, if you're dumb enough to not be afraid of her that would be your mistake.

Sprinting past me Drea has a smile of pure unadulterated joy on her face. My insecurity can't help but assess whether she has ever smiled like that for me, but I squash the thought. The woman opens her arms in invitation and Drea jumps into them slamming the woman with the full force of her. Embracing each other, their eyes closed, I'm moved by the genuine emotion in the movement. Though Drea is significantly taller than the Creole woman she looks like a child as she holds her in her arms, reduced to nothing more than the little girl sitting on the porch of her trailer. This woman was Drea's mother for all intents and purposes and as far as I could tell she felt Drea was her daughter.

As they move from the embrace neither fully lets the other go. Drea has her hands grasping the woman's face, and she returns with both her arms still gripping her waist.

"Petit mwen." She drawls and leans in to kiss each of Drea's cheeks in turn. "You have done so well as I knew you would; you are almost there."

Drea's face lights up with pride at this validation and she bows her slightly in thanks to her Master.

"Come, I am not just here for you, I have been given instructions." She makes a face as she says this as if it is a complete joke that someone would dare to give her instructions. I imagine there's nothing you could make this woman do if she did not wish to do it.

Drea nods and moves to her side taking her hand, not giving up the closeness but allowing her Master to address us all.

"You have all done very well, and I must say you seem to have been built from good character from your performance thus far. There has not been a group of so many perspective hopefuls that I wish to see success in more." I can't be sure but I swear she looks to me briefly as she speaks and my heart flutters. I don't even know the woman but from what I have heard, and this tiny snippet I have seen, I would feel honored to have her routing for me.

"My name is Adélaïde, and I am here to let you know you may only have one final trial but the powers that be, have decided to test you with a small interlude before we get there." My heart drops, what could this be, having one hurdle left was hard enough to imagine overcoming, having two makes this whole thing seem even more impossible.

Sensing the distress in the room Adélaïde holds her free hand up to steady us, I don't look to Drea I need to focus on what comes next completely and I know I will fall apart with distraction if I meet her eyes right now.

"Calm, none of you will die in this challenge, nor will any of you be eliminated. However, the winning team will go into the final trial with an edge. You will divide yourself into teams, each team will leave this room separately and undertake a … task. The winning team will be given an unspecified advantage going forward." She nods as she finishes.

Vague, it's all too vague. If we are allowed to split ourselves into teams then obviously, I will be with

Drea and Alice, but doing what? How can we ever be prepared to perform if they won't give us more notice or information. Grinding my teeth against the frustration I try to steel my rapidly increasing breaths. Regardless of this outcome, no one is going to die, and no one is going to be eliminated. So, in the end it doesn't really matter if we don't win, who needs an edge, we will be fine without it.

"Is there any point at all asking what the game is?" Nikolas says with attitude. I turn to glare at him, annoyance running through me that he is being rude to this woman. He doesn't need to shoot the messenger.

"Absolutely none my boy." She laughs in his face which makes him furious and gives me a little twinge of satisfaction.

Done with us she turns to Drea and places a palm flat against her cheek that she immediately leans into.

"Keep doing what you are doing Andromeda and we will go home soon hmm?" The action is so full of love and sentiment it breaks my heart. I immediately think back to the halfhearted compliment my Master gave me after the first trial, he didn't even bother crossing the room to me. And to think I was flattered by it; it was a slap in the face.

"I do hope so." Drea says smiling gently.

“Who knows ey you might even bring a souvenir with you?” Adélaïde turns and winks at me so quickly I almost missed it. Before I can acknowledge and return and sentiment, she squeezes Drea’s hand and moves to leave.

“Get yourselves into teams, they’ll call you when they’re ready.” She calls over her shoulder, hips swaying as she sachets out of the room and disappears down the hall to the right.

The room starts to spin slightly around me reeling from a world worth of information in a one-minute interaction. Another challenge, another game we weren’t expecting, and pitted against each other. Whether we will win or not I don’t know all I can hope is that we all come out the end in one piece. Honestly that isn’t what I’m focusing on. *You might even bring a souvenir with you.*

Am I completely off base assuming that I’m the souvenir, is she going to let Drea wrap me in a towel and stuff me in her suitcase on the way out? God, I hope so, I hope so with every fiber of my being. I don’t even care that she referred to me as an inanimate object, I’ll take it if it means I can go with them. I try to slow my breaths and my thoughts; I can’t get ahead of myself. She may well just have been joking with us, she might have no intention at all in bringing me with them.

Now it is confirmed however that they obviously are listening to and watching us, which means if Drea's Master knows I want to come with them, so does mine. I imagine him sitting in a little fancy room somewhere with the other familiars, drinking blood out of champaign flutes and being amused by our misery. What would he say when he saw me ask Drea to go with her, what would he do when he heard me admit life with him hadn't been living? I've never seen him angry but he's the kind of man you don't need to see angry to know it's something you want to avoid. The sheer presence of him is intimidating enough to keep me from upsetting the applecart.

My mind races through the possibility I could see him soon, face to face presented with the man who has given me this opportunity will I feel ashamed that I tried to throw it back in his face the first chance I got?

*

We aren't given much time to have an existential crisis as the announcement voice rings to let us know we have five minutes until the first team will leave. No discussion needs to occur for us to know who with whom is. Ash and Jared wouldn't split, and neither would us three. Nikolas is the spare, the ugly duckling, but lucky for him Ash and Jared don't really have a choice.

Regardless of how they feel they welcome him with them by shuffling slightly so the three men stand closer and that is all the confirmation he needs. Nikolas gives a nod of thanks to the men and drops his head, he almost looks ashamed. Perhaps he is regretting not making a strong enough attempt at friendship with anyone. His aloof persona won't win him points when it comes to popularity.

Juddering with nerves I hold my hands together, trying to keep my thoughts from racing so much that they overwhelm me. Alice is the absolute picture opposite and is rather thrilled she is getting to go on an outing that won't involve her possible demise. She seems to have convinced herself it will be fine because it was stated we can't die, what I don't say is that it doesn't mean somebody else won't. If this is another challenge that involves taking life, I don't know how she will cope. Repression is the tactic Alice has used for the trauma associated with the last trial and she has never again mentioned what she went through other than that initial wobble when I approached it. If she has to witness more death today, will she be able to keep up this façade? I don't even know if I will be able to.

"Who wants to go first?" Ash puts to the room. "I would usually say ladies first, but I don't think that would be particularly chivalrous in this situation." He laughs trying to make light of the dense atmosphere.

"I don't know, I honestly don't mind." I say looking to Drea for a suggestion. She just shrugs. "I guess we will go first if you don't mind, I think I would rather get it out of the way." I make the split decision.

"Of course." Ash says ever the gentleman, no one contradicts him.

"Familiar team one please proceed to the trial hall from trial two."

My stomach clenches and I grit my teeth. I didn't think we would have to go back there. Perhaps naively I assumed there would be a new space for each trial. Perhaps that is the scope of this building. Nerves may be swirling in my belly, but I don't let Drea or Alice see. Thoughts of my nightmare flash back to me reminding me what's on the line here. I will not be useless; I will not be the weak link. Today, if I can, I will save Drea for a change.

I steel myself and raise my chin in faux confidence. Grabbing Drea with one hand and Alice with the other I march forward before I can change my mind and storm towards the chamber of death from yesterday.

“I guess that means we’re off.” Drea laughs as her feet catch up with her and she matches my pace. “See you soon fellas, we will make sure to kick your ass at this.” She mock salutes them over her shoulder before we disappear down the hallway.

Each step toward the room becomes more and more stifling. My nose picks up the smell of blood though I can’t yet tell if it is my damaged psyche playing tricks on me or if they have genuinely not cleaned the room. Bile rises in my throat, I need to get a grip, I’m used to decaying bodies. I have moved them enough even if I wasn’t the one killing them. That doesn’t change anything, if I can move them without vomiting then I can go back into this room without doing it too.

I consider momentarily covering Alices eyes again but decide against it, she slit a man’s throat yesterday I think any ideas of remaining innocence would be a fallacy on my part and I’m not doing her any favors by sheltering her so much. If she has a total breakdown when we get in there, I will deal with that as it comes.

Rounding the corner and moving into the doorway my eyes are momentarily blinded by unending and perfect sparkling white. It has been cleaned. Thank the gods. I release a breath I didn’t even realize I was holding. Everything has been removed, the bodies, the blood, and the equipment to harvest and measure blood. The room is now an ominous blank canvas.

This is even worse.

I think to myself. I can't even guess what the game is because there's nothing to go on.

"Hello familiars and welcome. Today we will test your dedication to our cause."

As the announcement voice talks a small square in the middle of the floor hisses and begins to rise, revealing a hidden platform underneath. I can't yet see what it holds as I go to step forward, but Drea holds me back with a small shake of her head. W*ait.* She seems to say.

"Inside the box currently making its way into the room with you, are three vials and three hypodermic needles. Each vial contains a small amount of your Master's venom."

I blanche. Venom, that can't be meant to change us. Drea luckily already explained how that process worked and it wasn't this.

"This venom will slowly poison you, causing a delayed but painful death over the next 120 hours."

My head swings to Drea, did she know this, like she knew about everything else? I certainly didn't, I knew they had venom, and I knew it helped subdue a victim. Killing us? Somehow another important piece of information my Master missed.

"You will each inject yourselves with your Master's venom. After an initial ... set back ... you will then be unaffected for the first twenty-four hours before your condition declines. Therefore your performance in the final trial, occurring tomorrow, will not be affected. For each of you that injects the venom you will receive ten points, the team with the most points, wins." After a pause I can only imagine is for dramatic affect the voice continues.

"Fret not, if you win the trial and complete the change, your life will be saved. You have five minutes to make your decision."

As the voice clicks off a large LED timer appears on the wall opposite us counting down our minutes.

"Do we really want to do this?" I ask Drea. I already have decided I don't think Alice should. Who knows how ill this will make a child if its strong enough to kill us within days.

"What do you mean, what difference does it make?" She shrugs nonchalantly.

"Um, the difference is being poisoned or not poisoned. And I don't want Alice doing this anyway. The three of the men will definitely do it, so we will lose regardless. Might as well save ourselves the poison." I fling my arms in the air dramatically which elicits a small smile from her.

"Don't you laugh at me." I point in her face.

"Not laughing," She raises her hands in defense. "They said it won't affect us by tomorrow, by that point we will know who is and is not going to go through the change and we will be going through the change. We might as well take the advantage whatever it is." I know her logic is sound, but I don't fully trust the Masters that this won't have any negative effects on us, what if it kicks in in the middle of the trial, what if it affects children differently?

"And what if we feel weaker, slower? What then? The advantage whatever it is, won't matter."

"I think you're being a tiny bit dramatic, besides this isn't just about an advantage, they're asking us to prove our commitment." She repeats the words of the announcement and makes eyes at me as if I'm supposed to understand her. What is she afraid of that they will judge us if we don't?

"I would do it Drea, I would. But Alice is ten years old, I'm not injecting her with venom." It's a half truth, I wouldn't particularly want a slow poisoning regardless of the circumstances but it's an easy excuse.

"You don't have to. I will." We both turn, as if in slow motion, to Alice who has crossed the room and filled her syringe while we were squabbling.

"Alice." I warn. But it's too late, she plunges the needle into her tiny arm and empties the contents with a push of the plunger. Her eyes wince as she does so but she other than that her bravery is unbelievable. For a ten-year-old girl to not only inject herself, with the biggest needle I've ever seen, but to inject herself with poison. She doesn't make a sound; no cry or squeak escapes her lips. She merely winces again as she removes the needle and drops it to the floor.

The noise it makes it soul shattering. Silence disturbed by the clattering of plastic against tiled floor. Then without any warning she collapses to the floor and starts seizing.

"Alice!" screaming I run toward her and drop to my knees. Her head hit the floor on the way down which I'm also worried about. But the main concern is the fit, she trembles and shakes violently, her whole body somehow vibrating but stiff at the same time. No breath escapes her mouth that I can see but she has started foaming slightly around the lips. My mind whirls, I don't know what to do, I don't know how to fix this. I'm not a medic, I wouldn't know how to help a seizure anyway, but a vampire venom induced seizure is well out of my area.

All I do is try and provide her comfort, one hand cradling her head the other gently stroking her face in gentle circles.

"You're okay Alice, you're going to be okay." I realize I'm rocking back and forth as I cradle her, and I worry that I shouldn't be moving. White walls and white floors close in around me but my vision doesn't turn from the tiny body in my arms. Will they help her? Of course, they won't, why would these monsters come in here?

The longer I spend here the longer I resent them all, these vampires who think they can play god with our lives. A child should have never been put in here in the first place. Small, jagged breaths finally show through this girl's little stomach. She seems to be fighting her own body, trying to make it draw in and blow out life against its will.

How would I cope if she dies right now. Death has become a familiar friend these past few days, both by my hands and others. My mind has been able to compartmentalize it so far, the trauma, the deep mental roots that have begun to take in my psyche. I can feel them, the small tendrils wanting to break me down, wanting me to blame myself or others for what has happened. So far, I have been able to ignore it, but if this happens, if Alice dies …

Tears fall down my face in desperation, communicating what I'm unable to by words. Each drop a piece of the desperation I feel, so overwhelming that it demands to spill out and escape somehow. A tiny sob escapes my lips as I open them to try and say her name again.

Her movements are slowing down now and my heart speeds up in response. Is this her dying? Is this her body giving up against the venom?

Bile rises in my throat, and my stomach does flips. My breath completely halts while I wait to see if Alice's will return.

"Drea! Drea is there something we can do? You know more about this, what's happening? How can we help her?" the words sound choked as I force them out, not giving her the chance to answer one question before I start the other. My stupid racing thoughts didn't even think Drea might know more about this. But she didn't seem to be worried about Alice taking it? She was the one encouraging it, she can't have known this would happen.

When she doesn't answer I pull my eyes away from Alice for just a second to turn to find her.

"I'm sorry Sabine, you'll forgive me for this." I hear the words before I fully turn and before I have time to comprehend them, there is a sharp pain in my neck.

Fire burns in my veins immediately, starting in my throat and spreading outwards. It surges forward with each beat of my heart, seemingly moving in every direction. It halts everything, my words, my thoughts, and my vision. Pain unlike anything I have ever felt. Liquid fire licking inside me, it must be burning me. I must be being torn apart from the inside out and it's getting worse by the second.

Blinding white clouds my blurred vision and I frantically look around trying to remember where I am or what is happening. The pain is so overwhelming I can't grasp either currently. I'm unsure if my head is spinning or the room is but as I turn, starting to frantically claw at my neck a figure comes across my vision.

"Just relax okay, it isn't nice, but you'll be fine in an hour or so. So will she. I'm sorry, you weren't going to do it yourself." The voice is slow and distorted, I'm not sure who it is talking to me. The figure is tall but they're crouching over me blocking out some of the endless blank space around them. My eyes are working overtime trying to make the blurred figure come into focus, but it just sways more and I get another push of blinding pain through my head temporarily blacking my vision.

Who are they and why are they sorry, what did they do? Cold, solid floor suddenly meets my face and another, different type of pain, shoots through my head. The fire burning through my veins has spread all the way to my hands now and I feel them violently trembling out of my control.

If this is death, it's even worse than I imagined. Each moment more drawn out and torturous than the last I thrash in pain. Tormented I don't know where to focus on, every inch of me hurts and each second, I lie here the pain gets more and more intense. I feel my own ragged breaths, fighting to draw air through the agony. I wish for death, beg for it, whatever this infernal purgatory is I don't want to suffer it for a moment longer. If I had control of my limbs still, I would claw my own throat out, at least if I bled out then I might feel the sweet release of unconsciousness.

That mangled voice speaks to me again, but I can't differentiate any of the words anymore. My vision blackens with each passing moment, and I know that I'm about to pass out. If I am lucky, I won't wake back up.

CHAPTER FOURTEEN

"Hey princess there you are."

Each syllable is like a sledgehammer against my head. It races trying to piece together where I am and what is happening. I remember the last game, but the details are fuzzy, and my head protests at trying to be used while it recovers.

My eyes don't open, instead I scrunch them tighter together and I try to fight off the remnants of pain. The ghost of fire in my veins makes me cringe, no longer there but leaving tender scars behind that are still in the process of healing. I think back to a memory of my childhood, the first time I had the flu. The ache throughout my whole body, not just my skin but deep into my bones. I had stayed in bed and not moved for a full week; my mom had made fun of me after telling me I was a drama queen. I agree with her now, that was nothing compared to the pain I feel now.

Every square inch of my body feels like a traitor, punishing me for whatever I put it through. The second feeling after the widespread and intolerable pain is the awareness that I'm lying down. My head rests on a soft pillow and I'm covered with a downy soft duvet. Even those delicate fibers grate against my skin however, the smallest bits of movement creating a friction that my nerve endings scream against.

"Take your time, it looks like its hit you harder than the rest of us." A hand is pressed against my upper arm, and I hiss at the touch. The sensitivity makes me try and move out from under the touch but that causes a domino of pain at each contact point that moves against the bed.

My eyes take over and allow themselves to slowly open, the lights are turned off, good. I can make out someone sitting next to me, a blurred figure in the dark and my mind whirrs to remind me of the reason I'm in this state in the first place. An unsteady figure, an apology, the venom.

"You … you … injected me. With that venom." I put the pieces together. Alice was dying, Drea was apologizing to me, why was she sorry? Then the pain came. She injected me, before I could argue or fully make my mind up. She made it for me.

Alice.

"Alice." I repeat the word aloud.

"Alice is fine, recovering in her room. She had a

strong reaction to the venom but she's going to be fine. She's already asked for me to bring her some food." Drea snorts. I don't miss that she answered about Alice but ignore my first statement.

But Alice is okay, the relief that provides me even eases my pain momentarily. I had noticed her breath slowly returning but she was so still, the seizure so severe, I was convinced her little body wouldn't be able to survive that. The pain I'm experiencing must be nothing compared to what she is going though. How on earth could the tiny body of a child be coping with this, how on earth would we be recovered enough to undertake the next trial.

I knew this would happen; this hasn't given us an advantage this has absolutely ruined us. Whatever they will give us for the next trial it can't possibly make up for what we've lost. There is one day until the next trial, and I see no world where I am going to be back on my feet and ready to run or fight by then.

"You injected me." I repeat slowly, my words full of venom.

I turn towards her but in the dark I can't make out her face. She has her hands grasped together between her knees and she dips her head slightly as though she can't look at me.

Good.

I hope she feels as much guilt as I feel pain. I hope she's so ashamed of herself that she never looks at me with those eyes again. My pain is the second thing I feel now, it pales in comparison to the overwhelming betrayal. Her next words will be about the greater good I'm sure, she will tell me how she knew I wouldn't do it and she didn't want us to be disadvantaged. I don't care, it doesn't matter. She took my choice away, and I will never forgive her for that.

"Sabine." She starts, raising her head slightly but still unable to look at me. "Alice had already injected herself, if we didn't do it, that would have made what she did pointless."

"And?" I spit back at her. "I might have done it Andromeda, if you had told me that she would be okay. If I knew it was just a reaction that she would get over. Maybe I would have done it too and we could have all *decided* to do this."

"I was so scared you were going to still not want to." She whispered.

"So, you did it for me!" I scream at her then wince as my head throbs in response.

"I thought it might be easier, if you didn't see it coming."

"What the hell kind of justification is that? Don't you dare make this about me Drea, this was about you. You wanted that advantage, and I was in your way. You took away my choice. I trusted you." My voice breaks on the last words.

Drea's eyes fully meet mine now and they glisten with a wetness threatening to spill over.

"Please." She says, her voice trembling also "I did this for you too Sabine, we need to get out of this, together right? How can I try and take you with me if you don't make it through this? How could you forgive yourself if Alice has died in that last trial because you didn't do it? You would never forgive yourself. I know you princess." Going back to my pet name, silently begging me to understand.

"You don't know me at all, if you knew me, you would know that I would never have wanted you to make that decision for me." I've always wanted her help, I can't deny that, but *help* not control. I never wanted her to take things out of my hands. My stupid naïve ass actually started to think of us as a team. Drea the tougher one sure, but we were a team. Well, she has shattered that reality for me now I see her, just another Master.

"Would you do it again?" I prompt her when she doesn't respond to me. "If we were vampires, would you charm me too, if you didn't get your way?" That would always be lingering over us now, I don't see how I would ever fully trust her again.

"How could you ask me that?" She reaches for my hand, but I pull away. The shock of reality has helped me work through the pain and I drag myself up in bed with a grunt.

"Sabine, this isn't a normal situation okay, this is life and death. I'm trying to get us out of this alive." Her voice has turned begging now.

"This will never be a normal situation!" I throw at her exacerbated. "We are familiars, we might be vampires in a few days. Our entire lives are going to be life and death. You did this because you think I'm weak and you can't make decisions on my behalf."

"You are weak!" Drea shouts.

The silence stretched between us. Black shadows in the room become oppressive and I can feel my breath hitching. Part of me always knew she felt that way. I am weak, she isn't wrong. But to hear it from her, to know she feels that about me, it breaks something in me that I don't think can ever be fixed. So many parts of me over the past few weeks have been fractured but somehow this one hurts the most.

"I didn't mean that." She tries, but we both know she

does, and the lies feel empty.

"Yes, you do." I whisper. "Get out." more strength forced into those words.

"Sabine don't do this. We need to get through this next part together. We're going to leave together, you said that, you said you wanted to come with me." Her words come with the wobble of a woman on the verge of tears, moving from her chair she get on her knees next to the bed. Throwing her hands over mine and clutching so I can't pull away.

"I can't … I can't ever trust you, Drea." Her hands loosen their grip and slide from the bed, hanging limply at her sides.

She rises slowly, her head bowed. Each step she takes out of the room slower than it needs to be, as if she's giving me all the opportunity, she can for me to change my mind. Her movements still fluid and graceful as always. Then it strikes me.

"Did you, do it?" She stops, turning in the darkness to look at me.

"Did you inject yourself?" I say slower. The pain I'm feeling is going to keep me in bed all day, but here Drea is moving like nothing has happened.

"Yes, of course." Wrong. The words sound wrong. Is

she lying to me?

And with that. She slides the door open and leaves, closing it behind her. I'm left alone in the dark and in more pain that I can comprehend, I just don't know which hurts more, my aching bones, or my broken heart.

*

Tears don't fall in the hours that follow. I don't allow them too. Keeping the lights turned off, I wallow in the dark cell that represents the rest of my life. For a moment, just one, I could see a happy ending for me. Not just an ending where I was safe or protected, but happy. And Drea took that away.

My parents aren't a topic I think of often, its usually too painful, but I think of them now. They seemed so happy together until those final months before the crash. The kind of couple you see on TV who dance in the kitchen and say I love you whenever they can. A kind of childish love almost is how I would describe it, that initial excitement you see in shows where couples can't keep their hands off each other. I used to make fun of them, or make gagging noises, being too immature to understand. They would just laugh at me and say that one day I would find my own love and they couldn't wait to see my kid's making fun of me.

Love.

I can't truly say I loved Drea, that wouldn't be fair, I haven't known her long enough. Clearly, I didn't know her at all. But I honestly thought I was falling in love, I thought of her when I woke up and when I went to sleep. Between the nightmares here, I dreamed of her in small snippets, my mind desperate to create more time for us together in any way it could.

Each time I slid open my door it was her I was looking for, her I wanted to be close to. I would replay little bits of our conversations when we weren't together, imagining the way she smiled at me or the way her hand brushed mine, and ask myself what it meant.

The images I see are different now. My mind won't let me forget, as if it's telling me not to dare forgive her. Her voice echoes through me, her final *I'm sorry* before she stabbed me in the back. Or her finally snapping and telling me what she really thinks, *you are weak.*

And yet she maintains she did this for me, not to me. Do I buy that? I change my mind a million times over, telling myself she did this just because she cares about me so much too that she needed to see us win together. Then I quickly scold myself, poor little trusting Sabine, stupid Sabine who has never had any kind of meaningful adult relationship. I know that's what I want to be reality but what if it isn't, what if she just wants to win and I was ruining her chances. Ruining her opportunity to get what she really wants, getting out of here with her perfect Master to start her real family. Had she even considered taking me with her? Or was that just some lie fed to me to get me on board.

Perhaps I was just an amusing distraction for her in here, one that she was happy to eliminate if I got in the way. Even as I think that I don't really believe it, I have to trust that some of it has been real. I may be unexperienced in these things, but I know the way she looked at me wasn't a fantasy. The way her voice broke when she realised, I couldn't forgive her meant something.

Sliding my hands underneath me I push myself fully upright in the bed, I hurt less now, physically anyway. The feeling of overwhelming ache and weakness is lessening and fairly quickly. I will not admit she is right, but I begin to think perhaps that by the trial tomorrow I may be somewhat back to myself. Though I'm unsure exactly how much time has passed I know it's been an hour or so at least. The seconds and minutes dragging out into painful infinity, allowing me to wallow in my suffering.

At some point I would have to go out there and face her, if for no other reason than to check on Alice. Drea had assured me she was okay, but I would like to see that for myself. Those images of her seizing grip my mind and my stomach flips at the thought. My eyes scrunch close, and I take a few deep breaths. *She's okay, she's alive.* I remind myself. At least my anger doesn't extend to her, what she did was stupid and reckless, but it was her choice. Part of me wonders if she will choose to be changed at the end of this, I don't see what other choice she has.

When I was her age, I was in school like all the other kids. My mom would get me dressed in the morning and walk me down to the little bus stop at the end of my street, standing with me until the driver pulled up to let me on. I never had a lot of friends for some reason, maybe people could tell I was a little different. My English accent was slowly turning into an American one, but it happened slowly and for a lot of years when I was younger, I spoke in a strange hybrid of the two.

People made fun of me sometimes for it, so I kept quiet and didn't put myself out there. I knew enough people that I had someone to sit next to in classes sure, but I ate my lunch alone and I never got invited to sleepovers. My mom had always said it didn't matter because we could have our own sleepovers.

She would rearrange all the furniture in the living room, creating big wooden structures that towered over me as a ten year old, but in hindsight was just chairs piled on top of our dining room table and our sofas. Her constructions would then be draped in white sheets and fairy lights, I would run up and down the stairs gathering and depositing all the pillows and duvets into her tent as she made it. Our own personal little patch of heaven. We would disappear into our tent, and she would read me stories or plait my hair or paint my nails. Dad would act as our server for the evening brining us snacks or wine glasses filled with juice and I would giggle when he made his English accent posher to ask the "ladies" if they required anything else.

It may not have been perfect, but it was a childhood, filled with loving parents and happy memories. Alice didn't even have that. My hands grip into fists and I wince slightly at the motion, still slightly tender. This pity party I'm having for myself is allowed to last two more minutes then I am getting up and going to see Alice. No matter how scared I am she is probably ten times more scared, and she needs me to go tell her everything will be okay. Going into the next trial it might just be us two, but my promises to her still stand, I will do everything I can to get her out of here.

Fortifying myself, I throw my blankets off and swing my legs over the bed. The motion sets off a chain of aches and pains but nothing I can't handle.

My bare feet touch the cold floor and I take one deep breath before pushing myself onto them. Step one down, and that wasn't really too bad, I have the feeling the more I move around perhaps the more I will loosen off. Another reason to stop moping in here.

My hair falls loose around my shoulders and down my back, Drea must have unbraided it for me as I slept. A lump catches in my throat as I think about her, her hands gently unbraiding my hair for me as I sleep. Physically shaking my head to try and knock the thought of her out, I turn to brave the main room, but as I take a step forward the door slides open anyway.

"Hello little rabbit, how are you feeling?"

CHAPTER FIFTEEN

Nikolas steps into my room and slides the door shut behind him, I hear the lock turn into place. An uncomfortable vibrating noise comes from overhead as he flicks the light on and they struggle to illuminate the room.

Instinctively I take a step back from him creating as much distance as possible as he comes into view. In one hand he has a protein bar and the other a glass of water. He must see me staring quizzically as he raises both slightly and speaks.

“I brought these for you, I thought you might be feeling a little worse for wear.”

I say nothing, do nothing, I just stand there staring at him waiting for the other shoe to drop. The other part of this conversation where he says something snarky or throws me against the wall again.

“I’m not here to hurt you,” He sighs “I can do that in the trial if I want to. Just sit down and eat will you.” He takes a tentative step closer to me and it takes everything I have to not panic and take another step back. Why is he here, now, being nice to me? He may have done things to help Alice in the past but not me.

Contempt or possible physical attraction are the only two emotions I have felt from this man, conflicting though they may be. So, whatever he thinks he is here to accomplish, it isn't merely offering me kindness I know that much. I'll play his game though, even if it's just to see what he thinks he is here to achieve.

Stepping forward slightly I reach out my hand and take the protein bar, our skin gently brushing against each other as I slide it out of his hand.

"Thank you." I say as I take a seat back on the edge of the bed.

He sets the glass of water down on the floor next to me and takes a seat himself at the opposite end of the bed. In the light I can see the dark shadows ringing the underneath of his eyes. He moves more slowly than usual, even wincing slightly as he takes a seat. His usual intimidating and self-assurance presence is lacking today, instead he gives off the vibe of a broken man.

"You used the venom too then?" I guess.

He looks at me and huffs a small humorless laugh.

"Yes, I did, I feel like I've gone ten rounds with a

bear." He rolls his shoulder out as he speaks as if to loosen the pain from it.

"I feel better now than when I first woke up." I admit. He nods slightly, his head dipped, not making eye contact with me.

"The venom works to initially incapacitate you. Prey won't be able to fight back or run away initially, most people lose consciousness. It doesn't kill us quickly though; you go through a rebound stage for a couple of days where you recover."

"Then?" I ask, already knowing.

"Then your body can't keep fighting the toxin, the venom slowly degrades your blood cells causing widespread systemic collapse. You die a slow and extremely painful death." Okay I didn't know all of it, he sure knows how to paint a pretty picture.

"Oh good," I say, "I look forward to that." I fiddle with the bar in my hands, all sense of appetite thoroughly dissuaded.

"You won't have to if you can win this thing." I turn to look at him now, his words today sound softer. I don't know if it's because he is in pain or something has changed, but this Nikolas is not the Nikolas I am used to. I feel like I'm having an actual normal person conversation with him.

"Well, if the first two trials are anything to go off, I'm assuming we can't all win, and I'm certainly not the strongest or the smartest here." There is no point in lying to him or playing it big. I know and so does he that I'm useless. I've gotten by because of other people's help. Help I can't count on in the last trial.

"You have so little faith in yourself for someone who got herself this far." His eyes now meet mine as he tilts his head up slightly. His hair is loose and falls in tendrils down his quietly sad face.

"I have not gotten myself this far and we both know it." There's no malice or anger in my words, just resigned honesty.

"Yes, you have." He moves towards me slightly closing the gap between us on the bed "You have protected that girl and fought tooth and nail since you got here. You are the one who got Alice her flag, you are the one who led the pack to win the second trial, you are the one who held a knife to the man who was being a dick to you." He grins at the last part; obviously no hard feelings exist for him. I'm pleasantly surprised, threatening to slit someone's throat seems like the kind of thing someone would hold a grudge for.

"Don't give up just because you don't have the team you thought you had." My face drops at his final words and I don't realize until then I had been returning his grin.

"Drea told you then … what she did?" I don't know why, but I'm surprised. Why would she share that with everyone. Unless she wanted her side of the story out first before I emerged and gave her the cold shoulder.

"She did." Nikolas has a grim expression on his face, but he doesn't look away from me.

"It was out of line Sabine; she shouldn't have done that to you. But don't let losing her make you give up going into this next trial. You have a passion in you, a fire that I have never seen before. Especially in someone so tiny." He tries a small smile, but it falls flat. "If you want to get out of here, if you want to get Alice out of here, you can't let self-pity put that spark out."

He was getting somewhere with me until he said that. Self-pity? Who the hell does he think he is. He doesn't know me, nor has he made any attempt to, and now he comes in here and tells me to stop feeling sorry for myself? Screw him.

"I am not feeling sorry for myself." I spit. "I am not so pathetic that I would completely give up on myself, and especially on Alice, because some girl wasn't what I thought she was."

He raises his hands in defense.

"I didn't mean it like that, and you know it."

"Well please then Nikolas, enlighten me" I throw my hands up exacerbated. "You have hated me since the moment you got here, the only time you've ever spoken to me is to piss me off or intimidate me. Now you come in here to what? Make me feel small? Remind me to not be pathetic?"

Silence pounds between us, I can feel it oppressing me with each beat of my heart. The man before me looks broken, his shoulders hunch over in resignation. His eyes seem to be silently pleading with me, but I have no idea what for. He looks almost smaller like this; I can't believe the man in front of me is a man who I have been so intimidated by in the past.

"Did I ever tell you how I became a familiar?" his voice barely more than a whisper.

"Between your snarky comments and brooding? No, I don't think you have." He withdraws more into himself, and I almost feel bad for a fleeting moment.

"It was always just me and my dad, my mom died when I was tiny. Cancer. I don't remember her." Most of us here have lost our parents, there's a reason it was easy for us to disappear as a familiar. I feel for him in a way only a child who has lost a parent can, but if he thinks he can manipulate me with sympathy, he's sadly mistaken.

"My dad struggled to make money, he got real down after mom died, turned to drinking. He bounced from job to job, and we bounced from place to place because of it. When I was twelve, he met my *Master."* He spits the word as if it tastes like poison on his tongue. "He owns a casino in Moscow; one my dad had frequented on his drunken nights in those last few months. Racked up quite a bit of debt apparently. So, Alexandru approached him and gave him a way to pay off his debts. He sold himself and me to him. Two generations of service for whatever he had managed to rack up on the bar tab and the poker table" Now I could see Nikolas the child. The twelve-year-old boy with no real family and no real home, sold by his father.

He seemed to break a tiny bit more with each admission and I finally understood why he had never talked about it. We all had a story like this, our own trauma, our own reason we became a familiar. But Nikolas, he hadn't made peace with his yet. And he didn't want us to see his weakness.

"I'm sorry." I offer, we both know it isn't enough. He takes a deep steadying breath.

“My dad was crap, obviously, as he was with every other job. He forgot to do important things, he botched hunting for victims. The day a sketch showed up of him on the news in regards to an assault Alexandru hit his limit.” I know what’s coming. Nikolas has been talking about his dad in the past tense this whole time. He’s not around anymore.

“A vampire cant risk being exposed, not by a stupid, drunk familiar. Especially not when he has a more than capable back up.” His face screws up.

“I had been cleaning up after my dad for months, closing curtains and sun proofing where he forgot. I cleaned and maintained the house. I had even helped with cleanup of a few victims when dad left them to stew for too long.” The color drains from his face slightly.

I think of Alice, her blank traumatized stare when she saw her first dead body. Was that how little Nikolas felt? How could his father leave such a task to him. Disgust blooms within me.

“Alexandru had noticed of course. I was stupid to think he hadn’t been observing us. When that sketch came on the news I didn’t even have time to put the pieces together that it was another one of my dad’s kidnappings gone wrong. His neck was snapped, and he hit the floor, they can move so fast, so fast I didn’t even see it." I see him dissociate, he isn't watching me anymore but a replay of his father's not yet cold body and the sight of his Master standing over him.

"What choice did I have but to keep serving him, I had nowhere to go. So, I stayed, and I trained. I got strong, fast, smart." His hands curl into fists, gripped so tightly in his lap that his knuckles go white.

"Why?" I hear myself say. It breaks him from his trance and his head snaps up to look at me again. "Why are you still with him, why let him change you?"

I can see the indecisiveness in his face, the inner battle he is having with himself, about what I'm not sure.

"Sabine, I know I've been an ass and there's no excuse. But you seem like a good person. Like a genuinely and truly good person. If I tell you this, you have to swear to me that it will die with us."

I shift uncomfortably. Before today we had exchanged barely two civil words, yet here he was, spilling his life story and asking for my confidence. I should know better, I should have learnt my lesson in trusting Drea. But as I look into his face, the vulnerable face of a man who deep down is just the same hurt boy who watched his father die, I can't bring myself to tell him no.

"Tell me." Is all I manage.

He moves closer to me on the bed, so close our legs graze together and I can smell the coffee on his breath. He leans forward and for a moment a chill runs down my spine at the proximity. Visions of his teeth in my neck replay in my mind.

"I'm going to kill him." He breathes, no more than a whisper, as if he is terrified to say the words out loud.

My mind goes blank. Kill him? He can't be serious; he's going to kill his Master?

"You've stuck around all these years, put yourself through all of this, you are going to be changed into a vampire … to kill him?" It's unbelievable. He can't be serious.

"Oh, so that's less of a reason to be changed than yours? Being changed into a vampire because you have nothing else to do is fine, but doing it for revenge is stupid?" He growls. I don't know what reaction he was expecting from me, but I can tell I have thoroughly disappointed him. I change tactic.

"I just don't know how you have stayed with him, for so long, when you despise him so much. Back in the house you two seemed like you actually had a friendship!"

I had been so surprised when I met them, Alexandru spoke to him truly like a friend rather than a servant. The two seemed like they had a relationship, I had been so jealous!

"You get good at playing the game, at putting on a mask" He shrugged. "These vampires, these *things,* they are a plague on this earth Sabine. They murder, they ruin lives, they take us and they treat us like their slaves only to watch us die, or turn us into soulless monsters ourselves." Suddenly he is standing, pacing back and forth in the tiny cell of a room. "They need to be wiped off this earth, and I am going to be the one to do it." He straightens, trying to show pride and strength where I can clearly see fear and doubt.

"You're going to be what, a vampire who hunts vampires?" I try to work out his words.

"Exactly." He nods as if he thinks I finally understand. "They are too strong Sabine, too fast, we can't take them when we're human. But as a vampire, I can take down Alexandru in his sleep then hunt down the rest of the monsters until none of them are left." The fury that burns in his eyes now scares me. He's frightened of them yes, but he also loathes them with an intensity that could burn down the world.

If he is going to kill them all does that include my Master? More importantly do I care? Before I came here, I would have done anything for him, out of reverence, guilt, appreciation. He was this other worldly being who had saved me and given me a purpose but now? The more I had been here the more I saw him for what he truly was, a monster who had seen a young girl, who no one would miss, and he took me.

How stupid I have been, taking scraps of compliments or conversation from him, mistaking it for intimacy because it was the only thing I had ever known. What a good little bride I would have been for him. Not anymore, I don't want it, I have known for a while now. I knew the minute I had an opportunity to go somewhere better, Drea might be out of this picture now but that doesn't mean I have to go back to a life of empty mediocrity. I can still be turned; I might not be going with Drea, but I can make my own life like hers. Find my own place and keep it safe. I can become a guardian angel for the girls who don't have one.

"What about the rest of us then?" I ask him.

The fever dissipated momentarily from his view.

"I wouldn't kill you if that's what you're asking. You came here and made it your mission to protect that little girl. Even in the last challenge, you weren't going to let Alice do it, you would rather have lost the advantage right?" I nod, Drea really told them everything.

"You won't be a bad vampire Sabine, if you tell me you're going to do good with it then I'll let you go on your way. But I'm not sparing Melchior." My Masters name, I have barely heard it a handful of times. As a familiar we shouldn't use our vampires given names, that is reserved for other vampires.

"You can kill him." I decide. It isn't a hard decision; I want to leave anyway. I know now that I need to carve my own path, and after years of serving him, I don't owe *Melchior* anything else.

Nikolas looks visibly shocked at this, as though he would have expected me to put up more of a fight. His eyes wide and his mouth hanging open a little. Slowly the expression changes though, he becomes thoughtful, weary.

"What about the others though, Drea and her Master seem like good people?" I stress the last two words.

"Do you want to spare them because they're good people or because it's her?" he sneers.

"Don't belittle me," I warn him. "I may have feelings for her, they won't go away overnight. But they look after their town. They don't kill innocents. They. Are. Good. People." I stand now trying to look more intimidating than I feel.

"Listen," He holds his hands up. "Being here, listening to you all, I admit, it isn't as clear cut as I thought. Not every vampire may be a monster, I'll do my research. I will watch before I kill, I'm not going to wipe out vampires who genuinely are trying to live good lives. But trust me Sabine, I think they are few and far between." I nod and cross my arms, its good enough for me. If he is going to play judge, jury, and executioner then the least he can do is actually give them a chance to be judged. Though he doesn't specifically say it, I know Drea and her family will be safe.

"Sabine, you're not going home with him, at least not for long." We both know who he's talking about. "You could come with me?"

My arms, which were crossed defiantly across my chest, drop to me sides. This man is going to give me whiplash from how quickly his personality changes.

"You want me to come with you?" I ask incredulously, not quite believing what I'm hearing. He strides toward me and takes my hands in his.

"You are a good person Sabine, and I need help. Doing this, it won't be easy, I could use the help. Two vampires are better than one." He laughs.

I have no idea what to say, do I want to go with him? Do I want to be a vampire Van Helsing and decide who is worthy of living and dying? I've been playing that game for years now with the victims I select so I can't pretend that it bothers me, but still.

Do I want to be forever travelling, not putting down roots, putting myself in danger. And do I want to do it with Nikolas? It's an option I didn't know I had and honestly I can't fathom giving him an answer now. Part of me can't help still thinking about New Orleans and what I could have there. If I could forgive Drea, move on from what she did. Nikolas could still kill my Master and it would leave me free to go to her. Drea is where the possibility of family is.

What would I have with Nikolas? I didn't care for him in that way, and he had done nothing so far to make me think he would want to build a meaningful relationship, friendship or otherwise. Would I be trading one distant man for another? Spending more of my life in a shallow and meaningless relationship.

I close my eyes and step back, sliding my hands out of his grip.

"This is too much in one go Nikolas, I hated you yesterday. You've just turned my whole world upside down and I don't have the mental capacity to give you an answer right now." I can't bring myself to look at him as I speak so I bow my head and stare at the grey concrete floor.

"That's fair enough." He says but I can hear the disappointment in his voice. "But just so you know, I'll free you from your Master either way. And when I can, Ill free Alice from hers."

Guilt suddenly weighs heavy in my stomach; I hadn't even considered her in my possible futures. I look back to him and the kind man in front of me is someone who I don't recognize but would like to.

"If she gets out of this she will be changed, the winners will be changed back at their home, there's nothing we can do to stop it. But whoever would turn a child is a monster regardless, so I'll be coming for them. And if Alice needs somewhere to go, I'm assuming you'll be happy to take her?" He raises an eyebrow and his eyes sparkle playfully, as if he's expecting me for just a moment to say no.

"Of course, I will." the words come out shaky. I hadn't bargained to adopt an eternal child, but I have become attached to Alice in a way I didn't think possible. If she needs somewhere to go then I will always be there for her.

He nods, as if solidifying to himself that I am the person he thought I was. I wonder momentarily how that vision he has of me would change if I had told him no, to find somewhere else to put her. If I do decide to come with him, then he will have a perpetual child too. The thought makes me giggle to myself, I wonder if he considered that when he invited me to join him.

"Something funny?" He asks confused.

"This whole thing is such a mess." I admit.

He steps forward again, closing the gap I tried to create. A strong and calloused hand reaches out and caresses my cheek, my mind immediately compares it to Drea's soft touch.

"Everything's going to be okay, you just need to make it through this last trial." His hand drops and he turns to make his way to the door before pausing and throwing over his shoulder "Oh and do not discuss this again with me, there are cameras in the main area, not in the rooms. I'm sure the trials have cameras too for them to monitor us. I'll come one day soon enough after all of this to take the life of your Master. You can tell me then if you want to come with me." And with that he slides the door open and leaves.

I don't know how long I stand there, my mind a whirlpool of emotions. At least I no longer feel the crushing and inescapable feeling of drowning I had before Nikolas dropped multiple bombs on my life. Regardless of what happens next, I feel better. No longer will I have to worry about eternity chained to my Master, no longer will I have to worry about Alices future. Nikolas is going to take care of it all, all I have to do is decide what I want to do afterwards. Though that may be the hardest part of the whole thing. One thing I do know, is that I have to talk to Drea first.

My stomach does flips, and my nerves are wrought, more so that they have been before any trial. I'm glad I never ate that bar from Nikolas as I suspect I would be retching it back up by now if I had. I won't tell her what Nikolas has said, I'll keep his secret. But I need to see if I have it in me to forgive her and move past this. I need one hundred percent honesty from her.

I lift my chin and shake my hair over the back of my shoulders, I won't let her see how much she has ruined me. At least not if I can help it.

CHAPTER SIXTEEN

Alice has recovered surprisingly well; she has already been up and about well before me and eaten plenty. I guess kids do usually bounce back from things easier.

Though with her sunken eyes and slightly hunched shoulders I can tell she still isn't quite back to her normal self. The beating her system just took is written all over her posture and I wonder if every fiber of her is hurting from the seizure. Guilt is the first thing written across her face when she sees me, and perhaps a little fear. Like a child who knows they have done wrong and now must face the wrath of their furious parent.

A scolding isn't what I give her however, at the end of the day she isn't my child. And honestly, I can't tell her what to do, though it wouldn't have been my choice for her to take the venom. But then what kind of hypocrite would I be if I took her autonomy away when I was so hurt at the same being done to me? My main concern is that she doesn't truly understand the impact of what she has just done, I never did get a chance to have a talk with her about what it would mean for her to become a vampire. Did she inject that venom into her neck knowing that no matter what, she just made the decision to never grow past the age of ten?

By the end of this next trial, she would either be six feet under, or she would be an eternal child. Deep in my heart I always knew those were the only two options for her but hope had still festered like a deep wound inside of me. I had left it untreated to grow and now that hope felt like it would kill me as it was taken away.

The loss of a life, that's what I was feeling, the loss of Alices life. All the possible futures she could have were taken away in that split second decision. She would never grow up, never fall in love or go to college, never start a family of her own.

A silent tear escapes my eye and slides down my cheek as I make my way to her and embrace with all the force I have. Pain creaks throughout me in protest at the motion, all my nerves still alive and healing from the trauma. I suspect Alice felt the same as I feel her momentarily flinch before leaning into the cuddle and wrapping her tiny arms around me in response.

"I'm sorry." She whispers in my ear, her head buried in my loose hair.

"Don't be sorry." I squeeze her slightly with the words, "You did what you felt was right, I should have asked you what you wanted." A small admission from myself. I had spoken of Alice to Drea as if she wasn't even there. Her opinion and feelings hadn't even been a consideration from me and that was wrong. I remember being her age and having my parents make decision for me over my head as if I wasn't standing there taking in every word. It makes you feel small and unimportant. Perhaps my ignorance was what pushed her to take control of the situation for herself.

"I want to be a vampire Sabine." I pull back from her, shocked by her words. Her little eyes are set hard as if she is battling with herself to not give up.

"You … want … this? To be with the men who your mother traded you to?" She hasn't spoken much of them but she seemed to be aware they were bad men. When she first came here, she was so frightened. She knows nothing about being a vampire or the men she will be living with, how could she possibly have decided she wants this?

A deep and steady breath escapes her lips and she pulls fully out of my arms, crossing her hands across her lap. Her whole stance is comical, like she's about to tell me to take a seat and tell me her and my father are getting a divorce. I find myself pulling out a chair and slipping into it to face her, I reach out and place a hand over hers. I want her to know I am here for her, no matter what she decides.

"My mama, she worked for these men for a long time. She used to leave me with dinner in the fridge and not come back until morning. I had to get myself ready for school, sometimes had to walk myself if she was late." Sadness brims in her eyes, and I stroke a thumb over her hand in soothing motions. "She told me lots of stories about vampires you know, I thought they were real a long time before I came in here. The night she took me with her I knew something was wrong. That was when I met them, they looked like the vampires she had described to me in her stories, but I didn't want to believe it. Then she told them to take me." Her voice cracks. "I have nowhere else to go after this Sabine, I don't want to end up in one of those children's homes, and I don't want to die in here."

"You are not going to die in here." I say firmly. Her smile in response is shaky.

"If we win and the vampires make us into one of them then I'll be strong like you. I won't need someone to look after me ever again I will be able to do it myself." She squares her little shoulders as she talks, and it breaks my already shattered heart into more pieces.

"Oh Alice." Is all I can manage.

There's no point in me talking her out of it, she's made her decision. If she doesn't turn in the next few days, then she will die a slow and painful death. All the warning I have for her whirl in my mind until they blend into one, all of the things I want to tell her, to shake her for thinking this will solve all of her problems. But there I am again, the hypocrite, who came here, who wanted to become an eternal monster, because she had nowhere else to go. In essence Alice is a lot like me, and I think that is partly what makes me so sad for her.

"I'm sure they will look after you anyway, once you are their family. They might even let me come visit." I don't tell her about Nikolas, about his offer. How he will likely be visiting her well before me to put those men in the ground and free her. My eyes subconsciously sweep the room trying to locate any cameras that he had mentioned earlier. Even if I had wanted to tell her, I couldn't. Ratting out Nikolas is not on the top of my to do list.

I never really thought of vampires as monsters, my Master was the only one I had known. The fact that only bad people were drained by him kept me believing that it wasn't all so bad. The truth I had been ignoring was that he had no idea who those victims were, I could have brought him mother Teresa and he would have drained her indiscriminately like everyone else. I was the one upholding the morality.

Memories of the recent past flood me, they designed this, they decided to put us through this. Their familiars, the people who had lived with and served them for years. They had stood back and watched as we were slaughtered, our lives cut short in the most unjust way. No, they were not good people, and if Nikolas was going to cull them, more power to him.

In my daze Alice has taken my hand in both of hers and she holds on like she is terrified if she lets go, I will disappear.

"One more trial Alice, that's all we have to get through." I promise her.

"Do you think we can all get through it?" She asks, her gaze moving to where Drea is sitting about fifteen feet away from us. I had done my best not to look toward her when I came out and I battle with myself now to do the same.

"If we can, yes." and I mean it, I may not know if I can forgive Drea, but I don't want to see her die. She is the one person in here who I know undoubtedly deserves to live through this. The one familiar who has a life to go back to that will positively contribute to society instead of terrorizing it.

"Will we still be in teams?" the way Alice asks me

this makes me think that Drea has also told her what happened. I don't mind everyone knowing, but I would rather have left Alice out of it if I could.

"I don't know yet; they haven't told us the rules." The second part is an excuse and we both know it. Our first two trials said nothing about working together yet we still gravitated toward each other. As if our psyches knew that we were stronger side by side.

You are weak.

My mind betrays me and reminds me how little Drea has benefited from our so-called team. I'm the weak link, a hinderance to her.

Alice just nods knowingly; I suspect that she is much more emotionally mature than she lets on sometimes. For a girl who sounds like she has raised herself, she presents much more vulnerable than I would expect.

*

"Good evening familiars"

The announcement voice appears but I no longer fear it the way I once did. My stomach doesn't bottom out,

I don't feel the bile rising in my throat or my heart race. I have been waiting for this all day. All day whilst I sat in contemplative silence. Ignoring everyone around me as they stretched and drank warm tea, limbering up and loosening off their strain anyway they could. The seconds dragged by and with each moment my resolve hardened. I wanted out, I wanted to be done. This room was becoming more suffocating by the moment, surrounded by people I cared for in one way or another, people who I may see die or have a hand in killing. The end of this trial could not come soon enough for me.

"Based on the previous trial the advantage goes to familiar Aashutosh, Jared and Nikolas. Unfortunately the opposing team completed the challenge in a longer period of time leading to their loss."

I shoot a look to Drea hoping it can convey all I feel. *I hope it was worth it, you betrayed me for nothing.*

When I met her eyes however, she way already looking my way with a seething look of her own. *If you hadn't held us back, we could have won.* The announcement continues.

"That advantage will be taking one member from the opposing team, to strengthen your numbers."

Now my stomach bottoms out, so it is going to be set

teams, and we just lost Drea. Of course, we lost Drea, why would they pick anyone else, no one wants the child or the weak link. My emotions are a conflicting storm. My feelings towards her had left me untrusting and I was unsure whether I wanted to proceed into the next trial with her by our side, but having her so clearly taken away from us, we would lose. If one team was going to make it out of this, they would.

"The object of the final trial is to find a key and make it from one side of our maze to the other, without being caught, before the times runs out. Each of your Masters has been designated a familiar who is not their own that they are responsible for hunting. There are four keys in the maze and therefore we will allow up to four winners this year. If you are caught, you will be eliminated. If you cannot find your key, you will be eliminated. If you do not make it out of the maze by the end of the time, you will be eliminated.

Good luck."

"Alice, will you come with us?" My head snaps up to the sound of Ash's kind voice and tears immediately well in my eyes.

He's going to take her; he's going to get her out. Gratitude overwhelms me and prevents me from thanking him. My mind doesn't even think about the fact that me and Drea are now left together, I don't care.

“I don’t want to; I want to stay with Sabine!” My head rises and through my distorted tear filled vision I see Alice with sheer panic on her little face.

Moving with all the strength I can, I drop to my knees in front of her, clasping her face between both my hands.

“Alice.” I start.

“No, no! You and me Sabine, all the way through this.” Tears flow down her face now too. “You said you wouldn’t leave me, that you would get me out of here!” She pleads.

“Alice, I’m not strong enough, not good enough okay. I’m weak, and with a smaller team, even weaker. I don’t want to, but I’ll let you down. Ash is going to look after you now okay, he’s going to get you out of here.” Her tears pool where my hands meet her face and her body starts to rack with violent sobs.

“But who will protect you, you’re asking me to leave you behind.” Wailing the words.

“You don’t worry about me.” I shake her head slightly trying to get her to focus on my words. “You are going to make it out of here, and you’re going to keep on living okay Alice. Promise me.” I know as I say the words that they sound like a goodbye, that I have already accepted my journey is ending.

“I don’t want to go without you.” She chokes out. I feel a hand on my shoulder and turn to see Drea standing there, tears also silently streaming down her face.

“Don’t you worry Alice; I’m not going to let anything happen to her okay.” And in that moment, I don’t care that she injected me, I don’t care she took away my choices, because I can see the love in her eyes. She cares for me so deeply it hurts, and she cares for Alice just as much as I do. I haven’t forgotten what she did, I never will. It will the change the course of who we are forever. But though I may not forget, I can forgive.

Our eyes meet and I know that my heart is not the only broken one.

“Go with Ash, Alice.” I close my eyes and remove my hands from her face. “I’ll see you on the other side.” A kind lie, we all know it is, but it’s one we need.

“Come on Alice we’re going to look after you” Nikolas this time, I turn to him and see him with an outstretched hand.

Unfair. It’s all I can think, this is so unfair, they aren’t even giving us the chance to all get out of here. No matter what at the end of this, two of us will be dead. I take in each face as if it is the last time, I will see it. Ash, so kind and patient. Jared, so hardheaded and funny. Nikolas, deeper and more valiant that I could have imagined. Alice, so young and innocent. And Drea, so strong and selfless and loyal. Everything she has done has been for the greater good for us, even if I didn't like it.

Standing I place my hand on Alices back and give her a gentle nudge. She takes tentative steps towards them, as if fighting her soul with each bit she progresses forward. Her audible tears the only noise between us.

"Thank you." I say to Ash, he didn't have to do this, but I will be forever grateful to him for it. He simply nods back at me, and we wait for the lights to dim and the luminous floor lights to come on to show us the way.

When they do, none of us rush. No one here has an ounce of competitiveness in us, we don't want to see anyone die. By winning ourselves, we will be signing one of our friend's death warrants.

Slowly, one by one, we begin to march to our graves.

CHAPTER SEVENTEEN

The entrance to the maze is back outside in the forest, below ground. We can see a structure has been hollowed out and a mine shaft like space created for us to enter. Stood above it is each of our Masters, the ones whose familiars already lost not deeming to show up. Six vampires in total, some I now know the names of my own of course Melchior stands in a black corduroy suit with a purple turtleneck underneath. Alexandru, Nikolas Master throws him some finger guns, looking ridiculous in flared silver pants and a matching silver t shirt, it catches the moonlight every time he moves. Drea's Master Adélaïde hasn't changed from earlier and still wears all the colors of the rainbow. The other three vampires are all also men, I'm unsure who is the Master of who. Small nods and motions of acknowledgement are made but so quickly I wouldn't be able to match people up.

My eyes always stay on my own, he is the one who speaks anyway. No recognition toward me other than a gentle nod and small knowing smile. My brain replays the meeting of Drea and her Master again and again, noting the absence of all familiarity I experience.

"Good evening familiars. You have all done exceptionally well to make it to this point." His voice is like velvet and a shiver runs down my spine. I had forgotten how intimidating yet enticing he was.

"We vary how many victors we allow each time we conduct the trial. It was decided that due to population drops in the recent years, and the high caliber of familiar this trial has brought us, four of you will be allowed to succeed. If you can." The last words meant as ominously as they sounded.

"You will be given a ten-minute head start before your vampire begins hunting you, at that point you will have a further twenty minutes to find your key and the exit. Only four keys have been placed within the maze, and one exit. You have been divided into teams, but you may wish to split up as needed. We have provided you all with a watch to help aid your time keeping." Melchior lifts his hands and two of the unnamed vampires step forward and distribute stop watches amongst us.

"You will all accumulate in the entrance chamber and when you hear the claxon, start your watches and proceed."

Uncertain looks are exchanged amongst us, and I

reach out to take Drea's hand in my own. We haven't been able to talk, and this trial won't be the time nor the place. Before I die in there, I want her to know that I forgive her, I understand. She squeezes it harder than I would like in response. And with that we all make our way down into the maze beneath our feet.

The initial chamber is big enough to hold all of us comfortably with some wiggle room, fortunately it is at least well lit. Though somewhat dim, candles and braziers light the walls making it more than easy enough to navigate.

Two tunnels split off, one veering left and one right. Fire does lighten them however they go on for so long that I can't make out any difference between where the two would lead. Looking to Drea I see she is also squinting trying to find any difference between the two passages and evidently failing.

"How about one team goes left and one goes right?" Jared suggests, knowing what we are all thinking.

Drea shrugs at me and I answer, "That's not a bad idea actually, any preference?"

It is Nikolas who says, "You and Drea are already on the right might as well just make it random and stick to what's in front of us."

I nod to him. Hopefully keys will be evenly split

between the two directions and perhaps me and Drea will be able to find ours without any in fighting. My breath hitches as the thought crosses my mind. What if Ash's team doesn't find enough keys, will he let Alice have one?

Looking to her now, through the gaggle of people, she is clinging to Ash's side frantically. Snapping my head forward I shake it slightly, I can't let these thought distract me. Alice will be fine with them, better than she would have been alone with me. At least they will be able to keep her out of the grasp of any vampire who hunts her.

"Good luck everyone." Ash whispers. No one responds. We wait the silence stretching into torturous minutes until finally, the claxon sounds, and we all set our stop watches in unison.

*

We sprint down the tunnel together, not sparing a second thought to our advisories. Whoever built this did a fantastic job, its tall enough that Drea could likely touch the ceiling but only just, and wide enough for us to continue side by side. Fire burns in the braziers distributed on the walls every few feet and the cause an uncomfortable humidity in the underground space.

"You have any idea what we're looking for?" I pant as I struggle to keep up with Drea's long strides.

"No idea, gaps in the walls, boxes, something you could hide a key in. It's not going to be just sitting on the floor for us." Her words come out short and I consider for the first time that she may be angry at me.

"I'm sorry." I offer.

Drea stops dead and I run a good few feet past her before I realize she is no longer at my side.

"What?" She asks incredulously.

"I'm sorry. That I was … so … harsh with you." I mean it, I may still be broken from what she did to me, and I don't fully trust her anymore. I never will. But I understand why she did what she did, and I feel like I was unnecessarily cruel to her.

"You have nothing to be sorry for." Her voice breaks. "We don't have time for this." She takes off again, no longer running but as a steady speed walking pace.

Her words confuse me, is she mad at me or not? She doesn't want my apology but that was more than short. My heart wants me to tell her we need to make time but my head, and the ever-ticking stopwatch tells me she's right.

My little feet work overtime catching her up until we reach another crossroad. Left or right.

"We should have a system." I decide, "Start with every right and then if we hit a dead end we know how to get back."

Drea nods "Smart, let's do it"

Nodding I overtake her and head right trying to ignore how much I love hearing her praise me.

We continue this way until the timer tells me eight minutes have passed, until finally we find a dead end. Tears fill my eyes. I didn't think it would be that easy, but I am still furious and frustrated. Almost all our head start gone, and we've wasted it.

As if reading my mind Drea says "It's okay, that's one path ruled out, it's still progress."

She is about to turn and leave just as I spot something in the wall of the dead-end.

"Wait!" I shout.

Her head snaps back over her shoulder, her platinum white plait flicking out behind her. Just under the brazier there is an area of dirt that looks packed wrong, it sticks out more than the rest and is patted down far too smooth. Reaching forward I begin to claw at the packed earth furiously, it builds up quickly in my nails and they strain at the force of which they are being used.

"Hang on!" Drea's hand is on my shoulder and she's pulling me out of the way before I can stop her.

Pulling a knife from under her sweatshirt she begins digging with the blade, making far more progress than I had. Damn it, weapons, I had been so deep in my self-pity that I had forgotten we were stripped of everything when we showered after the second trial. I never rearmed myself. Stupid! One moment of scolding was all I was allowed however as I hear the sound of steel on steel. She has hit something.

Finishing off with her fingers Drea produces a small silver box from the excavated space in the wall. It reminds me of an ornate jewelry box with delicate carvings creating swirling patters all around it, now filled with dark mud caked in every crease.

"Is it locked?" I ask peering around her.

Her only answer was slowly opening the box, showing a red velvet lining, and a beautiful ornate silver key. A key. We had a key.

We almost missed that key, my subconscious tells me, but I ignore it. All I can hope is that in our frantic progression through the maze we haven't missed anything like this so far. I highly doubt we have time to go back, but from now, we need to proceed more carefully.

Drea reaches a long, elegant hand into the box and pulls out the key. She holds it in front of the light of the brazier and turns it over inspecting its beautiful design before handing it to me.

"Here." Is all she says.

I stare at her blankly, she's just giving me it, what if this was the only key?

"You found it princess; I was just helping the damsel in distress." She winks at me, and I melt at her teasing attitude. I missed this Drea; I want more of her.

Without argument I wrap my fingers around the piece of silver and close my fist tight. I'm not risking dropping this or letting it fall out of any pocket I could stash it in, its staying where I can feel it. If we find another key then Drea is home free, and if I need to I have a key I can give to Alice. I don't think too strongly about it, we still have twenty one minutes left and a lot can happen in that time. There's no point dwelling on an end I might not even reach. Instead, all

I say is,

“Let’s go get your key.”

She smiles and we turn back to retrace our steps. As we do I notice our clock tick over ten minutes. The vampires will be coming now. Neither of us discuss it but I see Drea quicken her steps, she now runs a hand along the wall to her right, I assume looking for inconstancies, so I do the same.

My heart begins beating faster and faster and I feel like the little rabbit Nikolas loves to describe me as. Down here, running through these tunnels I feel like I’m traversing the burrow followed by the fox. Which vampire is after us I don’t know, and I don’t want to know. Whoever it is, with their superior senses and speed, I imagine they are sniffing us out as we speak. Their nose picking up the scent of sweat and fear, their ears hearing our ragged breathing and harsh steps. How easy is it for them? I suspect if they wanted to, they could eliminate us all within a matter of minutes, so why hunt us down here? Is it part of their sick game, do they enjoy this?

I know the answer is yes as we take left turn after left turn. Suddenly Drea throws and arm out in front of me, stopping me in my tracks. I don’t move an inch, completely silent, trying to control my breathing. Has she heard something? Is this where it ends? With freedom so close. My hand clasps my key so tight I think it might break and sweat begins to slick between my palms and the metal.

"The lights are off down there." She says staring down to the right, it was the left turn on our way up here and so we didn't take it. I follow her gaze and see the tunnel descend into darkness, its end not visible.

"And?" I say, knowing her answer but wishing something else.

"We should go down."

I groan.

"Sabine." using my real name, manipulative move. "There's a reason that is the only tunnel in here that isn't lit up, we have to look."

I sigh, I hate to admit it but she's probably right. These people don't do anything without a reason, so either there is a key down there, or our demise.

Drea looks at me, pleading in her eyes. We don't have time to argue this.

"Fine." I look around a see a brazier just ahead of me on the wall, walking over I hold my key in one hand and with the other forcefully detach the torch from the wall. I turn to Drea and hold it up.

“Lead the way.” She beams at me, and I melt. This woman has one cracking smile.

Together we head down the darkened path, she can’t take my hand, both are busy. But her hand rests lightly on my lower back, guiding me forward. At first, I’m offended, thinking she feels the need to urge me on, but as her palm settles and I feel her steadying touch, I know this is just her way of telling me she’s there.

As we move I keep my ears on high alert for any movement around us, but none comes. Perhaps we’re being stalked, perhaps they want to watch the fear develop in us before they pounce. Being in the dark makes this so much worse, every shadow my torch creates becomes a new monster lurking in the shadows and I jump more than once at nothing.

Drea doesn’t tease me, I wonder if she is just as frightened as I am. Our watch counts down the seconds quicker than I feel comfortable with, and in the dark we move much slower than we did before. Until finally at only thirteen minutes remaining, we come to a dead end.

“No.” Drea whispers, realizing she wasted our time. “No, there has to be something down here, there has to be!” She turns to me, desperation in her eyes as if I can find the key out of thin air for her.

"Drea." I start. She falls to her knees and bangs her first against the dirt. We both here a gently pattering sound.

My brows knit together; it sounds as if dirt is gently falling, but I didn't see any. I look up and confirm that the ceiling is steady and not about to collapse on our heads. Drea bangs on the wall again.

"Yeah, let's not risk a cave in Drea." I don't want to scold her, but she is being reckless.

"Can you hear that?" She scrambles to the floor and starts inspecting the bottom of the wall.

"Drea its just loose dirt, it'll be falling from somewhere. We need to move on."

"No. We don't." She sounds sure, but there's also a terrifying undertone in her voice that sends shivers up my spine.

"Drea?" She stands and looks me dead in the eyes, any playfulness that was there earlier is gone.

"Sabine, I'm going to need you to crawl into a hole for me." She turns and I follow her gaze, holding the fire close to the spot at the bottom of the wall. The small one by one foot square that is sectioned out, leading into complete darkness. I swallow and look to her.

“You’re smaller.” Is all she says.

I close my eyes and try to take in deep calming breaths, in through my nose out through my mouth. It’s not that I am particularly claustrophobic but looking at this tiny space of freshly excavated dirt I suddenly cant breath. How far will I have to force myself in before I find what I’m looking for? What else will be in there with me. My skin pre-emptively crawls with the thousand tiny bugs I am imagining lining the cavity. But for her, for Drea I have to do it.

Saying nothing I hand the handmade torch to Drea, I won’t fit it in there with me, whatever I manage will have to come from touch alone. I look down at the key in my other hand, that tiny seed of doubt still planted firmly in my mind from her stunt.

“You can put it in your boot?” She suggests, understanding the look behind my eyes.

Again, I wordlessly hand her the key, taking an extra second we don’t have to brush my fingers against hers before dropping to my knees. Her eyes sparkle slightly as they threaten to brim with tears, she understands the decision I just made … to trust her. I strain my eyes as much as possible, I see nothing, just a never-ending blackness ready to swallow me whole. Creeping closer on all fours I realize I’m going to have to drop to my stomach and army crawl my way in. Laying down the dirt is cold against my skin, and I drag myself forward slowly. With each drag I pat the ground and walls gently in front of me trying to find anything that would indicate a hidden treasure.

Some small bit of lightly gloriously sneaks in past me where Drea holds the brazier to help light my way. It doesn't accomplish much other than reminding me I am not in fact in a grave, buried alive, but have somewhere to back out and escape to.

"Can you see anything?" Her voice echoes as it travels into the opening and around me. I open my mouth the answer, but no sound comes out, the anxiety compressing my lungs and keeping me silent. Like a nightmare where you open your mouth to scream, only to find silence.

Instead, I continue to feel blindly around, cringing at every piece of dirt that displaces and moves, feeling invisible creatures crawling over my skin. I push further and further in, the tunnel narrowing as I advance. Unaware of how far I have crawled all I can hope it that Drea is going to be able to drag me back out because as the walls tighten around me, I realize my arms are now lodged above my head, and I won't be able to back up on my own.

Wedged. I'm wedged so tight that I can't move forward or back, cant tilt my head upwards fully to see what's in front of me. The cold, oppressing mud clinging to me from all sides, sucking my heat and taking away my breath. This can't be it, we can't have come all this way for nothing. My heart beats in time with the ever decreasing seconds ticking on down on my stopwatch. If this doesn't work, if this isn't it, we're done.

In absolute desperation I force myself forward one more time, fitting even more tightly into the space and reach forward. I stretch every fiber of my arm, *please*, I think. My fingers pushing out as far as they will splay frantically search, *please.* My prayers are answered, my fingers touch something, its soft and fluffy, like a sock. I close my fingers around it and scream as loud as I can.

"Get. Me. OUT!"

Hands close around my ankles and I am pulled with all the force of a desperate woman. At first I don't move and I have the sinking feeling that the last push was one too many, that I'll be trapped down here forever, buried alive in my own grave of stupidity. But as the panic just about overwhelms me, I pop free and am dragged out with so much force that dirt is pushed up my sweater top and gets into my mouth. I squeeze my eyes shut in haste and clamp down on whatever is in my hand as Drea completes her final pull.

Immediately light shines through my eyelids and I know I'm free, Drea turns me over and starts wiping dirt from my face. Her motions are less delicate than I like but I realize she is probably panicking. Sitting up I make an outward snorting motion, pushing the contents of my nose free and clawing at my eyes to clear the debris.

Drea's beautiful blue eyes is all I see when I finally open mine, shining with concern and admiration.

"You good?" She asks, a smirk pulling at her lips. Now she has realized I'm alive she probably thinks I look hilarious. I don't reply, merely look around frantically for whatever I just recovered, my hands dragging around me.

I hit the fluffy item I found and hold it up proudly to see my prize … a rat.

I screech and fling it across the tunnel and it hits the wall with a soft bump. I found a dead rat. Which means … which means …

"No key." I whisper.

"It's okay." She says, but her face drops and she looks at her watch. We have seven minutes left.

"Let's try and find the exit" Drea stands and extends a hand to me; I don't take it.

"Exit? We can't go to the exit Drea we need another key!" I exclaim.

"We don't have time Sabine!" She snaps back, a hand dragging though the loose strands of her hair that have fallen around her face. "We need to find the way out, we might find something on the way" Lies, we both know it. But what other choice did we have.

I march over and stamp on the dead rat, needing to get some frustration out of my system. Slamming my foot down I feel the crack of bones and the mushing of rotten flesh and then … something hard. Not hard, solid. It jabs into the bottom of my boot, threatening to poke through if it were a weaker shoe.

Collapsing to the ground I grab the remains and begins tearing it open.

"What the hell are you doing have you lost your god damn mind?!" Drea puts a hand on my shoulder, but I shrug her off.

The smell is overwhelming, a smell of decay that I am familiar with but in this small humid tunnel its intensified in a way that brings bile in my throat and tears to my eyes. But as I tear and throw flesh away I see it, a glimmer of hope, a glimmer of silver.

My blood and flesh covered hands turn to Drea, a key clasped in them. I hold it up like it were the holy grail and her eyes widen in disbelief.

"They put it in a rat." She breathes.

She moves toward me, and I catch sight of her stopwatch swinging from where she attached it to her pants. Five minutes left. I explode to my feet and grab her hand; she doesn't complain about the demolished rat on them and clamps her fingers around mine.

Without another word we take off running back the way we came, we run until we find the first cross roads and try every left, instead of our initial every right. We hit the first dead end with two minutes left. The second with one.

My legs have never moved so fast, they ache, as do my lungs. But I push through, there is no stopping me as I fight with everything in my soul to just keep moving, just keep running. As I count the seconds in my head, I pray to whatever god I can think of that after all of this, we can get out of here. The injustice of it, to even have the key to freedom in our hands and still not make it.

Ten.

One more right, back the way we came, there's a turn at the end.

Nine.

The turn isn't that far, I speed my legs up.

Eight.

Each painful breath is a reminder that I don't have enough left in me.

Seven.

The turn is getting closer, this must be it.

Six.

Voices, I hear voices.

Five.

I squeeze Drea's hand possibly for the last time.

Four.

The turn is on me, I'm going too fast and almost fall as I round it.

Three.

Ten more feet and there's an opening.

Two.

I explode through the opening, collapsing to the ground, Drea crumbling on top of me.

One.

CHAPTER EIGHTEEN

"Just in the nick of time!" Alexandru, Nikolas Master.

W*e made it.*

I could cry if I had anything left to give, my body honestly doesn't have the energy left to even generate a tear. Drea rolls off me with a groan and I climb to my feet unsteadily. My legs wobble and protest at having to hold me up after the hard work.

"And do we have our keys?"

Keys? Keys! My brain is apparently shutting down along with the rest of my body as I hold out the rotten covered Key in front of me.

"Urgh, I believe you I don't need to hold it thanks." The vampire looks thoroughly disgusted at the sight of me and has a hand to his chest as if he is thoroughly offended by me offering it to him.

"Both of you though well done." Melchior, he stands further back from Alexandru, half hidden in the shadows. He doesn't move forward or approach me and from here I can't even see if he is happy to see me succeed.

“All four keys found.” He follows up.

Suddenly aware I snap my head up and look frantically around the room, Alice, Ash, and Jared all stand at the opposite end of the hall in front of another opening.

“Where Nikolas?” I say without thinking, he must be here somewhere, but I can’t place him, and my head is still reeling. Ash shakes his head and Jared just stares at the floor. Alice seems close to tears.

“Where’s Nikolas?” I repeat, my voice trembling.

“Oh, my lovely familiar?” Alexandru put an expression of mock sadness on his face. “He was hunted and found I’m afraid. He has been eliminated.”

My legs give out. I don’t know if it’s the shock or the exhaustion. Nikolas has been eliminated … he … he.

“He’s dead, you killed him.” I say flatly.

“Well, I didn’t kill him, whoever was hunting him killed him.” He sounds genuinely offended by my accusation and I shoot him a look that could kill.

When I first met these two, they seemed to actually be friends, how can he stand there completely unaffected by his death? How can he not care?

Rage overtakes me and my hands ball into fists, this monster is responsible for taking his father's life and now his. Two generations ended because of the whims of a vampire. In the end Nikolas was a good person, he had a purpose, was that why he was dead? Had Alexandru found out about his plan?

My stomach bottoms out. With Nikolas gone, I was stuck. No one would be coming for Melchior, no one would be freeing me from my Master. I went from having too many choices to none at all. Nikolas is dead, and I am trapped.

"Alas, very sad but onwards and upwards! We have five familiars and four keys here therefore our little game is not over." He waggles his finger at me and I strongly consider trying to reach out and break it. But … four keys.

Again, my head whips to my friends standing three abreast. Alice no longer clings to Ash and instead is standing back her head bowed in resignation. No.

The looks on Ash and Jared face tell me the same, they have the other two keys. Why would they give them up? Alice is a child, Ash already said she shouldn't be a vampire, it's an abomination. They probably think they are sparing her from an immortal miserable life. As Nikolas said, put her out of her misery. I don't even blame them, not really. These men are good and kind, and they have helped us where they can. But fundamentally, they don't agree with a child being turned, I have to respect that.

"Alice, you can have mine." I climb to my knees and begin to stagger towards her, key in my outstretched hand.

"No!" I hear Drea shout. But I don't listen, my eyes are on Alice. She moves slowly behind Ash edging out of my view.

"Alice it's okay." I promise, my voice breaking. Nikolas has asked what would happen to me if I made it out and Alice didn't. I don't know but I don't want to know. I wouldn't be able to live with myself, eternity wouldn't wipe away the sin of allowing her die to save myself.

Alice creeps behind Jared now and taps him on the shoulder.

"I need to tell you something." She says to him and motions for him to bend over.

"Alice." I try again.

She ignores me but keeps her focus locked on Jared, his face breaks slightly and I know it is killing him to do this to her. Yet he drops to one knee so that his head is in line with hers. A small kind smile at his lips.

"What is it, Alice?" He asks, his voice breaking on her name.

"I don't need her key; I can take yours." Her voice comes out as a hiss, as if a demon has taken over her body.

My mind can't process the words, is she going to try and mug him while he's down? It's a bold move but there's no way she can overpower him.

My question is answered however when from nowhere a blade appears in her hand and slices Jared's throat.

The world goes hazy. I sway on my feet, one hand still outstretched to Alice as her grinning face is covered in the splattering blood from Jared's neck.

All around me I hear screaming and shocked gasps, but I can't differentiate the noise. Alice just slit his throat.

The little girl, with her pigtails drenched in blood. She drops the blade and reaches down into Jared's pocket as he lies, collapsed, still bleeding out. Ash drops to bend over him and presses down on the wound, foolishly thinking he can do something to save him.

As the key slides out of his pocket and into Alices hand, the smile that overtakes her face is unhinged.

"See Sabine, I got his key! Now we can both go home." The words are ecstatic, she is so proud of herself.

"You!" Ask shrieks at me. "You planned this with her!?" His hand still clamped over Jared's throat, blood spilling between his fingers.

"No." I squeak. "No!" Finding more force, I scream. I would never have chosen this in a million years. I think back to the conversation we had with Jared when he asked if I would have sacrificed him to save Alice. I didn't know then, I do now.

"We took her to help, we were being kind!" Tears coat Ash's cheeks but I can't talk. Can't say more than my simple denial. I'm in too much shock I don't understand. Jared's thrashing movements are slowing and the gurgling noise coming from his throat are making me feel sick. Another good life, gone.

"No don't blame Sabine!" Alice scolds, "I knew she had knives, so I stole one while she was poorly and asleep! Don't pretend to be outraged, you were quite happy to let me die!" The way she looks at him I'm honestly terrified that she's going to pick that blade back up and kill him too.

Perhaps Ash thinks the same thing, or perhaps he feels guilt from her words, he was going to walk out of here with Jared and let her die. His head drops, taking in the sight of his now dead friend, all struggle ceased.

"Well, I never would have had bets on that!" Alexandru whistled.

"Alice." Her name comes out of my mouth one last time. I don't know what I want to say to her. I want to tell her she's wrong, that I never would have wanted this, that I'm sorry I got it so wrong, that she turned into a monster just like them.

Instead of any of those words, I just sob. A deep and hopeless sob. Alice is a monster, Jared is dead, Nikolas is dead, and I am about to spend all eternity with someone I have grown to hate. I will never see Drea again.

"Such dramatics." I hear from behind me somewhere. "Well let's get them all knocked out and back to whom they belong."

"Wait!" I scream, I need to say my goodbyes. I need Ash to know I didn't do this; I need Drea to know I would have chosen her. What about her Master? Would she take me if I begged? This can't be it!

But as I try to raise myself I see a blur of motion and feel a crack to the back of my head. Giving me

unconsciousness as a gift, sparing me this overwhelming grief.

CHAPTER NINETEEN

Not for the first time, I awake in absolute agony. Particularly my head. It throbs at the back with an ache I can't escape and I groan as I lift a hand to touch it.

The spot I find is so sensitive I hiss at the motion, quickly lowering my hand.

"Good, you're awake." Melchior. Do I still have to call him Master? I cringe at the thought of that word coming out of my mouth.

It takes me less time that I would have thought to gather where I am and what's happening. My old home, now a prison. All hopes of my future taken away in a moment of unfair cruelty. I want to swing at him, tell him just what I think of him and his vampire cadre.

If I weren't so small, so weak, I would end him here and now and go find Drea myself. New Orleans couldn't be that big?

But I am weak. And I know that no matter what I do, I

will never escape him, never beat him.

My mind wants to muse about Alice, do I still want to find her? Images of her with the blade against Jared's throat will haunt my nightmares for decades to come, I'm sure.

Shivering I use every ounce of strength I have to sit myself up in bed. My bed. I'm back in the house I have spent the last decade of my life in, and it doesn't feel like home.

Melchior sits in a chair next to the bed, each elbow resting on a knee. His eyes burn into me, and I wonder how much he knows about me wanting to leave. Perhaps that is what the venom trick was about, to test how much I was actually loyal to him.

"You have had a difficult time, Sabine." He starts "But I am extremely proud of you. You excelled in there, though I can't say I approved of your babysitting duties." His eyes flash and I revert immediately back to the girl so terrified and intimidated by him, shrinking into myself.

"You have earned your place at my side, today we start your journey to becoming a vampire."

I can feel my heart beating in my chest, I wonder how it will feel once it is perpetually slowed. This time last month I would have been ecstatic to hear those words from his mouth, now they ring hollow in my ears. I don't want to earn anything from him, I certainly don't want immortality from him. Though that isn't necessarily true, I just don't want immortality w*ith* him.

If he senses any unease in me, he doesn't acknowledge it, he presses on ahead in ignorance of the fact that I'm not responding to him.

"The process will be difficult for you, I will have to drain you of your blood first which may be … uncomfortable. But don't fret you will likely be unconscious for the rest. When you wake, you will feel exceptional." His eyes sparkle and he looks me up and down in a way he never has before.

My skin crawls as he drinks me in and for the first time ever I get the feeling he may want me to be his bride in every sense of the word.

"Our first order of business will be paying a visit to our dear friend Alexandru; he appears to have broken some rules." His words shock me out of my momentary panic. Nikolas Master?

"What rule?" I manage.

"It appears the vampire hunting dear Nikolas says he disappeared before he had a chance to find him." My heart leaps at his words, if they hadn't found Nikolas did that mean he got away? Did he find an out and run? I steady my breath and try to focus on Melchior, I wouldn't let hope take route just yet.

"Dear, silly Alexandru was so attached to the boy, it appears he didn't want to risk him not making it out." The vampire stands as he speaks and straightens the cufflinks on each side of his blazer.

"Which means?" I ask breathlessly.

"Which means," he snarls, "Nikolas is alive and well, and about to be turned. Without passing the trial."

He's alive, Nikolas is alive and so is the hope for my future. If he's already been turned Alexandru could even already be dead! And me, I still had a shot at freedom, if Nikolas was turned before we got to him.

"So, what do we do?" I ask tentatively.

"We will go pay him a visit and remind him of the consequences of breaking rules. But first my dear…" He towers over the bed; fear holds me in place when I know I should run. I wonder to myself if this is the charm Drea spoke of, hindering my good judgment. But I decide against it, I certainly do not feel calm, nor submissive, merely terrified.

"First we make you, my bride."

The world goes black as he moves in a blur and sinks his teeth into my neck. I gasp and scramble to push and claw at him, but he is an immovable force and before I can truly process what is happening, I black out.

The end.

UNDER THE BLOOD RED DAWN:

THE SECOND AND FINAL INSTALLMENT
IN THE BLOOD RED DUOLOGY,

COMING LATE 2023.

ACKNOWLEDGEMENTS

To my parents for always and continuing to give me the support and confidence to pursue my dreams. To my husband for always encouraging me no matter what way I need to follow my happiness. To my sister who has always been my biggest fan and best friend.

And finally, to all the amazing indie authors I have found and enjoyed this year for inspiring me to undertake this journey.

Printed in Great Britain
by Amazon